GRAVE

OF

SONGS

◇◇

CHAUNCE STANTON

ISBN: 979-8-6562-5787-9

www.chauncestanton.com

Dedicated to my hometown,
Annandale, Minnesota

Upon the Origin of What Really Matters

By Joseph Langland

And,
after a long journey,
we rose upon the pure white breast of winter
(O child, children)
in the fallen dusk of sun
tunneling into the moon.

There,
in Highland Township meadows,
a pine tree, somber in its head of boughs
(blue-green, gold)
drooped crystals from its stems
and called our shadows in.

Something
familiar in its arms
fragrantly lifted; it whispered to the dark
(starlight, starbright)
distance of sheds and barns
and ringed that forest field

With dreams
of strange illuminations.
But whether music, magic, games or stories
(forget, forgetting)
or the gnomes of old desires,
we all, it seems, forgot.

And
plunging through the snow
we came, once more, along those playhouse roads
(hello, hello)
upon men, women, and homes,
and a huge grave of songs.

Used with permission by
Paul Langland and Elizabeth Langland.

PROLOGUE

A train whistle is the song of the approaching horizon. It's the sound of big cities like New York and Chicago, gold fever, bison, and the oceans, too, all being pulled towards little towns like Annandale. Train depots on a line all the way to the Dakota Territory carried the wheat in rail cars back to the Minneapolis mills. They carried the hopes of farmers, blacksmiths, and shop owners. They carried teachers, bankers, and ministers. Sometimes, they even carried a boy who wanted only to find out where the train was going next, because everything on a train has a final destination.

$$* * * * *$$

Annandale, Minnesota

October 1888

The engineer peered down from the rail depot platform. Blood stained the steel rail under the thick iron cow-catcher apron. Dabbing his forehead with a dirty cloth, he tried to erase the coal dust pasted in every crease and cemented with sweat all the way up over his bald head. His eyes burned in the smoke curling around the hard, black bulk of the 12:05 train.

"There wasn't a thing I could do! I was slowing down already."

He was defensive, as if the depot agent had accused him of intentionally slamming the train into the boy.

The depot agent caught the slender gold-link chain of his dangling pocket watch from his vest. He flicked it open with a well-practiced pluck of his thumb and two forefingers.

"Twelve twenty-one," the agent noted. "He must have slipped."

The sign behind them read ANNANDALE in neat black letters that

1

looked fresh enough to be wet. Long unpainted maple boards ran east to west, parallel with the track where a hulking locomotive steamed after a run from Minneapolis.

"I couldn't even see him because the steam was blowing right over the front of us." The engineer reached into his bib pocket and pulled out his own watch. "What time did you say you had?"

"Twelve twenty-one," the depot agent answered. "Almost twenty-two. "

"That late?"

The agent nodded and exhaled.

"I've got boys of my own," he confessed.

"I've got one at home, too." The engineer's eyebrows rose and fell like a canvas sail tacking in the wind. "But this is throwing me off schedule!"

The boot heels of a tall, lean man in a long smock pounded the wooden deck of the platform. His hair was a tangle of bushy, brown locks coated in fine dust the color of bone.

"Howdy-do, Gus!" The depot agent offered the man a friendly wave, but the engineer shot him a hot look. The agent jerked his hand back to his side as the smile fled his lips. "Gus is the foreman over at the grain elevator," he explained.

"Little late today," Gus said by way of greeting. He plugged his stub pipe from a cloth bag of loose tobacco.

"Yeah, had a sort of…" The agent searched the engineer's face for a moment, seeing if a clue to the right word might appear there. "…mishap, I guess you'd call it." He dipped his chin, nodding to the mangled body crushed beneath the train.

Gus lit his pipe and looked down to the track and winced, waving off the swirl of white smoke that billowed from his bowl.

"Uh oh."

"Did you know him?" The engineer studied Gus's eyes.

Gus looked down from the platform and grimaced. "Looks like a kid. Hard to tell now, though."

"Yeah," the engineer agreed. "Hard to tell."

"Wasn't raining or nothing, though," Gus determined.

"He must have been daydreaming, then," the depot agent concluded.

"You know what they say," the engineer checked his watch again with a click of his tongue. Then he tucked his rag in the back pocket of his bibs. It hung out like a grimy gray tail. "You can't daydream around a bull, a mick, or a steam engine."

"That's right," The depot agent shoved a sack of mail away from the edge of the platform with his foot. "That's what they always say."

"We took on an extra car of plows and threshers, a solid ton, and she's been pulling sluggish, so I reckon we're already ten minutes behind."

"Sixteen," the agent corrected him, tapping the glass face of his watch.

"Yeah," Gus the elevator foreman agreed. "I'd say more like fifteen, sixteen minutes late."

"Running heavy makes it harder to stop, once you've been up to speed," the engineer explained.

The three men kept their vigil, eying the boy's body, but none of them moved. Gus broke the silence.

"I suppose he didn't feel nothing, so that's a blessing, at least."

The other men nodded solemnly.

"Yes, it's not a bad way to go when you get right down to it," the depot agent replied.

The engineer's eyes fired in anger.

"I'm sorry, but it is not a good way to go at all, seeing as it causes so much consternation for everyone else."

"Well, I suppose there's nothing for it but to get this over with," the depot agent sighed. "He's certainly caught under there."

"Clearing tracks is still the depot's responsibility, I suppose," the engineer suggested.

"Yes, that's true." The agent's face soured. "It's just that my boys are at the school now."

The engineer shrugged. "Wish I could help! My back isn't what it used to be. Besides, I need to write out a statement for the logbook." He looked at his watch again. "Damn! That late?" He wished the two men a good day and hurried toward the office.

"How about it, Gus?" the agent asked. "Can you lend a hand?"

"I got plenty to get back to at the moment…"

"I know, I know." The agent poked a finger in his pocket and removed a coin. "Look, I can pay you."

Gus laughed at the offer. "Five cents? Make it a dime."

The agent reluctantly agreed, and Gus took a long draw on his pipe before following the agent down the hook ladder to the tracks. They could taste iron mingled with coal dust.

The boy's left arm was gone, probably flattened under the wheels, but that was a problem for later, once the train pulled out. The boy's remaining arm was folded under his torso, and they tugged it free, unfurling it like the wing of a baby bird about to take flight for the first time.

"I sure hope this'll do it," the agent said, straining as the two men pulled hard on the dead boy's arm under the lidless stare of the 12:05's headlamp. "I'd hate to have to use the saw."

"I'm not using any saw on that boy," Gus said flatly. "Or an ax. You want me to fetch Mr. Dunton to help?" Gus offered, referring to the town's undertaker. "He could do any cutting you need."

"No time for that. This train's almost a half-hour off the timetable. It's you and me." The agent crouched low to grab the boy's sleeve, damp with blood. "Keep pulling."

CHAPTER ONE

THE STORM

June 1888

It was another steamy June day. The air already felt thick like it had yesterday and the day before. Mundy Nelson, still half asleep, propped his chin on his folded arms at the kitchen table. The smell of oats cooking on the outdoor stove made his stomach rumble.

Being only thirteen, Mundy was unqualified to judge the sunrise through the cabin window. Only his father, Lars, could gaze out from the cabin window and interpret the sun's corona or the movement of birds and know how that day would unfold on the Nelson farm. To Lars Nelson, the sky was a chalkboard, its secrets scripted in sun-gilded clouds. Only he knew its cipher: the angles of leaves, the color of the sky, and how each told the future.

They'd had a lot of rain early that year, on top of a winter full of snow, so the soil was pregnant with moisture from the early spring torrents, and it sweated into the oppressive afternoon air. These sunny days, all in a row, meant work from sunup to sundown to catch up with chores the spring rains had delayed.

Mundy wanted it to rain again, and hard, so he could work in the barn or help his mother in the garden—much better than yanking wild blackberry canes creeping in from the tree line in the far pasture. The blackberry thorns could hurt the cows and cause their wounds to fester, but those canes were within spitting distance of the troll mound in the woods.

Whatever work lay ahead, Mundy knew it would make him itch. He would want to quit in the glowering heat of early afternoon. His father would joke about the cows' milk boiling in the udder, but then their moods would sour, itchy with sweat and flies, so that by the end of the day, they wouldn't speak unless it was for his father to yell at him.

Standing at that window, Lars Nelson rubbed dust from the thin pane of glass with his fist and surveyed the outside world. He slowly drew his black braces over his broad shoulders. His feet were bare white gourds, toes wriggling free on the planks of the cabin floor. His boots—and Mundy's too—caked with mud and muck, waited outside the cabin door on orders from Mundy's mother, Brita. The worn bristles of a broom leaning next to the front door stood as a silent sentinel against the intrusion of the men's dirt.

"Well..." Lars murmured as he pondered the golden rays of dawn breaking over the homestead.

"Hmmm..." His father's head nodded, and Mundy lifted his head from his arms expectantly. The veil was lifting, nature's mystery would be revealed by his father. The day would be decided in his pronouncement.

"It is a good day," Lars determined. "...for clearing pasture."

Lars turned and smiled without looking at Mundy. Instead he opened the cabin door and filled his lungs with morning air. As he exhaled, Lars called to his wife who stirred the oats outside.

"Almost ready there, missus? We've got two hungry men in here."

If Mundy's mother replied, she'd done so with a glance or a flick of her hand. She had been very quiet for the past few months.

"Can't I help you fix the fence?" Mundy ventured. "You'll need extra hands."

"That's true, that's true," his father's words seemed to agree with him, but the tight smile returned, his father's eyes focused elsewhere. "Don't want to pull those blackberries, eh?"

"No, pa."

"Too hot? Too much work?"

For one wild moment, Mundy imagined a giant, terrible hand reaching from the woods and shredding his skin as it dragged Mundy toward the troll mound through the tangle of blackberry cane.

"No, it's just the thorns, pa," Mundy lied.

"Well, it's better you bleed than the cows. Besides, we're going to need more pasture if we're going to increase the herd, now that the train line is up and running." His father rolled up the sleeves of his tan cotton work shirt and muttered under his breath in Norwegian. Mundy didn't understand the words, but he understood what they meant. No point in arguing.

Brita Nelson appeared in the doorway, a shadow against the morning light that streamed in behind her. Her chestnut hair, knotted in a bun at the back of her head, glinted red in the morning light. She held the iron cooking pot by its handle, the steam rising from a thick slurry of oats, fresh cream, and butter. She lifted each foot, checking the bottoms for dirt, before she stepped inside. She set the pot on the little round table built long before Mundy was born by grandfather Nelson. Then she set out two bowls and a loaf of rye bread that she'd baked the day before.

His mother was a pretty woman, and his father used to say so. The tops of her high cheek bones were speckled with little golden freckles, and when she smiled, Mundy thought she was the most beautiful woman in the world, but Brita didn't smile much anymore.

Maybe she was just too worn out to smile. She'd been extra quiet for a few months now, ever since the neighbor woman died, Mrs. Koskinen. Before that, in the early winter, the Nelsons warmed themselves by the woodstove and listened to Lars's stories from the homeland. Sometimes the stories were dark and violent, and Brita scolded her husband for scaring Mundy, but Lars would shrug.

"This is just how the story goes," he would say.

Mundy thrilled at hearing about the terrible monsters and cunning heroes, but his father's stories would scare Mundy, just as Brita said they would. The monsters invaded his dreams to this day, so that he would wake up calling for his mother to climb the ladder to the loft where he slept and soothe him back to sleep.

But after Mrs. Koskinen died, Mundy's mother hadn't appeared to soothe him back to sleep.

Even though the Koskinens were Finns, Brita Nelson had shown the three Koskinen children as much kindness as the Nelsons could afford. Each day, Brita trudged through the snow to the neighboring farm each day to feed the Koskinen children—even Matias, who was a little older than Mundy and should have taken care of himself and his own family. She did this until Mr. Koskinen returned in late March from logging up north. Since then, Lars and Brita did not speak as kindly to one another. They did not laugh with one another. Lars hadn't mentioned how pretty his wife was since the first big snow of December when he'd wiped the big, wet flakes from her cheek.

The shadow of Mrs. Koskinen's death had crept into their lives like the spread of thorny brambles.

*****

"Mundy, you'll get to that pasture right after milking," Lars said. "We'll be in for rain later."

"Now why do you say it will rain?" Brita Nelson stabbed a wooden spoon into the glob of thick oats. Her question was a challenge. "The sky is clear enough. I could see the church steeple."

She exaggerated. They couldn't see a church steeple no matter how clear the weather. The nearest steeple was in the depot town, Annandale, three miles away, and between the Nelson farm and that new town stood trees twice as high as any building for miles.

"How can you tell about the rain?" Mundy asked.

"Look." Mundy stood next to his father at the window. His father pointed at the golden sun edging over the trees and fields in a cloudless blue sky.

"See that haze?"

Mundy noticed the translucent corona around the sun, like wisps of smoke.

His father pointed at the tips of rye stalks bowing with big droplets and the glistening black-eyed Susans in his mother's flower bed (the one concession to vanity allowed on the Nelson farm). The dew would soak through his boots, and his feet would be wet all day.

"See that dew?"

Mundy nodded.

"Good boy," his father said, gripping Mundy's shoulder. Then he sat at his place at the plank table. That was the extent of the lesson. Mundy tried to piece it together. Flowers, sun, dew. Somehow that meant rain, but he wanted to know why. Maybe one morning Mundy would simply wake up and know everything his father did. Then he would be a man.

His father, sensing his confusion, patted Mundy's shoulder.

"You're trying too hard, Mundy," he said. "Nature comes to a person naturally."

"I guess so."

"You'll see." His father tore off a corner of cheese from Mundy's plate and ate it. "And the best way to learn is to do. We'll get the milking done, then you water the herd. Keep a tether on the big one. Otherwise she'll drown them all."

"Yes, pa."

In the summer, they led their milkers to the pond to drink their fill, which was a lot easier than pumping the water three or four times a day, especially during the winter, when your skin could stick to the iron pump handle. Each cow needed three or four gallons of water every day, more when it was hot, like today.

"This will be good practice for you—for when we have a bigger herd. You think you work hard now! Wait until we have twenty milkers! Forty!"

That was his father's plan: increase the herd of Ayrshires and sell the cream and cheese to shops and townspeople in Annandale and maybe even in Buffalo, a larger town on the rail line to the east. Cheese would travel all the way to Minneapolis markets. Mundy couldn't imagine working more than they already did with four cows. Six, if the two calves lasted the next winter.

"So, let's get our work done before it breaks loose," his father suggested. "Water the cows. Then you can start clearing the blackberry cane."

Breaks loose. Mundy fought the smile teasing the corners of his mouth. Even if it meant an itchy hot morning in the pasture, at least—maybe—they would finish the day's work early, before sunset for a change.

"Missus, you'll bring our lunch to the orchard today when you hear the train whistle."

Mundy's mother shrugged her assent and dropped scoops of oat mush for the Nelson men to eat.

His mother broke the silence by clearing her throat, just as Mundy filled his mouth.

"Rub some *kattemynte* on your skin to keep off the mosquitoes," she said. She called the plants by their Norwegian names, but she meant catnip. "And don't make me come looking for you two at lunch," she added, sweeping breadcrumbs and stray bits of cheese into the chicken bucket. "I don't have time for hunting today."

✶✶✶✶✶

Maybe it worked on mosquitoes, but his mother's catnip salve had no effect on the deerflies. They assaulted Mundy as soon as he stepped into the pasture. He snugged his field hat low on his forehead to keep them from getting tangled in his thick brown hair. Some of them were as big as his thumb, but they were easy to crush with a quick slap or by rolling their soft bodies between his thumb and forefinger until their guts exploded. They lived along the edges of woods and tall grasses, but once they found their prey, they were relentless.

Next to the tangle of woods, tentacles of wild blackberry cane arched out of the earth, clawing their way forward to conquer the pasture's clover, wild rye stalks, already heavy with seed, and the tufts of tall buffalo grass. It was only late morning. The sun had many miles to travel before noon, but already Mundy was hungry again.

There was nothing to do except get started. Mundy took a deep breath and tugged on the deerskin work gloves that his father had made. Soon he found the rhythm of his work. Within an hour, the pile of canes was nearly to Mundy's waist. He toted a few bundles to the drying shed next to the house, because cane made good kindling for the kitchen fire. When he returned to the field, he lamented how much cane was left to clear. Most of it was first-year growth and wouldn't produce berries, but deeper in the patch, older canes bent with little plump berries. He picked his way toward them, his arms raised overhead so as not to tear his flesh with thorns. He wedged one gloved hand in the pit of his arm and slid his fingers free. His hands smelled like oiled buckskin from the gloves, but he picked a berry for inspection. Just as he thought: each berry had a bumper crop of seeds waiting to be spread by birds.

No bugs hiding on it and no greenish-white fungus. He popped the berry in his mouth, letting the concentrated flavor, potent and floral, coat his tongue. Wild blackberries were as delicious as they were invasive. He tasted another, and then another, until the tips of fingers were stained carnelian, and he wiped his mouth in hopes that his lips wouldn't give him away with his father.

A branch snapped and the weeds rustled in the nearby towering poplar trees, their leaves babbling in hot gusts. Mundy felt a chill. He stalked to the edge of the woods, lifting each foot waist high and setting it down as quietly as possible. He was trying to convince himself that he wasn't scared. He held back the low branches to peer into the sun-dappled world within the woods, and he could see nothing unusual. Lady slipper flowers nodded to him, their white and lavender petals glowing in the understory like angels' eyes. A little further in, the only remaining hill on the farm lurked in the shadows like a huge gray beast with its back turned to Mundy. Ridged with sumac and wild plum trees, the troll mound was taller than his father and twenty feet across.

Mundy's dad knew all about trolls. He had seen a troll in person, although he didn't want to talk about it, especially when Mundy's mother was around. Trolls buried in the mound would dig their way out in search of their first meal in a thousand years. They liked nothing more than finding children wandering around on their own—just as Mundy was doing right then—and the trolls would eat them. They tunneled all over the earth and across oceans to make new homes in the thousands of mounds along the rivers and across the prairies of North America.

Stop it, Mundy tried to calm himself. Stop thinking about it.

He didn't want the nightmares to come back. They could scare him awake: dreams of the farm overrun by trolls, eating the Nelson family's supplies, slaughtering their cows, clubbing his mother and father with branches and big field stones while he tried to run, but never fast enough.

He reminded himself that there were any number of real dangers: renegade Sioux warriors, or a ravenous great cat, or wolves, or wild dogs.

There's nothing there, he thought. He stepped out of the woods, the sweat beading on Mundy's forehead and streaming into his eyes. He was wiping his face with his sleeve when he felt a sharp sting on the back of his neck. He whirled around. Over him loomed Matias Koskinen, from the neighboring farm, clutching a long stalk of stinging nettle. His hair was so blond that it looked pure white. He was fourteen and as tall and as strong as a grown man, and he lived to torment Mundy.

"I bet that's going to burn," Matias grinned. Mundy knew the smile well. He'd seen it often enough because Matias never missed a chance to shove Mundy down or to swing him by the ankles in circles and send him flying into a pile of cow manure. It was as if the loss of his mother had no effect on Matias, nor did he credit Mundy for any of the ongoing kindness shown to the Koskinens by Brita Nelson, but the Koskinens were Finns. The kind who throw their broken implements and putrid animal carcasses over the fence without remorse.

Mundy dodged away as Matias raised the nettle for another strike—this one aimed at Mundy's face. Mundy scrambled into the pasture with Matias following, whooping like a Sioux brave. Matias's glowing blue eyes assessed Mundy's escape routes, ready to cut them off, but Mundy managed to rush past him, screaming into earshot of his father in the barn.

"You get away from here you rotten apple!" Mr. Nelson shouted like a bear about to charge.

The sight of Mundy's father emerging, pitchfork waving wildly in the air, sent Matias laughing back across the property line.

"Watch out for the storm," he shouted back at them.

"Just look at him," Lars told Mundy. "Running around without a care in the world. Ignoring his own chores and disturbing yours. To look at him, you wouldn't know his mother died."

Lars gripped his son by the shoulders pinning his arms to his sides. He spun him to the left and to the right inspecting for damage.

"Nothing torn, nothing broken. Some welts just here on the back of your neck. And bug bites, but I don't see any blood. Now get back to work. You and your friend can play another time," A little smile curled on his father's lips.

"He's not my friend! I hate him!"

"I know," his father laughed. "I was only teasing. I thought you might need a little humor to get your mind back on your work."

Even though Mundy was sweating and exhausted, he couldn't get out of his chores. He returned to the edge of the woods, gloves on, tugging cane out by the roots, until his shoulders ached. The skin on his neck still burned. Soon he was daydreaming that it was Matias Koskinen—not Mundy—whom the trolls dragged, screaming and crying, by the feet into the woods where they would roast him alive over a fire.

That was a good story.

$$* * * * *$$

A rush of coal-black billowing thunderheads entombed the morning's blue sky. The long, roiling horizon above the fields flashed purple. The sun would set unseen. It was night already further west in the prairie.

Lars sprinted toward Mundy across the pasture as the first flash of lightning sizzled the air overhead. Moments later, the ground growled beneath them in the reverberation of rolling thunder, like the tolling of a giant bell, tipped with deep, booming echoes.

"Let's get those cows back in the barn right now," his father yelled as he ran past. "I'll meet you there!"

Mundy knew better than to ask questions. By the time he reached the grazing pasture, the cows were trotting toward the barn on their own, their lowing panicked, their eyes bulging with terror. He ran alongside them, but another round of powerful thunder made them break into a gallop, leaving the two calves lagging behind.

The first two cows reached the barn door at once, scraping the posts with their flanks in their desperation and sending buckets and tools clattering on the ground. Soaked to the bone, Mundy and the calves reached the barn as the hail began cracking against the roof as if the sky were dropping rocks. He pushed the straggling calves through the opening and dragged the door closed behind them. The calves' baying chorus of fear punctuated the roar of the storm as they huddled under their mothers' muck-splattered legs in the center of the barn.

His father was inside already, bundling old, dusty canvases into a pile on the workbench.

"Get over here! Hurry, Mundy! Damn it!"

He'd never heard his father curse in English before. This was a bad storm. Mundy ran to the workbench, and his father told him to put his arms out. Soon he held a pile of canvases and wool blankets they used to cover new-born calves. His father told him to take the canvases and run back to the field shed.

Mundy froze, blinking. The field shed was half falling apart, a relic from the original farm better used for firewood.

"I said go!" His father shouted. "Now!"

Mundy wanted to ask why? Why would they put themselves in danger for a rickety old outbuilding? His mother burst through the door, a black wall of rain blocking the view of the yard. Her long brown hair, undone, was sopping wet and matted against her head.

"What are you doing out here?" She yelled. "We need to get to the cellar."

"Missus, you take the lamp and blankets and go to the cellar! Mundy and I will be there soon!"

She turned to Mundy and through gritted teeth commanded, "Come with me now."

"No!" His father shoved Mundy toward the open door and the storm beyond. "We've got work to do! Get to the shed, Mundy!"

Mundy ran with his bundle as fast as he could into slivers of freezing rain that bit his face, lashed by wind from the north and then from the west. He looked back to the barn. The figures of his mother and father were illuminated by hot white flashes of lightning, their faces gnarled in angry words. His father raised his hand, about to strike Brita, and then the scene went black in a single roar of thunder.

Mundy hunched over the stack canvas, pressing forward toward the field shed that swayed like a pregnant heifer with the whipping wind pulling at the wooden shingles. A maple plank snapped off the north wall, exposing the building's skeleton of red oak posts. His father caught up with Mundy.

Mundy ducked through the doorway of the shed and pitched his bundle on the ground. The timbers overhead creaked as they shifted under the force of the wind. His father stumbled in moments later, breathing hard, his arms full of more blankets and canvases in various states of repair. They stood in the darkness for a moment catching their breath in quick rasping gulps.

"Spread out the canvas on the ground," his father instructed. "This wind might take off the roof."

They tugged each corner of canvas and blanket, stretching them in a haphazard patchwork on the shed floor, which they weighted down with disused fence posts and ancient scythes with thin blades, rusted and gouged. They hurried back to the house as a lightning strike charged the air around them and immediately gave birth to the loudest clap of thunder Mundy had ever heard. A poplar tree snapped, falling in a whoosh of branches where only hours before Mundy had stood pulling cane.

His father pulled open the swing door to the root cellar and waved Mundy in. He ran down the stairs, his teeth chattering, straight into his mother's arms. She wrapped a blanket over Mundy's shoulders. The sputtering lamp light revealed the stone wall and the ends of tree roots pushing their way in. Her cheek was red where his father had hit her.

The wind and rain did not weaken for an hour. More trees crashed, their roots tearing loose from the saturated ground. Brita wrapped a blanket around herself and Mundy, rocking them back and forth for warmth. His father joked about whether any of the apple trees would have any fruit left, but Brita hissed at him to stop joking.

"You put Mundy in danger, Lars," she hugged Mundy tightly. "I won't forgive you for that."

The storm eventually broke, leaving only the patter of cold rain and night. Lars opened the cellar door and called down to them.

"We can go up now," he declared. He clutched Brita's arm to steady her up the old wooden ladder, but she shrugged off his hand, glaring at him and saying nothing.

CHAPTER TWO

GREASE THE WHEELS

Mundy's mother wasn't at breakfast the next morning. The outdoor cookstove they used in the summer was cold to the touch. The empty skillet hung on an iron hook on the wall, waiting her sure grip.

"She's over at the Koskinens again," Lars said, pulling a half-eaten loaf from under a thin, white cloth. He tore it in two and offered a chunk to Mundy and dipped his in a bowl of milk still clotted with cream. "We'll never starve with a milk herd, even without a woman!"

Mundy knew better than that. His mother milled the wheat for the bread that his father was chewing. The cows kept them from starving even during the long winter, but only because Mundy's mother churned butter and set cheese every week in the spring and summer. She had to come home soon. The cheese rounds in the cupboard hadn't been flipped for two days.

"And for lunch," his father continued. "More bread. More milk. More cheese. And you know already there are plenty of berries." He rubbed Mundy's wild hair like Mundy's mother might have done.

If she were there.

"I don't want any more berries," Mundy said, pulling away from his father. Mundy didn't care about breakfast or lunch, either.

"You're troubled," his father said as he chewed, the bread catching in crumbs in his thick brown beard. "Go ahead. Ask."

"I don't understand about the field shed and why…"

His father let out a long, slow breath that stopped Mundy's words.

"Buildings do more than just stand around and rot. Someday you'll know."

Another thing unknown to Mundy. Someday. Eventually. When

you're a man. You'll know.

The door creaked open and Brita Nelson appeared, awash in morning light. She paused at the threshold without entering, her eyes downcast at first and then trained on her husband, her nostrils flaring. Her thick brown hair was no longer the tangled wet mess Mundy had seen the night before, but it was combed out long, hanging down to her waist.

She stepped inside, leaving the door open behind her.

"Are you telling Mundy nonsense stories again?" She rubbed Mundy's head. "You know he'll have bad dreams."

"Helping out the Koskinens again, I suppose?" Lars said without looking at her. "Generosity begins at home, Brita."

"Not now," she shook her head and closed her eyes.

His father's neck muscles tensed as he slid a chair—Brita's chair—away from the table with his foot and nodded for his wife to sit down.

"Mundy, go start the milking," he commanded. "It's run day, so you'll help your mother load the cart."

Mundy had forgotten it was run day—the day his mother delivered cheese to town.

"Come to think of it," his father added, balling his fist into the palm of his other hand. "You look over those cows, too, to see if any of them got hurt last night."

Mundy didn't have his over-shirt on yet, but he sensed that he needed to leave quickly, so he thumbed his suspenders over his shoulders, grabbed his chunk of bread, and fled the cabin. As soon as he shut the door, low hissing erupted, indistinguishable as words, like steam rising from a teapot just before it boiled.

*****

The ground was all muck from the storm, sucking in each step in a mud trail from the house to the barn. Mundy wondered about the road to town, and if they'd be able to get the wagon through some of the roughest parts. Poor Cloppie would have to work hard to pull them, and they'd be heavier on the way home after they loaded salt and cloth and whatever else Brita bartered for cheese.

After he finished milking, he set the milk pans in a stone alcove that stayed cool. He covered the pans with cheese cloth to keep the flies out. The cream would separate from the milk, and then his mother would skim off the cream for the butter churn and add the milk to the week's collection for her next batch of cheese. Then he helped his mother wrap a dozen cheese rounds in thin cloth. She held back two each time so that they would have enough cheese for themselves to last through the winter. She thanked him for his help with a wedge of cheese from the cut round. It was pale, not quite white and not quite yellow, but it smelled and tasted like butter. He ate it all, and she laughed.

"There's a growing boy," she said and rubbed his hair so that it stuck in all directions.

"Ma!" he complained, patting his hair down flat.

"I guess we better go," she said. She took a piece of paper from the table and tucked it into her purple velvet clutch bag with wooden handles, a wedding present from her sister and brother-in-law in Spring Grove. Mundy set the cheese rounds under the buck board so their legs would keep the cheese from bouncing off when they hit holes.

Brita pulled herself up on the board of the wagon and said she'd be happy to let Mundy drive.

"You've got such a way with Cloppie," she said. "She likes you."

"She likes you, too," Mundy assured his mother as if it mattered what the horse thought. "I spend more time with her, I guess."

Mundy didn't have to do much once Cloppie was on the road to town. She knew the way all on her own, so he relaxed his grip on the reins and shifted himself upright. The breeze rustled the oat field in cool, gentle waves. The seed heads were green, but the stalks were starting to brown. Mundy and his father would be out scything soon.

"Your father is a good man," his mother announced. "Or at least he means well. You know he wants to add to the herd, but we can't keep up the way it is, just the three of us, and we can't afford to hire help."

This was his mother saying something important to him. He let her words sink in. He paused, offering, "Maybe we could afford to hire help once we get the new milkers."

"More cows! That's all you two ever think about!" Her hands rose and fell on the fronts of her legs in exasperation. "It's not as simple as buying more cows or even hiring someone and—poof—all your worries are over. You have to pay for the cows, and you have to pay for a farmhand or two. Then you have to feed them all, the help and the cows. And there's a pretty good chance the hands will steal from you—or worse—

not work so hard after the first few days."

From the turn onto the lake path, they could see wisps of smoke tickling the sky with light-gray fingers of smoke from the town's forge, smoldering tree stumps, and cook fires, all reaching up to the golden day, turning substance into air, a sacrifice to the great God of pioneers.

Brita tried again to convince Mundy as if words would win over Mundy to her side.

"It won't work, Mundy. You've got to believe me. Your father won't listen to reason. This crazy plan could be the end of us."

This was the first time he'd heard his mother share her opinion on the matter openly instead of sneaking in stinging barbs at her husband at meals.

"Maybe you could talk to him? He'll listen to it, coming from you."

Mundy didn't believe that. He didn't know enough about anything to make Lars Nelson change his mind.

"But we should try," Mundy countered. "What with the railroad running regular. The town is growing fast."

"You sound like him, but you don't know. Before you came along, even before I met your father, back in Spring Grove, I always thought I would sew and cook, yes, and have a bright little boy..."

"I'm not little."

She ignored him. "...a bright little boy, maybe more. But I also imagined there would be time. Time to visit. To read. To sing. This is what my family did in Spring Grove, together with people like us, but here, there is nothing but toil." She held out her hands, considered them sadly and shook her head. "I used to have pretty fingers. Soft. The kind to set rings upon."

"But that's dawdling!"

"It may be dawdling, but it is wonderful. I miss it. I miss my family."

Mundy felt very uncomfortable with this information—information that his mother should have kept to herself. As far as Mundy was concerned, the Nelsons already were a family. His brow furrowed worrying that they weren't good enough for her.

"I am posting a letter to my sister today, your Aunt Helga."

Brita lapsed into silence, not elaborating on what she had written, and they spoke no more until the cart rounded upon the firmly packed path that was Annandale's main street.

"At least there's no dust, because of the storm," he said.

＊＊＊＊＊

Flat carts rolled down Annandale's main street carrying lumber, the air ringing with hammers driving nails into shingles for the new school or framing milled lumber into walls for the town's second hotel, going up across from the railroad depot. Tethered horses stomped and twitched their tails, impatient and fly ridden.

Mundy eased the cart along in front of the building distinguished by whitewash lettering announcing WELLS FAMILY GENERAL, SAM WELLS PROPRIETOR. He liked Mr. Wells, who was a fair dealer and very kind to Mundy whenever he visited with his mother. He always asked Mundy about the cows as if he were fascinated by them, and then he gave Mundy a butterscotch or a peppermint stick.

Up and down the main street, men exploded through doors in bursts of laughter or curses, their hands full of slats, barrels, tools, and crates, in and out from long carts. Usually, Mundy recognized a few faces in town, but these boisterous, back-slapping men were as new to him as the grain mill, the two-story school, the newspaper office: wooden buildings rising fast, pressing their flat faces against main street and the new rail line.

A massive Friesian stallion tethered in front of the tack shop on the opposite side of the street pulled hard at his tether, big and powerful like a storm. Mundy wondered if he would pull out the post. At sixteen hands tall, the stallion stood over the others around him, with his jet-black coat and a long, glistening mane. "Isn't that Vahva?" Brita asked Mundy, pointing to the stallion.

"Who is Vahva?" Mundy asked.

"The horse! Kauko's—I mean, Mr. Koskinen's horse!" She scanned the street, but for what or for whom, Mundy couldn't tell. "Ah! There he is!"

Mundy couldn't hate any beast strong enough to pull a timber wagon on its own, even if it did belong to their Finnish neighbor, Koskinen. The Finn claimed he earned the stallion from the logging company as part of the wages, but Mundy and his father suspected he stole it.

Kauko Koskinen leaned against a horse tie-up, and Mundy's face crinkled in disgust. He lifted his chin and smiled at them, brushing dust from a sack coat sewn by his dead wife. He propelled his lazy, lanky frame towards them. Like his son Matias, Koskinen's eyebrows were light enough so as to be barely perceptible, but his steel-blue eyes burned hot with a wolf-like will, and they were trained on Brita Nelson.

"Well, hello there! I thought I might find you here."

Koskinen nudged his felt hat upward until its brim pointed skyward, in danger of slipping off the back of his head. He grabbed Cloppie's bridle and guided her forward, even though Mundy was trying to hold her in place.

"Where are you taking us?" Brita asked. Her voice was warm and unconcerned, in spite of the fact that Mundy was still drawing hard on the reins, forcing Cloppie's head back. Brita gripped Mundy's arm without looking at him. "You can let go now, Mundy. Mr. Koskinen has her."

"I thought we could picnic and watch the train pull into the depot," he said, turning to them with the ends of lips tickling a smile. "Have you ever seen the train pull in, Mrs. Nelson?"

"That's very kind, Mr. Koskinen," she laughed. "Isn't that kind, Mundy? But we couldn't possibly. Not today."

"Maybe just a quick snort, then?" Koskinen patted the rear pocket of his pants and removed a brass flask, dinged and well-worn.

"Mr. Koskinen!" Brita Nelson's eyes widened in shock, but her mouth belied her pleasure. "We are not a drinking family. Shame on you!"

"I admire temperance in others," he unscrewed the lid and took a gulp before returning the flask to his back pocket. "A man needs a woman like you to keep him on track. Now that my Hilma is gone, there's only this…" he waved the flask in the air. "And your kindness, of course."

Still seated in the wagon, Brita stretched down her hand to him. He pressed the flask into her grasp, and she sat upright before tipping the flask and letting the whiskey spill to the ground.

Kauko Koskinen grinned. "Now there is only your kindness left."

"Ma!" Exasperated, Mundy slapped down the reins hard against the wagon. "We have to get going!"

"Be polite, Tiddemund," she warned him with her lips pressed in a straight line. "Say good morning to Mr. Koskinen."

Mundy grumbled something that must have passed for good morning, for Koskinen and his mother chatted as if he was no longer there.

Koskinen extended his hand to her and helped her down from the wagon. She swept back the hem of her skirt so it wouldn't get caught on the step. Mundy gathered the cheese and hopped down into the rutted street.

"Mundy, hold that sack open." She pulled out one of the cheese rounds and pressed it into Koskinen's hands.

"No!" Mundy dropped the sack and was about to snatch back the cheese when his mother stopped him from moving forward by putting a hand on his chest. He was almost as tall as she was now, and strong, but it felt like he'd run into a wall.

"I can almost taste it now!" Koskinen sniffed the rind, his eyes rolling to the back of his head in mock ecstasy. "And what did I do to deserve this?"

Brita said nothing but set her hand on Koskinen's sleeve and patted him.

"We must go," she said announced more loudly than she needed to. "Our list is very long today."

"Alright then." Koskinen straightened his hat with one hand. They watched him saunter off a few steps before he turned around and addressed Mundy. "By the way, Matias is looking forward to playing with you again." He winked and then walked off toward the impatient stallion.

Once Koskinen was out of earshot, Mundy barraged his mother with questions right there on the street. How could she give away cheese at all, let alone to that Finn? But she glowered at him by way of answer, and then when she'd had enough, she slapped him across the face.

"You listen! I make the cheese! I cook. I clean. I mend your wounds. If I choose to be generous with our bounty, when we have so much, then that is my concern. And if you so much as mention one word of this to your father, I will tan your hide."

She turned on her heel and marched into Sam Wells' grocery. Mundy was far too old to cry, and yet his mother's sharp, painful rebuke stung hot on his cheek. He lowered his head, hoping no one had seen him being struck by a woman. He tied Cloppie up, taking an extra-long time so he could collect himself. By the time he entered the store, his mother was well into bargaining the price for the cheeses that she had stacked on the counter. Mr. Wells was saying they were very nice, as always, but he couldn't give her as much as usual because she hadn't brought in enough rounds.

"But we need sugar. Six pounds. And a tin of the yeast."

Many of the men in town that day were young, but Mr. Wells was old, maybe fifty, and portly.

"You can have the entire stock, if you have enough cheese to trade or money," he said.

Ever a shrewd bargainer, Brita Nelson feigned interest in a batch of brooms, then in the door. "Well, I'm sure you'll get cheese from some-where just fine. Come on, Mundy. Let's collect these rounds and leave Mr. Wells to his business."

"How about tomatoes?" Mr. Wells leaned forward with his knuckles on the counter next to the cheeses. "Canned tomatoes. Fresh from Cal-ifornia."

"We don't eat those," she declared. "They are poison."

"Sure, sure," Sam Wells looked down, adjusting his apron. "I ate some last night. Maudey ladled them over a piece of chicken, and by God if I didn't eat them all down, but I'll probably die later."

"Mr. Wells, if you want to slowly poison yourself with nightshade, that is your concern. But my family will eat only as the Lord intends, the fruit of our labor."

"That's a head-scratcher right there, Mrs. Nelson. What about the sugar? And the packaged yeast? Those aren't the fruits of your labor."

"Papa wants some cigars, too," Mundy pointed to a big round jar where tall, tightly wrapped cigars stood bundled in groups of six.

"That's right, and six cigars."

"Mrs. Nelson, I am in this business to make a little something for myself and my Maudie and little Pokey, and Johnny, too. Now I don't aim to get rich doing this, but I can't lose money on this cheese deal, either."

"Charge more for each one."

"I'd have to! But then no one wants to pay more for cheese than they have to, not a penny more."

"I have six more cheeses ready at home. You can have those for a little less. I'll send Mundy back with them."

Mundy was shocked. "Ma, those are for the winter!"

"We need supplies now, Tiddemund. Keep quiet."

Soon Sam Wells loaded the sugar, coffee, yeast, cigars, and two shriv-eled oranges into a wooden crate. He set a ten-pound sack of flour over

Mundy's shoulder like a pack mule. Then he counted out coins, some of which Mundy's mother put in her handbag and some of which she kept in her hand. As Mr. Wells offered Mundy a red-and-white striped peppermint stick, Mundy plainly watched his mother slip those other coins into a small leather satchel she wore around her neck, tucked under the bodice of her plain brown dress. The peppermint burned his mouth as it melted, turning his teeth and tongue red, but Mundy didn't even notice. His mother had given away cheese to Koskinen and hidden money. Something was wrong, but Mundy didn't know what it could be. He sure as heck wasn't going to ask her about it and risk getting slapped again.

"Take this letter to the depot and have it posted," she pressed two Indian-head pennies into his palm for postage but only reluctantly released her hold on the envelope. Mundy did as he was told, although he took his time. The depot agent wasn't keen on being bothered during sweeping the platform, and he made Mundy wait. After the swoosh of the broom stopped, fine, gray dust from the mill still floated in the air.

Mundy gave the man his mother's letter and the money. He peered at the address.

"Only sending it to Spring Grove? That's not very far! Why not send it to New York? Or to London? Should we send this letter to London, son?"

"No. My aunt doesn't live in London."

"That's hardly the point, is it? It's a big world! Think big!" The agent looked down at the envelope again. "Ah! You're the Nelson boy, eh? Good thing you came along. Stay here." He disappeared into the depot and emerged with a different envelope, and it was addressed to Mrs. Brita Nelson. "Looks like your mother already received a reply! These trains are getting faster all the time!"

Mundy brought the letter back to his mother at the cart, and she cried when she saw it, pressing it to her chest.

"That is wonderful! Wonderful!" Brita exclaimed. "Let's get going, and I'll read it to you on the way back to the farm."

While he untethered Cloppie, Brita carefully pinched off one corner of the envelope and then used her thumbnail to score a line down the side. She opened the end only enough to remove the letter. Brita began reading aloud even before Mundy was seated, and her voice was fired with the excitement of receiving a message from her sister, Mrs. Helga Ingegaard, of Spring Grove, Minnesota. As she read further, however, her voice registered concern.

Dearest Brita,

O, sister, my heart is full. I might tell you that the weather has been fine and that the children are well, but our circumstances have changed for the worst.

You would not recognize the gentle town that once cradled us in its arms. The people of Spring Grove have turned on us and speak ill of our family. Halvar's congregation is demanding that he stop preaching the truth of the Lord's Word. Among them is Deacon Gronvold, who has doused his soul in liquor for the eternal flames to consume. But my Halvar will not be swayed from his path, even though that path is now uncertain. His path is ours. We now must seek a flock in need of a bold shepherd, unafraid to rebuke those who stray.

The Lord says in the Book of Jeremiah, 'For I know the thoughts that I think toward you, thoughts of peace, and not of evil, to give you prosperity,' and it is the Lord's wisdom upon which we must depend.

How I long for the occasion of our next meeting, sister. I pray that your Tiddemund is well, and perhaps we shall meet him soon.

Your devoted sister,

Helga

Brita pressed the letter to her lap and clicked her tongue.

"Oh, the poor dear! I just wish I could help them!"

"Does Uncle Halvar raise sheep?" Mundy asked.

Brita's face softened into a smile as she explained that the sheep were people.

"It's just the way the Bible talks. The Lord is my shepherd, I shall not want…"

She told him more words from the Bible about how people were sheep, but Mundy thought he wouldn't like to be led around through rivers and valleys, especially when there were cows to be milked.

"What is Spring Grove like? Are there many people?"

"More than here! And Norwegians like us, too."

A spark returned to Brita's voice as she told Mundy about the town, about her family's home, and all the friends she and Helga had made.

Her name was different then—Brita Lund. She told him the funny story of how she met Lars there.

"He nearly knocked me over! He was walking so fast and I was just turning a corner, talking to Helga and not paying attention. But he was so kind and so handsome."

Before Lars convinced Brita Lund to return with him to the Nelson farm two hundred miles to the north where they would find their fortune, Lars was simply a stranger in town. He'd come to Spring Grove seeking a former soldier with whom Lars had been corresponding. Anders Nilsen had fought alongside Lars's brother at the Battle of Missionary Ridge, where Jarl Nelson had been killed.

"You could say that the war brought us together," she added.

Mundy's mother sometimes spoke of returning to Spring Grove, but Lars always reminded her there was no good time to leave the farm, and so Mundy never had met his mother's family.

✳✳✳✳✳

Mundy had just brought Cloppie out into the pasture when his father called, waving a hammer over his head from across the field. It was time to repair a section of fence where the posts sat at new angles and a rail lie snapped in two from the cows' panic during the storm.

"Put your shoulder against that post."

Mundy did as he was told. He could tell from his father's gruff tone it was not a day to ask questions. His father hammered the top of the post with an eight-pound sledgehammer twice and then paused.

"You've got to put more into it, Mundy, if we're going to straighten it!"

Mundy strained his shoulder into the post, his feet beginning to lose ground in the dewy grass. His father struck again and again, the *whoomp, whoomp* of each blow made him flinch. He could feel them reverberating in his chest.

"Push harder!" his father barked. The combined force of the hammer and Mundy's weight couldn't straighten the post. It hadn't moved at all. His father threw the sledge to the ground, panting with exertion.

"You can stop now, Mundy."

His father sat on the ground, defeated, his face in his hands. Mundy sat next to his father. They faced the crooked post. They needed to straighten it before they could replace the old cracked rail.

"You might want to fix that fence!" A man's voice startled them. It was Kauko Koskinen, the Finn neighbor, striding up and judging their progress on the fence to be unsatisfactory. He looked pleased with himself, probably full of their cheese.

Lars Nelson rose to his full height. He retrieved the sledgehammer and let the length of the handle slide in his grip until the head came to rest against his hand. He was shorter than his neighbor by half a head, but he was more powerfully built.

"What do you want, Koskinen?"

"I want what we all want. Enough food for our families and a little silver for our funerals." He sucked on a blade of grass. "The hogs are looking good this year. I could put up a side for you, if you like."

Lars remained silent, but Mundy knew what he was thinking. They had never taken a thing from the Koskinens, and they never would. Unlike Koskinen, Mundy's father never left his family and farm for five months every year—and over the winter, when a man was needed more than ever by his family. Mundy couldn't conceive of a man leaving his wife and children like that during the darkest, coldest days of the year, no matter how much pay he got. It was risky. Too much could happen to the man felling tall trees in the north woods. Too much could happen to the man's family, alone, huddled against banks of snow with dwindling supplies. In fact, when men disappeared from their families, people said they'd gone logging, even if they'd been murdered or had fled to a life of immorality and drink elsewhere.

But this was how it was for the Koskinens. They butchered their hogs each fall before Mr. Koskinen abandoned them to work the high ball logging camps way up north. They called it high ball logging because winter was so cold in northern Minnesota that loggers' testicles shrank bank inside their bodies, or so Lars had told Mundy. Maybe that's what made Matias such a bad seed.

"I have other business with you," Koskinen's voice was like a sawblade, whirring, quick and sharp. "To be plain, I want to buy this plot, here..." With one hand cupped against the sun, he used the other to indicate the land they stood on all the way to the Koskinen property line. "...And there."

His father snorted. "I knew you wanted something. Coming here to talk about hogs!"

"It's a fair deal for the both of us, Mr. Nelson. I think your family has a little too much ground and not enough silver."

Lars tightened his grip on the hammer. "Last I heard that big paycheck of yours from the timber company wasn't even good. What would you even pay me with? Beans?"

Koskinen shrugged.

"It's true, the companies don't back the money until June. That's just their way. They need the time for selling their logs to mills and to the railroads. But look around Nelson. It's past June. I have the money."

"And what would you do with my land?" his father asked, but even Mundy knew the answer. The Koskinen land was mostly swamp and scrub. All the mosquitoes in the county came from the Koskinen farm.

"That's my business," Koskinen's thumb hooked into his pants, very near a leather sheaf that held a bush knife. "Now I have enough money to buy your land, so I won't have to go logging for the winter and freeze my fingers."

"It's not your fingers you should worry about," Lars retorted. "We choose our fates."

"Choose?" Koskinen folded his arms over his chest. "That isn't a very Christian point of view, Nelson."

"Perhaps not, but it is a proven truth."

"Well, let's discuss your atonement from your heathen ways. Help a good Christian brother by selling him your land. I want the easy life of a farmer, like you have."

Mr. Nelson's jaw tightened.

"It's not for sale, and it's definitely not for sale to you, Koskinen."

"Think of what's best for the land." The Finn laughed, a low dry chuckle that showed his uneven front teeth. "I need the land for pasture, and I might fill more of the low parts to get it ready for plowing, something you haven't gotten around to because you don't have enough children to work the land you have."

Lars Nelson's voice pitched high and fast like strangled birdsong. "You will leave my farm right now!"

"There is no need to be impolite in the face of hard truths, Nelson. Perhaps if you spent more time with your very lovely wife and a little less with your cows, you would make the children you need, but for now…"

Mr. Nelson took a step toward him, hammer at his side, ready to strike.

"You don't talk about her."

Koskinen nodded as if agreeing.

"She seems to think you should sell it to me," the Finn said.

Rushing like a wolf at Koskinen, Lars Nelson's eyes burned with hatred, his head lowered, but the Finn danced away, exultant.

"We'll discuss this again and soon." Koskinen's back was to them, but the warm breeze floated his voice like a noxious cloud of coal smoke. "I think we are in for a hard winter."

*****

Mundy arose earlier than usual to be in the barn before being told, and before the sun had even begun painting the horizon. He couldn't sleep anyway, not with the tension between his parents. They weren't speaking to each other, going about their daily chores with their brows furrowed, jaws clenched. Then there was the cheese and the coins. Secrets.

The tension between his parents were black clouds on the horizon before a storm. The storm was coming, and it wasn't something he could change.

If his father was pleased to see Mundy in the barn early, he didn't reveal it. He didn't offer his usual, friendly good morning! before doling out instructions.

"Go get Cloppie ready. We're going to town for some boards and nails."

Mundy stood the hay fork against the stall he'd been mucking, knowing the unspoken word was now. He snatched a short coil of rope from the hook inside the barn door, and he went in search of the old roan mare.

During the warm weather, the Nelsons left Cloppie to her own devices in the pasture. She didn't mind being outside, even when the flies were bad. She wandered under cover during the heat of the day, but otherwise she grazed until they needed her for pulling or riding. That morning, Mundy found her standing in the pasture facing the sunrise, chewing on clover, her jaw mashing side to side.

He called her, and she whinnied but did not turn to face him. She didn't want to be bothered until the sun made it above the horizon. She was older than Mundy by at least ten years, so you'd think she'd know how sunrise would turn out, and he told her so.

"No time for lollygagging today, Cloppie."

She stamped her foot and put her head down for another tug of clover.

"Not today," he cautioned her. "We're going to town again, and that means you, too."

Unlike Mundy, she didn't like going into town. He patted her flank, and she ran a nuzzle against his chest and pushed him away. Her self-determination made Mundy laugh.

"If I have to go, you're definitely going! That's only fair."

He drew a quick loop with the rope and threw it around her neck. She eyed him coldly, disappointed that he would resort to such violence against her, but she turned, ready to face the inevitable, and herself led the way back toward the barn.

His father was waiting with the harness and collar for Cloppie, and then Mundy helped his father turn the small wagon that they would use to haul the supplies.

"What are we getting the boards for?" Mundy asked.

"We're going to patch up the field shed."

Mundy blinked but said nothing. That field shed started the problem between his parents the night of the storm. His mother wouldn't approve of them spending money to repair that rickety heap of splinters, as she called it.

Sensing Mundy's hesitation, Lars arched his eyebrows.

"The Good Book says you should obey your father and mother."

The Good Book was the Bible. Maybe they were Christians after all.

***** *****

The trail was soft from the torrential spring rains, and Cloppie's shoes caught clods of earth in each step along the narrow track that meandered between the woods and the lake. She pulled them slowly. She was tired out, getting old.

Lars sputtered and wiped his mouth when mud struck him in the face. He wiped at it with his fingers but succeeded only in smearing a streak from his lower lip to his chin. Mundy laughed, and then Lars laughed, too.

A branch snapped nearby. Mundy swiveled his head in time to see a blue jay screeching as it arced from the branch of a linden tree to the low boughs of a jack pine. A lone, hulking figure—bigger than any man Mundy ever had seen—stood among the trees. A shadow, but solid. Mundy blinked, and when he looked again, it was gone.

"Pa, I just saw an Indian in the woods!"

Clenching the reins, his father slowed Cloppie and scanned the woods.

"How do you know it was an Indian?"

"He was in the trees, that's all. And I think he was big."

"Not likely to be an Indian around here," his father explained. "They all got pushed out years ago. They know enough not to come back."

"What else could it be, then?"

"Think about it, Mundy. If it wasn't an Indian, what else could it be?"

"A troll?" Mundy almost whispered it, giving himself a chill of fear as he spoke the word.

"That's right." His father nodded. "Could have been a troll. But don't tell your mother."

✳ ✳ ✳ ✳ ✳

Dunton's funeral parlor was a single-story shed made of new wood boards and a bay door that pulled open on runners. As Mundy and Lars walked past the open door, Mundy slowed his gait, straining to see in the dark interior, past the work bench with the unlit oil lamp and a mallet and all sorts of chisels scattered across its surface. He was hoping to see a dead body and, at the same time, hoping not to see one. Living on a farm in the middle of fields and woods, Mundy had seen plenty of animals die, and that was never easy. The year before, Molla, a very friendly milk cow, died giving birth. That had been difficult, and even his father had remained quiet long afterward. But Mundy never had seen a dead person before.

Mr. Dunton appeared from the gloom with his arms full of planks. Mundy looked down when Mr. Dunton wished them a good morning. He was the man who dealt with the dead. He had touched the dead and put them in the wooden caskets he built. He was a carrier of death, and he was just as dangerous as a poisonous snake.

Mr. Dunton smiled like other men. If Mundy didn't know that he was the undertaker, he might think him to be pleasant.

"That big wind the other night sure did some damage on the roof," Mr. Dunton said. "You can't hide shoddy workmanship from the power of nature."

"That is very true. I could help you patch it up," Mr. Nelson offered.

Mr. Dunton laid the boards in a pile and wiped his hands on the back of his black trousers.

"Oh, no, no, no. No need for that."

As Mundy's father exchanged pleasantries with Mr. Dunton, Mundy's eyes found a casket stood up in the corner, and Mr. Dunton noted his interest.

"Would you like to get inside?"

Mundy shook his head and took a step away from the workshop door, causing Mr. Dunton to laugh.

"Don't you worry! You've got plenty of years before you need to see the inside of one of those."

"That's a real nice one," Mr. Nelson offered. "Nicer than most I've seen."

"Well, thank you for saying so. That one is not for sale, but it is my finest work yet! You could say it's a custom piece for a very special client. Me!"

He explained he had built it early so he would be less of a burden on others when he passed on, which meant die, Mundy knew.

"It would be kind of difficult to build a casket for myself after I'm already gone, if you catch my meaning! Well, I can tell you, having that stand where it is gets some of the locals to thinking. Caused more than one of them to pre-order their own caskets, just in case."

He placed a hand on Lars Nelson's shoulder.

"Now don't be troubled when I ask you this..."

"Yes?" The smile froze on Mr. Nelson's face.

"…but have you made arrangements for your passing?"

"No."

"…because you don't want to be a burden to your loved ones, do you?"

"No."

"You know, in their time of grief."

It was Lars Nelson's turn to step away from Mr. Dunton, be tripped on the planks that lay on the floor but righted himself against the bay door.

"Careful!" Mr. Dunton chirped. "Small accidents a big man's corpse can make! Just a little saying we undertakers share."

Lars chuckled. "You are not wrong. I will bear it in mind. Good day, Mr. Dunton."

Mr. Dunton picked up the planks in the half shadow of the undertaker's workshop.

"Don't delay too long, Mr. Nelson! Tomorrow is not promised!"

Lars waved good-bye to him without looking back.

Mundy asked his father if they would buy caskets, and how much it would cost, but Lars explained that caskets were only for people who didn't have their own land.

"You only need a fancy box if you want to get planted in a cemetery with strangers," he explained. "But we have land. We'll go back into the soil, like real farmers."

Mundy wondered about the Nelsons in Norway, generations of farmers and fishermen, and Viking warriors before that. Did burying your kin give you a claim to the land, like planting a flag on a new continent? Maybe someday Mundy would sail to Norway and reclaim the family land like a king retaking the throne.

*****

John Buri ran one of the two hardware stores in town. Although Mr. Nelson didn't care for Buri, he was better stocked than the other one. Buri was a man no older than Lars Nelson, with a tidy beard trimmed to a sharp vee down his neck, but you'd have thought he was much older than thirty judging by the way he had his hands in everything in town.

His eyes peered out at the Nelsons over blue-steeled wire spectacles as he discussed politics with a customer, but he did not pause his conversation to greet them.

"...and that is the extent to which Governor McGill was willing to take it for the session. But, mind you, come autumn, you're going to see movement on the issue in the Senate. I have it on very good authority."

The man speaking with Buri noticed the Nelsons, waiting quietly behind him. His lip curled—it was a subtle sneer, automatic and uncontrolled. Mundy's father nodded to the man, but the man ignored him.

"I'll tell you what I wish your friends in the Senate would attend to is all these foreigners here, taking sections of good land and running it to ruin. They're as dumb as their cattle."

Buri smiled and nodded.

"Well, our families were all once new to this nation at some point. We must be patient and help them as best we can."

The customer, who looked no better or worse than the Nelsons, looked over his shoulder at them with disdain.

"There at least ought to be a law that they bathe once a month."

Mundy's father removed his hat, clenching the brim with both hands.

"Kindly excuse us, gentlemen, for we are counted among those foreigners that you are talking about who have taken some good land outside of town. My brother and I would have split it—he was a foreigner, too—only he died at Missionary Ridge in the war with the Confederacy."

Buri laughed in a low small breath, and the other man stood straight, unwilling to look at the Nelson directly.

"I, for one, have too much to do to be wasting time in here," the man grumbled as he shuffled past Mundy, heading out into the street. "But I expect you'll give me a full account of the legislature's actions next time I'm in town."

"Of course, Mr. Lowry. Good day."

Then, as if no venom had been spat, John Buri beamed at the Nelsons.

"And what can I do for you folks today? Need a new manure fork, do you?"

Lars Nelson said his fork was fine, but they were interested in boards and nails.

"Building a rabbit hutch, I suppose."

Why Buri was playing such a guessing game, Mundy couldn't fathom, and he could see his father was on the verge of telling the man to mind his own business. Instead, Lars told Buri that he wanted 10-foot boards and a half-keg of penny nails.

Buri scrawled some figures on his slate, tallying numbers aloud as he wrote. "…carry the one. There. Do we have any cash today?"

"No, sir. I was hoping we could carry it on account until harvest."

Buri snorted as if Mundy's father proved the point to some argument he had recently made, and he turned his attention to the ledger that lay open on a table, transferring the figures from the slate with the stub of a thick pencil. His gaze fell on Mundy, he said, "And what about you? Looking forward to school?"

Mundy was old enough not to be shy, but something about the man's direct manner made him sheepish. He pretended to look at a pile of plow points.

"Sadly, no. He is not going to a school when there is work to be done. He is my only son."

Buri paused in his writing and looked over the tops of his spectacles at them.

"My parents farm forty acres, you know, over in Albion." He pointed over the depot, over the new hotel. "Not too far from Maple Lake."

"Oh?" Mr. Nelson's eyebrows raised. "I didn't know that."

"Certainly. Of course, they're getting older now. Slowing down."

Mr. Buri exhaled through his nose, staring hard at the ledger, lost in thought.

"I will extend you the credit you need," he said, his face softening in his own benevolence. "Yes, sir, I grew up on the farm, but I went to school. Still helped out on the farm, though. Little one-room shed. Just me and four other children. I ended up teaching the little ones even then! Yes, sir, school is what each child needs."

The thought of school did not interest Mundy in the least, and he almost said that to Mr. Buri, but his father answered.

"Thank you for your concern, but no."

As Mundy's father sorted through a keg of nails looking for the best ones, Mr. Buri looked Mundy over like a hawk on a post sizing up a field mouse.

"You tell that father of yours that we sure could use his help finishing the school. Walls are up, got some windows in. Shingles need some work after that storm. I don't care what language he speaks, just so long as he works. Help offset the cost of the first year of books and teacher's fees. That's a good deal, isn't it, son?" Mr. Buri nodded enthusiastically, trying to get Mundy to ape the gesture, but Mundy blinked at Mr. Buri, not knowing how to answer or if to answer.

"A house divided, Mr. Buri, cannot stand," Lars Nelson stated.

Mr. Buri set down his pen in the fold of the ledger and sat himself upon a stool he kept in front of a rack of sawblades.

"Oh, come now! I'm not asking the boy to fight the Confederacy! There is a new war on now, Mr. Nelson. A war on ignorance." Buri raised his hands pointing in all directions with his upturned palms. "Forty lakes within ten miles from where we stand. You can't farm lakes. People are going to come here to hunt, fish, and recreate to get out of the squalor of their cities, all right on the rail line. That's why I got this shop up so darned fast. Seize the opportunity. This railroad is going open up the world to us." Buri pointed at Mundy. "We need young men like little what's-his-name here to be versatile. Willing to shift course when civic need arises."

"And yet our family needs him on the farm even more. But I do not doubt what you say. I see the potential…"

Mundy knew his father wanted to mention about his plan to increase the dairy herd, but Mr. Buri interrupted him. "Well, Mr. Nelson, I can tell you, the school board, of which I am a member, will be most interested to prove you wrong on that count."

"On a school board too? Aren't you busy enough tending to your store and dabbling in the politics?"

"Oh, come now, Mr. Nelson. As a hard-working immigrant I'm sure you appreciate the fact that men with initiative like us can have several irons in the fire simultaneously!" Buri now copied the numbers from the ledger to a sheet of newsprint he cut from a long roll. "School board member? Guilty. Purveyor of your shingles and plowshares? Guilty. Mayor of this new-born burgh? Also guilty. But I atone for these crimes by helping organize the new Methodist Episcopal church, where, incidentally, immigrants certainly are welcome."

"So busy!" Mundy's father feigned astonishment. "I commend you for all those irons in your fire. I'm sorry to say the boy is needed on the farm so we can settle our accounts."

"Suit yourself. You won't be able to avoid it much longer. And the longer you wait the harder it will be for the boy. Can he even read?"

"Yes, he can read just as well as his mother."

"And you, Mr. Nelson? Can you read, or would you like me to read this lading bill out loud for you?"

Lars Nelson snatched the paper from Buri's hand.

"Let us conclude our transaction so we all can get back to our work. I think we are all very busy."

Mundy helped his father load the wagon with three dozen boards stored under an awning on the side of Mr. Buri's store. Mundy lifted the far end of the stack as his father guided them on the wagon. Some of the boards his father would cut into shingles, Mundy supposed, but the others would replace whole rotting lengths of the field shed that his father wanted to protect—maybe because his own father had built it, or maybe it was Norwegian stubbornness.

With the wagon loaded, his father announced that he'd ordered flour for Mundy's mother, and they needed to go to the train depot. They left the loaded wagon tethered in front of Buri's store and walk over to the train depot. Mundy knew that his mother bought flour at Mr. Wells grocery only the day before.

Mundy looked east and west but did not see a train coming. The next one wouldn't come through for another two hours at 12:05, but he'd heard special trains carrying government dignitaries or federal troops, even, sometimes took over the rail line, heading off to fight Indians or explore new land, or to see all the new towns and depots sprouting along the rail. There was nothing but swamp, field, and woods shimmering around the tracks in the summer heat.

Mundy's father greeted the depot agent, Arthur Stern, and the two men talked like old friends, their heads nodding, easy smiles on their faces, which surprised Mundy who knew his father didn't have friends. In fact, Mundy had never seen his father behave so strangely before: all his teeth exposed to the elements, shaking hands (using both of his hands like a vise), and making jokes! Usually if his father made jokes, they were made for Mundy's benefit, father to son, or at the expense of the neighbor, Koskinen. The agent, however, made no note of anything unusual about his father's friendliness, which proved that the two men didn't know each other very well.

Soon enough, Mundy understood his father's enthusiasm: a new creamery was being built in Buffalo, about twelve miles east, right along the rail. That meant that the Nelsons could sell their milk to the creamery and get top dollar.

"As it is, we sell a small amount here and there," Lars explained to Mr. Stern. "But selling a load of milk on contract, that is the plum. I'll not lie to you, getting our cream to them would be a welcome source of income."

"Why not try the new creamery in French Lake? Much nearer for you."

Mr. Nelson nodded and waved off the tail end of the depot agent's sentence.

"Yes, yes. I tried there, but they told me they weren't taking on any new farmers. I knew what they meant. They weren't taking on any immigrant farmers, which isn't even true. Plenty of Finns on their books."

"Oh dear," the agent stated flatly. "Must the immigrant forever be abused?"

"At any rate," Mr. Nelson looked Mr. Stern directly in the eye. "It's Buffalo for us."

Mr. Stern opened his hands to the sky and shrugged, his eyebrows rising. "Everything comes at a price."

"I imagine it does, but the price needs to be fair."

"Oh, I agree! If I'm to see your butter and cream safely aboard and manage the paperwork, then it indeed needs to be fair."

"I wouldn't have the patience for paperwork," Mr. Nelson agreed.

"I'll do you one better," Mr. Stern replied. "Between you and me, the real money for you will be once the passenger line gets up and running. They'll need food for the dining car in a year or two. That's the contract you want." He smacked Mundy's father on the shoulder. "You'd be drawing your pay from me regular, no waiting."

"Yes!" Mr. Nelson patted Mundy's back. "That's the contract we'd want! We want all the contracts, don't we, Mundy?"

Mundy offered a half-hearted smile, his shoulders sent jostling side to side by his father's playfulness. He didn't say anything to his father. His thoughts had strayed to what his mother had told him on the wagon ride to town the day before.

He is being unrealistic. You know he wants to add to the herd, but we can't keep up the way it is.

Maybe she was right. Mundy certainly wasn't looking for more chores to be added to his day. But maybe she was wrong. Maybe they had to try it to find out.

"Of course," Mr. Stern dipped his chin and spoke in a low voice, confidential-like. "I'd expect a slightly increased finder's fee for that contract, when the time comes."

"Of course!" Mr. Nelson shrugged. "When the time comes."

"Greasing the wheels of commerce, you could say."

"You make the wheels turn and I will apply the grease, eh?"

The two men laughed, but not Mundy. He didn't think his mother was going to find this sort of commerce nearly as amusing as they did, and that was going to be a problem.

Mr. Stern suddenly look startled. He drew his pocket watch from his vest pocket by using his index finger to lift its gold chain. He flicked open the cover with his thumb and two forefingers and squinted at the time.

"I make my first grease now then, yes?" Reaching into the sack, Mundy's father pulled out two cheese wheels—another two meant for the winter supply.

"Oh, my!" Mr. Stern exclaimed as he lifted each cheese to his nose. "Smells like a woman. A beautiful woman!"

"Plenty more where that came from!" Mr. Nelson said, but Mundy knew that wasn't true. Now there were only three left.

Mundy hadn't smelled any woman other than his mother. She had smelled like sweat more than once, and sometimes like bread, but more often than not, she usually smelled like wood smoke. Maybe she was immune, because she made the cheese? But that didn't make sense. When Mundy and his dad spent a day mucking out the barn, they definitely smelled like manure when they came back to the cabin.

Mundy decided he would definitely start sniffing more women when he got the chance.

CHAPTER THREE

FULL STEAM AHEAD

Cloppie strained in the heat with the wagon full of lumber, so Mundy and his father walked alongside her. Lars urged her forward by slapping her flank with the back of his hand and encouraging her in snatches of Norwegian. They were heading north, making their way back to the farm, and Mundy broke the monotony of the creaking wagon and Cloppie's outraged snorts by asking his father questions.

"Why couldn't we take the cream ourselves to Buffalo on the wagon? Then we wouldn't have to pay that man at the depot."

His father shook his head as if to say, you just don't get it.

"First of all, that man at the depot is helping us. He's got inside information for us to better our situation. Second: can't you reckon figures? Twenty miles round trip, three times a week? With the train from here to Buffalo, we need only travel a fifth of that every week. And even that's too much for this sorry old horse of ours."

"So, what happens if Cloppie breaks a leg or gets sick?"

"Well, I suppose we'd need to find another horse. Probably should be thinking about getting a different one before too long anyway."

Mundy thought of the Koskinen's stallion, nearly three times as big as poor Cloppie. The Nelsons sure could use him more than those Finns ever would, but then what would happen to poor Cloppie? She had some life left in her.

"Maybe we could get a big Friesian. Or maybe even a big Belgian?"

"And where would we keep a beast as big as a Belgian?" His father sputtered.

"They can haul tons!" Mundy countered.

"Yes, they can haul tons, but they eat tons! Maybe I should send you to school, to learn math at least."

"You didn't go to school."

"There wasn't a school when I was young, but I learned from your grandfather about math. He was plenty smart with numbers. When you're running a farm, you've got to do the math every day: what do you need to do to improve your position? How much time and toil will it take? Do you need to pay a blacksmith to make a new tool, or beg a neighbor for a fair trade on a cow? How far a haul to market? What price will you get for it at the end? Will that price shift with the wind, and how soon will it pay off?" His voice trailed off leaving only the sound of the wagon creaking and Cloppie's hooves on the path.

Lars capped his hat with one hand to keep it from blowing off when a wind gust came off the lake and caught them broadside, stinging their eyes with dust. Mundy pressed the corners of his eyes until tears moistened away the pain, and just as he blinked his vision back into focus, he noticed, ahead of them on the trail was a lone rider on a big mare, bigger than Cloppie, but not as big as a Belgian. Her coat was golden chestnut, but her mane was long and white.

"Pa!" he pointed to the rider, and his father called out to Cloppie pulling hard on her reins, bringing the wagon to a creaking stop.

"Hello there!" The rider called from his perch. They had never seen the man before. His sunbaked face bore a friendly expression, but Mundy knew you couldn't put much account into appearances. Even a friendly old milker could pin you in a stall and crush you to death.

"Is that a palomino?" Mundy whispered to his father.

"I don't know," his father replied under his breath so the other man couldn't make out what he was saying. "Just let me do the talking."

"I see you're admiring Isabel," the man stroked the horse's man. The horse shook its muzzle side to side making the various clasps and buckles jingle on her harness. "She's a beauty, isn't she? I rented her from the Army down in Omaha. I'm told she comes from Texas stock. Blood from the Spanish royal herd."

"You don't own her?" Lars asked.

"No, in my line of work, traveling like I do, I prefer the railroad where I can find it. But horses like Isabel have seen me right over the years, up and down this wild land of ours."

"And what line of work would that be?"

"Land survey work." He touched the brim of his hat, adding, "The name's Lewis."

Mr. Nelson straightened himself, like a rooster. He handed Cloppie's tether to Mundy and approached Lewis and his rented mare as cautiously as he would a nest of wasps.

"The last time we saw surveyors around here was when the Washburn-Crosby mill people sent them out from Minneapolis in the dead of night like a band of gypsy thieves to sneak in the railroad. Are those scoundrels building a spur line to Clearwater?"

Lewis shook his head. "I wouldn't know about that," he said, straightening his hat by the brim. "Not a railroad man."

Mundy knew exactly why his father asked. A few dozen farmers who lived north of the Annandale rail stop had been more than disappointed when the Washburn Crosby milling company hadn't laid tracks to Clearwater, as expected. It soured the opinion of folks like Lars Nelson. But if there were to be a spur line that ran to the north from Annandale, that would bring the train near the farm, and that meant the Nelsons might have even less ground to cover to deliver their milk to the creamery, and less time traveling meant more time milking. More milking meant more cream, and more cream was the guarantee of the farm's prosperity.

"But you are a land surveyor?" Mr. Nelson asked.

"That's right. Only I work for the Minnesota Geological Society," Lewis brushed the side of his face to spur on a horsefly before it bit him. "I'm traveling the state to record the land as it is now. Historic sites. Points of interest. That sort of thing."

Mundy's father was perplexed. "If you're a surveyor, where is all your equipment?"

"I suppose you mean my Gunther chain, theodolite tripod, and range rods?" The man noted Mr. Nelson's suspicion. "Yes, sir, I am a real-life land surveyor. But smart enough to keep that bulky equipment on the site I'm working on." He climbed down from his horse and patted his coat pockets until he found an object that looked a little like a pocket watch. He held it out for Mundy to examine.

"You know what this is?"

"It's a time piece," Mundy answered sheepishly.

"Look again."

The face, instead of having numbers on it, instead had letters: N, NE, E, SE, S, SW, W, NW, and a load of tick marks separating each letter.

What Mundy had mistaken for an hour hand on a clock was actually a pointer, and it remained steady even as Mr. Lewis turned it.

"That's a magnetic compass, and it's about the only piece of equipment I carry around with me—mostly because I'm afraid of setting it down and losing the damned thing. Pardon my language. But it helps me find my way to and from places, and it is indispensable in survey work."

"You see Mundy," his father began. "The compass always points due north no matter which direction he faces."

"More or less, Mister...?"

"Nelson." The men shook hands. "The name's Nelson, and this is my boy, Tiddemund."

"Well, Tiddemund, your father has got that just about right. Did you know that a lot of people think this here compass points due north, but it actually pulls toward a different place called magnetic north? Look." Mr. Lewis closed his fingers and hid the compass. "I bet you both can point out due north without a second thought, am I right?"

Both Nelsons nodded, and Lars pointed ahead of them on the path.

"Yes, that is north," he affirmed.

"Right you are! And you wouldn't need me or this little contraption to tell you that. Why, you could figure it out any number of ways. On solstice, for example, it's the point exactly in between the sunrise on your right and the sunset on your left. That's true north. But here's the thing. This compass doesn't figure true north. It suggests a different north, called magnetic north. And magnetic north isn't exactly the same in one place as in another. It gets close, but it's not close enough. It's a little different here than it would be, say, in Nova Scotia or in London."

"Or Norway?" Mundy asked.

"Is that where your people come from?"

Mundy nodded.

"Yup. Norway, too. Have to take careful measures of different points. We surveyors use poles, compasses, and Gunther's chains, and we find corners, pick landmarks, sketch maps, and eat a lot of venison jerky that's as tough to chew as a moccasin."

"But you don't work for the railroad?"

"Precisely. I suppose, though, that it's the railroads and farming that are changing the lands most around here. It's timber up north. I'm commissioned to record the ancient structures before they disappear. I've heard that there may be a great many of them in the area."

"What type of structures?"

"What we're looking for are little round hills where there oughtn't to be any hills. Sometimes they're only three or four feet across. Sometimes they're bigger than a barn. Farmers don't like them because who wants to plow a contour when flat ground is easier?"

"*Trollskur*," Mundy almost gasped it out.

"What's that now?" Lewis cocked his head, looking at Mundy almost sideways, like an owl.

"Oh, the boy said *trollskur*. It's Norwegian, from stories about the giants who live under little hills. It's folklore. I tell him many stories, and his mother doesn't like it."

"In Norway, too, eh?" Lewis pondered a stand of pines. "Well, sir, I don't know anything about these trotskers or whatever you called them, but I do believe them to be Indian mounds."

"Mounds?" Mundy asked, thinking of their own troll mound in the woods. If it had been there a long time, maybe the Indians had known about the trolls. Maybe they fought wars against each other, tribes of natives, their faces streaked red with warpaint, firing flint-tipped arrows at the giant trolls who swung trees like wooden clubs. Or maybe, like his father claimed, the trolls had come later, following the Norwegians to America, to keep them humble.

"That's right. Small hills," Lewis explained. "Some people call them barrows. Like the kind prairie dogs make, only bigger. I've seen some as big as that new town."

"Ah!" A glint of recognition passed over Lars Nelson's face. "So, you're looking for buried treasure!"

"No, I am no digger!" Lewis laughed. "I'm doing what they call an archaeological survey of the region. My only interest is to record the locations and dimensions of all these structures. Then, farmers and railroad men can do as they wish. Maybe you could help. I came an awful long way to track down a man over in French Lake who died before I could get here. I thought I'd check around before I move on. Do you know of any of these mounds in the area?"

"Mounds?" Lars was quick to reply. "No, we don't know of any of these mounds."

That was the first time Mundy had ever heard his father tell a lie.

45

"Now I've also heard there might be some on a farm nearby—"

"Nowhere around here," Lars interrupted.

"Apparently, they're just about the only Norwegians out this side of the railroad, other than yourselves, I guess." He stared down at Mundy. "Know of any other nice Norwegian families around these parts, Tiddemund?"

Mundy shook his head, and that was true. Mostly there were Dutch, Germans, and Swedes north of town. And then those rotten-apple Koskinens.

"Maybe I could ride with you a-ways and talk to some of your neighbors. Someone around here has got to know where those other Norwegians live."

"You wouldn't want the trouble. We live past Clearwater, and we best be on our way now."

"With that nag? Well, that's just cruel, if you ask me." He nosed his horse north. "I reckon I'll ride with you a-ways, just the same."

Lars found himself trapped. He looked to the lake as if the answer would float across to them on the sun-tipped waves that made the lily pads dance.

"You say you're looking for those little hills?"

"That's right. Mounds."

"Now that I think of it, there is a little group of them. Maybe a half dozen. Right along the north shore of the big lake."

Mr. Lewis swung a leg over his saddle and jumped down, unstrapped a worn leather saddle and removed something that, once unfolded, Mundy recognized as a map, creased and torn.

"The big lake?" Lewis held the map up to them, his finger on an oval drawn in black ink surrounded by broken lines labeled with numbers. "You mean this one? Clearwater?"

"Yes, that's the one. Just up the trail here. Then follow the shore…" Mundy's father leaned forward and tapped a point on the map. "To there."

"Do you know who owns that land?"

"Certainly. Christien Olsen."

"Do you know Christien Olsen?"

"Of course."

"Perhaps you could introduce me to him?" He patted the map with the back of his hand before refolding it and returning to his pack. "Seems like a lot of folks around here aren't partial to strangers."

"That's true. We like to keep to our own business."

"Well, it's not that far out of your way, judging by the map."

"Any other day, Mr. Lewis." Mundy's father turned to his son. "Oh, Mundy! Didn't I tell you we needed to pick up that flour for your mother! Oh, I apologize, Mr. Lewis. My stupid son here neglected to get the flour like I told him to! We need to return to town."

"You must hate that poor nag! But your business is your own." He pulled himself back onto his horse and he and his horse turned their noses north. "I thank you for the guidance, just the same." Lewis bid them a good afternoon and rode off.

Lars scratched Cloppie's snout as they waited until Lewis was well ahead before they cajoled Cloppie forward.

"Why did you lie to him about the mound?" Mundy asked.

"It's not for strangers to know about."

"And was it true?" Mundy asked. "About the little hills on the lake?"

His father nodded.

"Are they troll mounds, like ours?"

His father shrugged.

"How many cheeses did your mother sell in town?"

"Six, I think," Mundy replied. He didn't mention the cheese Brita gave to Koskinen.

Lars nodded.

"You will need to ride back to town with whatever cheese is left. Deliver it to the Mr. Stern at the depot. Tell him it's a little grease for the wheels. Tie Cloppie up near the new church and walk to the depot. Don't draw attention to yourself."

✳ ✳ ✳ ✳ ✳

Within ten minutes of his arrival, Mundy became the talk of the town.

He walked up the main street toward the depot when John Buri stepped out to dump a spittoon. He wore a leather apron over his clothes, a long-sleeved white cotton shirt done up to the neck with a black bow tie bobbing below John Buri's dark beard, all of which looked too hot.

"Came back to sign up for school, eh, boy?"

"No sir."

"Come on in. It won't hurt to add you to the student roster now. That way, after harvest, you'll have a seat waiting for you, just in case your father changes his mind."

"No thank you, sir! I have to get going."

"Boy, I didn't ask you. I'm telling you to come in."

John Buri clapped a meaty hand on his shoulder, the other swinging the brass spittoon. Mundy froze right where he stood unsure of what to do next, but Buri yanked Mundy into the store. The smell of sawdust and grease in the hot air made him dizzy. Buri's hand slid off Mundy's shoulder, down to his torso, so that he was snugly drawn next to the leather apron. They navigated past wooden crates full of horseshoes and nails and pulleys and tackle blocks, past a pile of rope, past empty window frames that jutted into their path and beyond that, uncut sheets of glass. Mundy could see oil marks on the apron and yellow-white chips of wood like little teeth.

"Now let's get you signed up."

He shoved Mundy toward a desk piled high with ledgers and loose bills of lading.

As Buri slid his chair out, about to sit down, Mundy swiped a handful of upholstery tacks from a nearby barrel and scattered them on the seat just before Buri's behind made contact with the chair. Buri spun like a dog after its tail, pulling tacks from his backside and howling in pain.

Mundy dashed outside and nearly bowled over several onlookers straining to see what caused the commotion inside the hardware store. Buri yelled for them to catch that boy, but Mundy dodged the feeble efforts of Mr. Dunton, the undertaker with his own casket on display, who looked more bemused than intent on foiling Mundy's escape.

"Run, boy!" Mr. Dunton shouted after Mundy had passed. "It's after you!"

And Mundy did keep running, the cheese sack banging against his leg. He was breathing so hard he thought his heart would explode. He could see the depot even as he drank in deep draws of breath. Behind him, John Buri vented his anger at the undertaker for not catching Mundy. Gasping for air, Mundy walked the rest of the way to the depot. He found Mr. Stern in the depot office, making notes in a book as big as the table it sat on.

"Hello, there! Did you get lost?"

Mundy hand Mr. Stern the sack containing all of the Nelsons' remaining cheese. "My father says it's grease for the wheels."

Mr. Stern a accepted the cheese with a wink, ruffled Mundy's hair.

"You tell your father it's full steam ahead!"

The agent dropped the sack to the floor and went back to his book.

Mundy took one last look at the cheese lying on the floor, wondering if he could be hanged for tacking the mayor's behind.

✳✳✳✳✳

By the time Mundy made it back to the farm, his legs quivered from exertion, and he bet Cloppie was feeling the same way. He looked for his father in the barn and then in the pasture beyond, finally spotting his father at the field shed, already sorting the new materials for the repair project. When his father noticed him, he set down a plank on the sawhorse, and came marching toward Mundy.

"How'd it go?" his father called.

"Full steam ahead," Mundy answered.

"Good, good. Let's keep that our little secret from your mother. I don't want to trouble her just yet."

"Yes, pa," Mundy agreed, but there would be no way to keep the missing cheeses a secret for long. His mother knew how many cheeses were supposed to be on the shelves.

For the remainder of the afternoon, no boy was as hardworking and helpful as Mundy. He even volunteered to muck out the barn, a chore his father usually had to threaten him with a belting before he'd even consider it, but today Mundy didn't mind it. It helped him to keep from fretting about events in town, only he hoped his father wouldn't get the wrong idea and expect Mundy to volunteer every time.

Hours passed, and Mundy's occupation had brought him out to the yard where he notched timber for fence stiles until his shoulders were sore. The afternoon heat broke as the sun beat a path towards the horizon. A fleet of thin clouds tinted violet and pink lingered in the late afternoon. His mother rang the dinner bell, the one forged in Norway by her great grandfather, and the smell of chicken roasting filled Mundy's nostrils. He reckoned he could eat the whole bird himself.

After supper, Mundy crawled into the loft even though it was light outside. He could hear his mother and father talking, watching the sunset from the upended logs they used for stools. They spoke to one another quietly, but angrily. Even as Mundy started to doze off, the cabin door creaked open, and his father kicked off his boots at the door.

His father pulled himself up the ladder and into Mundy's loft.

"Are you awake?" The sloping roof forced his father to sit crooked.

"Where's mother?" Mundy asked.

"Not to worry. She's picking slugs from the potatoes. It's full moon and those slugs are having a parade. I need you to promise me not to tell her about today."

"About the cheese?"

"Yes, the cheese, but also about our arrangement with the depot agent." His father held out his hand. "Deal?"

"Yes. Deal." They shook on it in silence, then Mundy asked, "What about the land surveyor? Is that a secret?" It was hard to know what was meant to be spoken about and was meant to be bottled up.

"Nah! That was nothing!" Mussing Mundy's hair, his father disappeared down the ladder. "Don't let the trolls get you in your dreams!"

$$* * * * *$$

The sound of men talking and the neighing of a horse out in the yard interrupted afternoon milking.

"Mundy!" Lars hissed. "Peek through the slats! Who's out there?"

"It's the land surveyor from yesterday," Mundy announced. "He's with Koskinen."

Lars rose slowly from the little single-legged milking stool, wiping his hands on the front of his bibs as he pushed through the barn door.

In the drive, Koskinen stood next to Lewis looking like he'd won first prize for smiling.

"Good afternoon, neighbor!"

Lars shot Koskinen a warning glance, but he nodded to Lewis.

"Good day, Mr. Lewis," he said. "What do you want, Koskinen? "

"There seems to be some confusion," Koskinen said. "This man thought there weren't any of those funny little hills around here. He thought there might be a different Norwegian family in the area. That's strange, isn't it?" Koskinen chuckled. "Well, I told him straightaway that there was only one Norwegian farm north of town, so here we are! Is the missus around?"

Mundy's father took a step forward, and Lewis, sensing trouble, stepped between the men.

"Good afternoon, Mr. Nelson," he extended his hand and, as if by habit, Mundy's father shook it. "I'm sorry to impose on you like this."

Lars Nelson dropped his chin, his eyes averting Lewis. "I'm sorry you troubled yourself to come all the way out here, and I am sorry for…being cautious yesterday."

Lewis' eyes gleamed. "Not at all. I certainly don't blame you for, uh, being cautious, so please, let's not have any discomfort between us. Why, I once met a man who pretended to be his own wife just to get out of paying me for a boundary map that I'd drawn for him! Kept saying he couldn't open the door because he was in his unmentionables. Then his wife turned up on my side of the door with a basket full of chicken eggs and gave him what-for. They didn't have any money, but I did get the eggs and this story, so it was well worth it!"

Lewis ran his hand along Isabel the palomino's flank and unfastened the steel square buckle on a saddle bag. He motioned for Mundy.

"Put out your hand."

Mundy looked at his father, and, not seeing any prohibition in his expression, slowly extended his hand. Lewis dropped a stone Indian arrowhead, cool and smooth, in his hand.

"That came from the lake shore site you told me about yesterday," Lewis explained. "On that account, I am grateful. You didn't steer me wrong. You may have obfuscated a little bit about your own circumstance, but you didn't fib about those mounds. There are at least six, even a big one. Must be where the chief is buried. That's where I found that arrowhead, and I thought the boy might like it."

Mundy turned the arrowhead over in his hands. It was as long as his little finger, a triangle with a stem on the wide end, with jagged edges that led to the point.

"Was it buried in a mound?" Mundy asked.

"No, I found that with just a little boot-scraping in the topsoil. So, it's not so old. The deeper in the ground, the older, usually. By my reckoning, that one's only fifty, maybe a hundred years old."

Only a hundred years! A hundred years before, his family had been in Norway. There were no white loggers and farmers in the area, only Indians and maybe a French voyageur hefting a pack full of pelts on his back. Mundy slid his finger against the edge, wondering if it had killed a bear or flown in the wars between the Sioux and the Chippewa.

"Tiddemund, give it back to Mr. Lewis," his father ordered.

"I'm happy to let him keep it," Lewis began, "There will be plenty there. And maybe even more interesting items."

"Like what?" Mundy asked, but Mundy's father interrupted him.

"That's very kind, I'm sure, Mr. Lewis, but the boy has no need for the relics of savages."

Mundy ran his finger over it one more time, clasped it briefly, feeling the arrowhead press into the soft flesh of his palm. Then, heeding his father, he returned it to Lewis, who cocked his head, his eyebrows knitting in thought.

"I hope I haven't given the impression I am a treasure hunter or common grave robber, Mr. Nelson." Lewis placed the arrowhead in his shoulder case. "Far from it: I am no digger."

"I see," Mr. Nelson replied.

"No, sir. Slows a fellow down, digging holes and hauling chunks of rocks around. That's for others. I only measure and map the mounds before they all disappear."

Mr. Nelson shrugged, prompting Lewis to continue.

"And that brings me to my purpose. My assistant, if he sobers up, will arrive in the area tomorrow or the next day, which is why I'm anxious to come to terms with you on the matter of your site. As it happens, we are making our way south before the winter. When we have finished at the lakeshore site, I would appreciate the chance to record the features of your site, if it is indeed an ancient native site, as Mr. Koskinen asserts."

"I'm certain of it," Koskinen averred, his voice slow and brimming with vindication.

"You keep out of it," Mr. Nelson growled.

"If I could just take a look around…" Lewis took a step forward, but Mundy's father put a hand on the surveyor's chest. Their eyes locked.

"I could point you to it," Koskinen said, beginning to raise his arm. "I've seen it myself back in the woods."

"Any finger you point I will personally cut off," Lars retorted. "Leave now. And if I ever see you on my property, I'll send a warning shot past your head, but I have terrible aim."

Lewis stepped back. "I'm not here to rob you or cause you any grief, Mr. Nelson. Far from it. In fact, I can help you level off a piece of land and even pay you for the time. We are cataloging the artifacts we find in these barrows before they all disappear to the plow for good."

"No."

"Let me at least tell you the terms."

"No!"

"Isn't that little hill on the parcel you're going to sell to me? Let me buy it from you, and then I will deal with this man," Koskinen smirked, and not knowing when to stop, as Finns were known for, he added, "I'm sure Brita would like to finally get that new spinning wheel."

It was shocking to hear Koskinen use his mother's first name. Lars grabbed the Finn by the collar. Koskinen's eyes glistened even as Lars shoved him against a tree.

"You have abused her good nature, Koskinen!"

"She's a grown woman, Nelson! She knows her own mind."

Lars punched Koskinen in the jaw. Koskinen sprang back and pushed up his sleeves. He threw a wild haymaker that caught Mundy's father on the side of the head. Lewis stepped between the neighbors and gripped them both by their shirts.

"I feel like I've stirred a hornet nest! Neither of you is under any obligation to me or to the State of Minnesota. I'll take my offer and go quietly, Mr. Nelson, but I should warn you: there will be other men who will come. Their interests differ from mine, and they won't leave, and they won't take no for an answer. It might not be this year, but they will come. You have very talkative folks all along the rail line, and they seem to know about this place. Every nook and cranny. No matter how much you'd like to keep it secret."

Mundy's father waved off the suggestion. "I don't have time for this. Follow that bastard off my property and both of you can go dig up all the holes you care to on his damned land."

"You tore my shirt!" Koskinen was outraged, holding out his arm to show them the frayed thread and the gap between his cuff and the sleeve. Then a cruel smile crossed his face. "But I'm sure I can get your missus to mend it!"

Lars started after him, a burning rage in his eyes as Mr. Lewis hurried Koskinen away, but Koskinen kept the arm with the torn sleeve over his head, his fist clenched, as if he were holding a flag.

✳✳✳✳✳

The next afternoon, the Nelsons had another unexpected visit when Mr. Dunton, the undertaker, appeared in the yard on his sulky. He caught sight of Mundy and waved him over.

"Is your father nearby?"

"I'm not sure," Mundy, who wasn't used to being guarded with the truth, felt a redness flushing his cheeks. "I think he went to town."

"Is that right? I suppose he walked there?" Mr. Dunton pointed to the pasture. "I can see your old nag from here. Maybe he hitched a ride with his neighbor? I hear they're very close friends!"

"Yes, sir, that's it." Mundy agreed. "He hitched a ride."

Mr. Dunton backhanded Mundy across the jaw, not hard enough to loosen teeth, but enough to snap his chin to one side and make him realize that lying wouldn't pass muster with Mr. Dunton.

"Young man, you are in a heap of trouble with Mr. Buri. Go fetch your, father."

Mundy held back the tears. His breath came shallow, afraid of his father's anger. Lars appeared from the cabin with breadcrumbs in his beard. His cheeks turned ashen when he saw Mr. Dunton, and his chewing slowed.

"Who has died?"

"No, nothing as dire as that, thank the Lord," the undertaker laughed. "Serious, but not fatal. I'm on town business, as an intermediary. If you'll just give me a few minutes of your time." He glanced at Mundy, adding,

"Alone, I think, would be best."

His father nodded for Mundy to leave, and Mundy decided he'd look for his mother in the garden and see if she needed help, but he hadn't crossed more than half the distance from the yard when he heard his father calling for him to come back, and his voice was angry.

There was nothing to do but face it and have it done with. He returned to the yard in time to see Mr. Dunton riding off on the sulky, looking back with a satisfied, mirthful expression. He touched the brim of his hat when he caught Mundy looking.

"I sent you into town on an errand, not to stir up trouble!"

"Yes, sir."

"Do you know how angry Mr. Buri is? I guess you thought it was a good thing to do, trying to upholster him yesterday. And do you know what else?"

Mundy shook his head. He couldn't look at his father directly. It was like staring at the sun. Too hot, too bright.

"He is angry not only at you, but also at me. Me! Because you are my son. And now you have sealed your own fate with your crooked little adventure. Now I need to pay the town and their school for your education, or I will be arrested for what you did."

"Just say no!" Mundy could see how easy it would be to ignore the problem. The town was far enough away, maybe people there would just forget about the Nelsons and their farm.

"It's not as simple as that, Mundy."

"But I don't want to go to school, and you don't want me to go, either!"

"Look, Mundy, I am not free if I am forced to do something, am I?"

"But they wouldn't arrest you. Not for something I did."

"Probably not," his father conceded. "But there are other considerations, even if it is just to keep people in town friendly to us. If we lose those connections, suddenly my account is no good, and we can't get supplies. Maybe the depot won't let us load milk for the creamery. Maybe we sit right here and starve like Indians."

"But I want to help on the farm!"

"You should have thought of that yesterday. Now I not only lose cash, I lose you to school for part of the workday."

Mundy's eyes blurred so that he could see only the light blue of his father's shirt, the color of the noon summer sky. His father drew Mundy to his chest and held him, Mundy's tears dampening his father's shirt and soaking the breadcrumbs caught in the folds of the cloth.

"I thought we were free people, pa."

Lars exhaled and looked off into the distance.

"There are moments when we stand alone in the woods or in the field, with no other person around for miles—that is the moment we are free."

"Like an outlaw?"

"Yes, like an outlaw. You are my little outlaw, aren't you?"

Mundy smiled and nodded, wiping his nose with his sleeve.

"But you got caught!"

Brita appeared in the drive. She was holding Koskinen's shirt in front of her, considering the tear. She slowed when she noticed them, but she said nothing and passed them.

Mundy and his father watched her shut the door to the cabin.

"I'm sorry to say, Mundy," Lars sighed. "The only true freedom for a man is death."

CHAPTER FOUR

FREEDOM

The field shed wasn't worth saving. Its shingles scattered across the field, the roof sagged like an old swayback cow, and the gaps between wall planks wouldn't keep out a raccoon.

The little building creaked as it rocked side-to-side in a breeze that fluttered the front of Mundy's shirt. Another strong storm could topple it into a pile of kindling. He couldn't understand why they would bother to put any amount of effort toward repairing it, but they were. They dressed shingles with the adze, bundling them into groups of twelve with baling twine. They left a loop on each tie-off as a handle. Lars tested a ladder he'd fashioned from fallen branches for the two rails, and the rungs, yellow and sticky, from the milled lumber they had purchased from town. Satisfied that it would hold, Lars climbed it and soon was crouching on the roof.

"Hand me the hook-pole," he directed.

Mundy hoisted a long, smooth pole with an iron hook on one end, and his father grabbed it, rotating it so the hook end dipped beneath the field shed's eaves. He hooked the first bundle by the loop and lifted the shingles by raising the pole, hand over hand, until the bundle rested next to him on the roof. Likewise, his father lifted a pail of nails by its rope handle.

"Good, now bring the hammer and come up here."

Mundy tucked the hammer, which had come with his grandfather from Norway, in the waist of his trousers and climbed the ladder. It was the hammer that built the field shed to begin with, and the roof of the cabin, and the barn. It wasn't their only hammer, but it was his father's favorite.

"Why are we fixing the shed, pa?" Mundy asked. "We hardly use ever it." It seemed a reasonable question, but his father, with a half-dozen iron nails wedged in one side of his mouth, shook his head. He took one of the nails from his lip and drove it through the shingle in three blows. The wood beneath was soft from dry rot.

Lars finished nailing a line of shingles until no more nails dangled from his lips.

"My brother and me helped my father build this rickety old building, Mundy. We had to clear woods first. I know you work hard, but you haven't had to clear woods. And then there was the little hill right where the shed is now."

"You mean like a *trollskur*?"

His father drove another nail. "Twice as tall as you, had maples and the elms growing out of it, and my father wanted the land flat for pasture. We busted our backs and with a team and a shaver plow we borrowed from the Olsens, we finally leveled that little hill, and then we built this shed right on top of the spot."

"Did you find anything, like arrowheads or anything?"

Hammering was the only response. The first shingles were in place, and his father hooked another bundle, drawing it up to the roof, but the rope caught. Mundy scurried up the ladder, prying the rope free so that his father could pull the shingles up.

"The way you climb," His father shook his head. "I'd swear you're part squirrel!"

"Why won't you tell me about the trolls, pa?"

"You're here to work, not listen to my foolish tales. Your mother would be angry that I even mentioned the little hill, let alone what we found in it! Now hand me those nails sitting there behind you."

"Just one question. Please, pa!"

Lars laughed.

"Just hand me those nails!" His fingers wiggled impatiently. "Then maybe I'll answer one of your questions, but just one."

Mundy's thoughts raced as he handed another round of nails to his father. He had so many questions about trolls and treasures, it would be difficult to choose just the right one.

"Have you ever seen a troll?"

Lars smiled. "No. Not exactly."

"But you told me once that you saw a troll!"

"Did I?" His father crouched down to straighten another row of shingles.

"Yes, you did!" Mundy could barely contain his curiosity. "So? Where did you see him?"

"I saw him right here!" his father growled playfully, throwing his arms over his head as he broke from his crouch to scare Mundy, and it did. Startled, he tried to find his footing, but his body was out of balance. Mundy felt himself falling backwards over the edge of the roof.

Lars's smile change to a widening expression of horror, and then all Mundy could see was blue sky. Mundy's father reached a hand in time to grab the front of his shirt and part of Mundy's belly, and he yanked him away from the edge. Mundy was safe, but just barely. He dropped low on the roof so he wouldn't stumble a second time.

"That was close!" Lars panted. "I thought you—" His words were lost in the sound of cracking wood. In an instant, Lars's legs disappeared through the rotted slats. He cursed in Norwegian as he strained to lift himself back to the roof. He rolled onto his side, wincing, and gripping his leg where the cloth on his pants was torn. A little pool of blood seeped between his finger. His calf muscle had been gashed by a nail in the fall.

"Are you alright?" Mundy asked.

"Yes, yes." His father let out a long breath, his eyes closed tight. "Are you alright?"

It was all so foolish: the dull point of a rusty hand-forged spike, his father's unsure footing on the roof, and that rickety old pile of bleached basswood that somehow had withstood almost forty winters thanks to Norwegian stubbornness.

"Yes, pa, I'm fine." Mundy didn't know what to do. "Should I get ma?"

"No, no. I'm alright, Mundy." He clasped both hands over the wound and grimaced. "Everything is going to be just fine."

But everything wasn't fine, and his father was not alright. These were words that proud people said to mask their own fear. There was a secret now in Lars Nelson's blood—a very small secret—that entered his body through the jagged cut where iron and wood had broken the skin.

Lars climbed down the ladder and leaned on Mundy for support as they limped to the cabin. There, Brita cleaned the gash on his leg and pressed the feathery leaves of yarrow against it.

"The *ryllik* will stop the blood," she said.

"I think you are a *heks* with your herbs," Lars quipped.

She scolded him. "Don't even joke about that!"

The bleeding did stop, but a match was lit, and its tiny spark spread flame through Lars Nelson's blood.

The first sign that Lars was unwell came that evening. They were seated on the log benches outside, swatting mosquitoes in the humid evening air, when Lars cried out and gripped a cramp in his leg just above the knee. He dropped to the ground writing, but he waved them off.

He was breathing hard through clenched teeth.

"I better wash your wound again," Brita decided. She told Mundy to fetch a basin with water.

"I'm fine! Just let me just lie here a moment."

After unraveling the cloth, Brita poured water on his calf as gently as she could, but he howled in pain and crawled away from her.

"That water is boiling hot!" he declared, but Mundy had just brought it straight from trough, and it was no warmer than the air around them.

Within two hours, Lars was shivering uncontrollably.

"I've never seen anything like," he murmured. "Winter has come in July." it

* * * * *

The next morning, his parents' bed creaked as his father tried to stand, but his father roared in pain and collapsed, rigid. Mundy's mother lifted herself on her elbows over him and called for Mundy to bring a cup of water.

Several minutes later, as the pain subsided, his father again tried to raise himself, in spite of his wife's warnings.

"You'll just make it worse, Lars! Stay in bed!"

"There's too much to do."

Brita was able to press him back into the bed, and he was too weak to resist.

"Mundy can help do the chores today. I'll help, too." She pulled up the leg of his night pants and lowered her head to his father's wound, sniffing. Her head shot back, and her face contorted in disgust.

"What are you doing, Missus?"

The color had drained from her face.

"Get going, Mundy."

Then Mundy began the morning milking, but he was distracted by his father's distress. He spilled more than he should have. It was man's work, and he was doing it all alone.

He was one step closer to something, he just didn't know what it was.

✳✳✳✳✳

In the afternoon, Mundy returned the herd from the pond and closed them in the pasture for the evening. He returned to the cabin, curious to see if his father was up and about.

Brita sat on the log bench under the porch awning. Strands of hair had loosened from the plaits trailing over his mother's shoulders so that her forehead and eyes were hidden. She shelled brown beans into the front of her dress between her knees, catching the smooth tan beans that were destined for winter baking and to sow next year's crop. They were seed for early harvests that his grandfather brought from Norway. When simmered, they made a creamy sauce, which was just about the only food he looked forward to in winter.

Mundy could see only the worry lines of her mouth. She was talking to herself as she cracked open each pod but then froze when she realized Mundy was near. She slowly rose, clutching the front of her dress to keep the beans steady. She angled herself over the big Indian willow basket Lars had gotten her from town one Christmas, and she let the beans drop inside.

"What are you doing?" she asked.

"I came to see how pa is."

She nodded to a pile of discarded pods. "If you want to do something useful for him, throw those shells in the fire. We're letting him sweat out his sickness."

Mundy gathered the dry pods and pushed the door open. Sweltering hot air flooded from the cabin, and he could hear the crackle of wood burning in the stove. Lars was in bed, tangled in sheets. His bare chest glistened with sweat, and the mattress cover was soaked in a dark ring. He told Mundy to give him water.

"I think your mother is trying to kill me," his father's voice came in shallow, raspy breaths.

"We're going to sweat the sickness out of you, pa."

He shook his head. "It's in my blood. It's too late."

Mundy dipped a tin cup into the water pail he'd brought in, and he leaned over his father, guiding the cup toward his father's trembling lips.

"Have some water."

His father turned from the cup.

"Did she give this to you?"

"No, pa. I poured it myself." He used his hand to steady himself on the bed. It was damp, and when he pulled it back, he realized the moisture came from—not sweat—but from blood, the poison blood that oozed from his father's dressings.

"Ma!" Mundy yelled. "Ma!"

Lars gripped Mundy's arm. "No matter what happens, I don't what you to go spreading any rumors about anything, do you understand?"

Mundy did not understand, but he was supposed to, so he nodded anyway.

"I'll tell you what your grandfather told me. We were the first Norwegians here and we don't want to be the last."

"Just rest, pa. I'll find her. Everything is going to be fine. Then she'll fix your dressing..." but his father's grip tightened on Mundy's arm hard enough to leave bruises.

"Just listen!" His father's eyes were wild and distant. Sweat dripped from his forehead. "We built everything here. From nothing! We flattened that little hill, like I told you. Flattened it with a team and a scraper." He signaled frantically for Mundy to give him another sip from the cup.

"Remember when we thought we were finished, and Jarl said what's that?" Mundy didn't respond, confused. Jarl was the name of Lars Nelson's brother, the one who had died long ago in the war with the Confederacy.

"...He said what's that? Poking through like gleaming daffodils. Those skulls, the top of them. We dug at them like badgers. And then father...Caught us...He was angry. Twice the size of a normal man! And do you remember the teeth? The teeth. You said you could eat a tree with jaws so big."

"Were they troll skulls?"

"Eat a whole tree with those teeth. Even father was scared."

Gasping in pain, his father's his eyes widened.

"I've been waiting for Jarl," he said, the fever having weakened his voice to a wheezing whisper.

"Pa!" Mundy yelled.

His father's mouth trembled, and his head rolled to one side. "Now we dig them." He gripped Mundy's arm weakly, but his cloudy eyes bulged at Mundy. "And all that gold and teeth, just waiting in the ground!"

Mundy's father lapsed into incoherent mumbling and then fell asleep. Mundy pulled his arm free and went outside to tell his mother about the bleeding, but she was gone. Not in the barn. Not in the orchard. She must have gone to check on the Koskinens.

✳✳✳✳✳

In spite of Cloppie's resistance, Mundy got a saddle on her and made her trot into town. Remembering the recent run-ins with Mr. Buri and Mr. Dunton, Mundy kept to the edges of town instead of traveling down main street where the young Dr. Ridgway lived in a two-story clapboard house that the town had built for him.

He knocked on the door, and Dr. Ridgway himself answered, still chewing his supper. All the doctors Mundy had ever heard of were old men with thick white beards, but Dr. Ridgway was younger. He was in his mid-twenties with gleaming black hair, straight, combed back to reveal a widow's peak. Gold wire-rimmed glasses peeked from the pocket of his gray vest, which was unbuttoned.

Mundy explained the situation, imagining that the doctor would dash for his leather kit at the news and insist they rush back to the Nelson farm. Instead, he told Mundy to wait for him in the yard.

"If he's going to die anyway, he won't mind if I finish my dinner," he said, closing the door on Mundy. Ten minutes passed. Just as the sun dipped below the horizon, the doctor reappeared carrying a leather bag big enough to hold a goose.

Mundy helped him onto a big chestnut steed, another gift from the town. Seeing as the doctor had never had cause to visit the Nelson farm before, Mundy led the way, warning the doctor of low branches on the trail that cloaked themselves in the purple twilight.

When they dismounted at the farm, Mundy's mother leaned against the corner of the cabin, watching them.

"Who's that?" she asked righting herself.

"It's the doctor," Mundy said.

Dr. Ridgway introduced himself, and she scolded Mundy.

"You should have told me you were going to fetch the doctor. I'm afraid you've come out for no reason, doctor."

"If you don't mind, Mrs. Nelson, I would like to be the judge of that. Seeing as I'm already here and all." To Mundy, the doctor added, "I might need your help. Will you be my assistant?"

"Yes."

"Good. Now let's have a look at the patient."

They went inside.

The doctor swore as soon as they entered the cabin, noting the blazing heat.

"Kill that fire, Mundy," the doctor instructed.

"But we're trying to sweat the illness out…" Mundy offered.

"Kill it. I can assure you, whatever is wrong with your father, Indian cures won't help him."

Mundy opened the stove door and removed a glowing ember with the tongs, laying it on an iron ledge to save over in case they needed a fire later. Then he used the poker to break up the fire and mound it with ash to help smother it out. He propped open the cabin door to let out the heat.

Dr. Ridgway told Mundy's mother to light candles so he could see. "If you have any to spare, that is."

"We have candles, and plenty," she huffed. She lit one from a glowing ember in the stove and then lit others until amber light chased shadows into the corners of the cabin. It was clear that Lars hadn't moved, but he was awake. His jaw was clenched, tight with pain, his breathing shallow and rapid.

Dr. Ridgway peeled away the cloth bandages and inspected the wound. He looked at Brita and shook his head.

"I'll need to amputate this leg."

"No!" The word exploded from Brita's lips.

"Cut it off," Lars whimpered.

Brita placed her hand on Lars's forehead. "I am sorry you are ill, Lars, but what good is a one-legged farmer?"

He closed his eyes and nodded.

"You will have to think of another cure," Brita told the doctor.

Dr. Ridgway searched his bag and pulled out a flat glass bottle and uncorked it. He poured a brown liquid onto his father's wound—whiskey, like the men in town drank. His father hollered and kicked as if the doctor had poured molten steel on him.

"Do you have any more whiskey in the house?" the doctor asked.

"Certainly not!" Brita retorted.

"I'll leave this bottle, then, but I'm adding it to the bill. Pour some on the wound, just enough to coat it, every hour or so. Try to get him to hold still when you do it. We want to burn the infection out from the inside."

"Is he going to get better?" Mundy asked, his eyes flicking between them. But they didn't answer, and that was an answer of sorts.

"Oh, pa!" Mundy lay his head on his father's chest. He had so many questions: questions about how to do and how to be. Questions about the past and the future. All the answers burned in his father's blood and evaporated with his father's fading life.

He felt his father's hand press against his neck.

"Mundy," his father strained to speak.

"Yes, pa."

A wave of pain surged through his father, and his body shot rigid. Mundy yelled at the doctor to do something. Brita stroked Lars's face, calming him.

"All is well, Lars," she whispered. She bent down and kissed his cheek, tears dropping from her to her husband. "You must rest now."

A hard knocking sounded on the cabin door. Dr. Ridgway asked Brita if she would like him to see who it was, but she wiped her eyes and opened the door to the purpling darkness of twilight. There stood the silhouette of Koskinen, tall and lanky.

"Sorry to bother, Mrs. Nelson," he said. "You had mentioned you might bring some bread over for the children, and when it got so late…"

"Now is not a good time, Mr. Koskinen," Brita replied between gulps for air, her chest heaving with emotion. "Lars is not well."

"Is that the medicine man in there? What is wrong?" Koskinen tried to peer into the cabin interior, bobbing his head, but Brita pressed him outside and closed the door behind her.

Dr. Ridgway placed his hand on Lars's forehead. "We need to take that leg off," he told Mundy. "Can you talk some sense into your mother?"

Mundy didn't answer. What she said about a one-legged farmer was a harsh truth. He'd seen his father recognize it, too. A one-legged farmer still has a mouth to feed. They barely could make ends meet as it was, and winter was only a few months away.

"Son!" Dr. Ridgway gripped Mundy by the arms and shook him. "Do you hear me? Your father is as good as dead if we don't get that leg off!"

Mundy pulled away from Dr. Ridgway and yelled for his mother.

"I'm deciding for you!" the doctor reached into his bag and pulled out a handsaw whose teeth glowed gold in the candlelight. "Mr. Koskinen! Get in here!"

The cabin door flew open and Koskinen burst through even as Brita tried to hold him back, telling him to leave it alone. Koskinen paused when he noticed the saw poised over Lars's upper leg as Brita tried to drag him from the cabin. He swatted away her hands.

"You're going to take off his leg?"

"The infection has spread too much!" Dr. Ridgway explained. "I need you to keep hold of his shoulders in case he comes to."

"Kauko!" Brita screamed, her face flushed with emotion, and her eyes streaming. "If you help this man, I will not speak to you again!"

Mundy tried to shove Dr. Ridgway, but the doctor's feet were planted. He was intent on performing the amputation. Their attention fell on Koskinen as if he held the power in that awful moment to determine a man's fate. He stepped to the bedside, grimacing when he saw the wound exposed. He exchanged a look with the doctor. They both understood the next few minutes would decide whether Lars Nelson survived without a leg or died with two legs. He grabbed the saw, pulling it easily from the surprised doctor's grip.

Koskinen placed a hand on Dr. Ridgway's shoulder and led him out of the cabin.

"You just signed that man's death sentence," Dr. Ridgway sputtered.

"It is up to God, now."

✳ ✳ ✳ ✳ ✳

Mundy didn't leave his father's side all night. He dozed off, but he had terrible dreams. Trolls savaged his father and burned down the cabin. He started out of sleep in a panic, feeling momentary relief that his dreams couldn't touch his waking world. Then the reality of his father's condition returned to him, and he felt the helplessness of despair. He gripped his father's hand and pressed his lips to the flesh burning with fever.

Dawn didn't find Lars Nelson yawning like a bear, nor did the bed creak as he sat upright and planted two feet on the ground. Instead, the cabin was quiet except for quick, wheezing breaths—uneven and shallow—the rasps of a dying man.

Brita lie on the floor at the foot of the bed. She pulled herself up when she heard Mundy stand. Her face was haggard with exhaustion.

"Did you sleep?" she asked.

"A little," he whispered. He wanted to tell her about the dreams, but she would be angry, because he wasn't supposed to be afraid of trolls anymore. She would be angry with Lars, too, for telling him stories about monsters so often. Now there would be no more stories.

"He's so gray," Mundy declared.

"You do the milking and I'll fix you some oats," Brita said, brushing a wisp of hair from her eyes.

"I don't want to leave him," he replied. "Besides, I'm not hungry."

"I'll stay with him," she forced a smile. "You go."

The fresh air of dawn reawakened a new round of anguish in Mundy, but there was no one to hear his cries except their little milk herd. His father, his strong father, who stood against the sky hoisting heavy bundles of shingles, now was disappearing from their lives. In his place, there was a shell of a man.

His mother met him at the door and folded her arms around him, walking him backwards, like a dance.

"Don't go in there, Mundy," she told him. "He is gone."

There was one person less in the world who loved Mundy. He felt so weak, his legs, his arms. He couldn't stand. They fell to the ground and wept together.

✳✳✳✳✳

It came time to discuss practical things much too soon. Brita told Mundy they would need to bury Lars, but the thought of putting his father in the ground made Mundy's stomach tighten as a wild anger took root. He refused to fetch Mr. Dunton, the undertaker. He told his mother what Lars had said, that there was no need to spend good money for a boughten box when they owned land. She grew sullen, her mouth tight.

"He can't stay in here," she warned. "I've written a letter to your aunt asking if she can send her boy to help on the farm. He's a little older than you."

"We don't need any help!" The words spilled out of Mundy's mouth, but he didn't mean them. Mundy and his mother needed all the help they could get.

She ignored his outburst and handed him a letter addressed to the Ingegaards of Spring Grove.

"Post this with the depot agent." She pressed two pennies into his palm. "Don't lose those. This letter needs to be delivered."

Brita Nelson née Lund, a woman in her thirties with a twelve-year-boy, had forty acres in the middle of nowhere, a herd of hungry cows, and Finns for neighbors.

CHAPTER FIVE

A FUNNY THING

A funny thing. That's how Mundy would have described it. After arriving at the depot, Mundy spotted the agent, Mr. Stern, talking to Koskinen. He ducked into the shadows where chickens in wooden crates squawked and ruffled in protest.

"...but the real money for a fella like you, Mr. Koskinen, is in the contract with the railroad company when they get that passenger line running. And I'd be more than willing to support your case, when the time is ready."

"If the price is right, eh?"

"Well, one hand can feed the other, if you catch my meaning."

Koskinen undid the string of a small sack hanging from his belt. He reached in and removed two coins.

"I do catch your meaning, Mr. Boynton." He was about to drop the coins into the agent's outstretched palm when he held it back. "But this contract. It must be for me alone, yes?"

"Of course, Mr. Koskinen!" The agent nodded. His eyes focused on the coins in the Koskinen's pinched fingers. "Why, this arrangement is solely between you and me!"

Mundy made himself known to them by shuffling his boots against the deck of the platform.

The agent tensed for a moment, startled that Mundy was so near.

"Got a letter to send," Mundy mumbled, stretching his arm out to them as if it were a branch and they were a writhing coil of snakes.

"Got a letter to send," Mr. Stern mimicked in a falsetto voice. "Too bad your father died before he could teach you manners!"

"Say please to the nice man, boy," Koskinen added.

"Please," Mundy added, not looking at them. The agent took the letter and read the address.

"Spring Grove again? Isn't that where all those dumb Norwegians come from? I suppose you'll want a stamp for this here letter."

Mundy, recalling the coins his mother had given him, handed them over to the agent who closed his palm on them without counting and hooked his hand on Mundy's shoulder before the boy could pull away.

"I reckon your mother will get pretty lonesome soon," Mr. Stern said. "Without a man around."

"No, sir," Mundy responded quietly.

"Mighty big responsibility, all that land and those cows. I suppose your father's plan to increase the herd for the creamery will have to fall by the wayside. So many dreams die with a man."

Mundy shifted, uncomfortable. He felt tears coming, but he was pinned in place.

"Not to worry," Mr. Koskinen added his hand to Mundy's other shoulder. Mundy felt like one of the milk cows trapped in a stanchion. "Your mother has been very kind to me and my family. I'll be around." Mundy tugged his shoulders free.

"Look at that," the agent said, consulting his pocket watch for the time. "No one can stop the hands of God."

To the agent, God was Time, exacting cruel justice with each tick of a clock hand. To Mundy, God was an invisible string, a string tied to the letter from his mother that would travel in a dingy bone-colored canvas mail bag on the train to Minneapolis, stretching sixty miles, and then knotting, turning, heading another hundred miles to the southwest corner of the state to the Norwegian settlement in Spring Grove. How tightly that string would close around him was yet unknown to Mundy.

*****

A soft lingering caress on his face awakened Mundy in the morning. Nothing like his father's rough hand compressing Mundy's chest or jabbing him in the stomach until he submitted to waking. Mundy opened his eyes only long enough to see his mother peeking into the loft from the ladder.

"No dawdling today, Mundy." She said it softly, but there was iron in her tone that meant: that wood won't split itself and stack itself. That had been his father's job.

Even though winter seemed miles away, it was on the move towards them. It now was up to Mundy to build their wood pile, so they wouldn't freeze to death. Three felled trees needed splitting, but there wasn't a full cord of wood among them. He would get very strong by November using the saw and the ax.

There was nothing for it but to get the day started.

"It's late," he rubbed his eyes.

"You needed the rest," Brita said as she disappeared down the ladder.

By the time Mundy climbed down after her, she already was on all fours using a rag to wipe the floorboards. A blanket crumpled on the little wooden chair suggested that she had slept contorted next to her husband, whose body, gaunt and gray, lay dead. His mouth hung open as if he were in the middle of a song.

She stopped wiping and offered to make him some food, but he still wasn't hungry. He hurried out to begin chores and stared into the morning sun, which would no longer be judged through the kitchen window. Mundy walked through the wet buffalo grass without understanding what the beads of dew meant, into the barn where there was no cheerful whistling to calm the herd during morning milking. The whistler was silenced, and the cows were sullen, bleating even after they'd been milked, as if they, too were grieving.

$$* * * * *$$

Using the flat side of a hatchet, he tapped a wedge into the end of a maple log. Then he hoisted the eight-pound hammer waist-high with both hands. His forearms strained with the weight, but that was the one his father would have used. He lifted it over his head, but the weight jerked his arms behind him, and he let the hammer drop. How was he going split wood over and over again if he couldn't lift a hammer?

The sound of a horse striking the drive and the strain of wooden wheels alerted Mundy to visitors. Patting his eyes with the backs of his hands, he tried to see through his tears. A shimmering cloud of dust in the horizon formed into a long buckboard wagon that turned down the drive. Pulled by Koskinen's powerful black Friesian stallion, the wagon was driven by Matias Koskinen, sitting straight, his chin in the air, like a dog pretending to be a man, but he was not alone. Seven other neighbors, looking grim, as the wagon swayed and creaked over rough ground. Mundy called for his mother, and she appeared, wearing her fancy lavender calico dress and a clean apron, as if she'd expected visitors.

Three men, representing the other farms surrounding the Nelsons and Koskinens, descended from the wagon, each wearing a black coat that looked so similar to the others that Mundy wondered if they had come from the same roll of cloth. The coats hid patches on the work shirts of Piers Kersten, Jonathon Engleman, and an Englishman named Garret Lowell, a bachelor with sixty acres that he won in a wrestling contest with a Sioux war chief.

The men helped down two women, Mrs. Engleman and Mrs. Kersten, and her little girl, Mariel.

This was a burying party, and Mundy wanted nothing to do with it. He drew back, taking up a position at the sawhorse, far enough away that he didn't have to worry about looking people in the eye or pretend to listen. The Kerstens had only three months before buried their son Roy, the closest friend Mundy ever had. Roy had drowned in the spring torrent, and they didn't find him for two days. Mundy wondered if Mrs. Kersten even missed him, because she had six other children.

The visitors couldn't help themselves from stealing glances at the barn, at the cabin, straining to see the cows in the pasture. The men were taking stock, assessing conditions, passing judgments—all this before they even removed their soiled felt hats in feigned bereavement. The two women gathered Brita into an embrace.

"It was too soon for him to go," Mr. Engleman told Mundy's mother, resting his hand on the side of her shoulder.

She nodded slightly but turned her torso so that his hand found only air in its grasp.

Mrs. Kersten, the first woman to speak, used a voice so strained with tension that Mundy thought it might snap in two.

"We've come to help you with your husband."

She cinched her lips shut after she was done talking. She had a long, deer-like face but with a pointed chin where the deer's mouth should be. Unlike deer, her eyes were long and narrow, two slits set close together like a bird of prey. She wore a cotton dress that looked newly made with a powder-blue body and a white stitched front with a scalloped collar that crept up the neck. She had one arm slung over her youngest, the gimpy daughter. Mariel's head was covered by a bonnet made from the same cloth as the dress, but her mother's bonnet, tied across her shoulders, was lumped under the bun of her blond hair high on her back. Like her mother's dress, Mariel's dress looked newly made. This was probably the first time the mother and daughter had worn them out of their cabin.

"Is he inside?" Mr. Engleman nodded toward the cabin. Mundy's mother said he was laid out on the bed.

Mundy kicked a rut into the ground, wishing he could find a good throwing rock in the dirt to wipe the curiosity from Mariel's face. He felt a hot rush of shame for thinking such a cruel thought.

Matias climbed back on the wagon and passed a basket to Mrs. Engleman that was covered with cloth. She was a young bride with gold-blonde hair who came from Denmark to replace the previous Mrs. Engleman who had died giving birth two years previous. She offered her condolences, her head low so that Mundy couldn't see her face past the confines of her bonnet. She gave Brita the basket, explaining it was only two loaves of seed bread and some sausage.

Matias leaped down again, which would have been good timing for a twisted ankle or impalement on a pick blade. Instead Matias landed on sure feet and waved for Mundy to help with the horses.

"What do we do now?" Lowell asked. Engleman shrugged, looking to his young wife for guidance.

"Where would you like the hole dug?" Kersten asked. His wife shot him a scowl.

"It's a man's grave, Jonathon," she corrected, smoothing her mouth into a smile. Kersten shrugged, pretending to look for burrs on the shovel handle.

"Maybe under one of those trees?" Mrs. Engleman suggested. "Such a nice place to look out over the fields, the sunrise." She pointed to the Nelson's small orchard, three rows of apple trees, next to the cabin.

Mundy's mother shook her head, setting the food basket down. "I don't want him buried that close." She shaded her eyes with one hand. "Put him out by that old shed. That's what killed him—that shed and his stubborn streak."

Kersten looked to the pasture and stuck the point of his shovel into the ground, leaning upon it.

"Missus," he said to his wife. "You seemed about to say something about that. Speak your mind."

Mrs. Kersten didn't like being put on the spot. Her eyes widened at her husband even as she struggled for words.

"It's just that, well, that is so far away from the home."

"He is dead," Brita said flatly. "He has no home."

"But his soul lives on with God."

"He is dead, and we live on. Memories of him will not feed my boy or keep my fire burning."

"Pardon me," Kersten spoke. "But the body away from the light of God is corrupted. Maybe we should take him to the lake cemetery. Our little Roy is there, and Ellen's sister, too."

"We have plenty of ground right here," she looked to Mundy who nodded his agreement. "That's what he wished."

Becoming restless, Mariel Kersten tried to pull out of her mother's grip, but Mrs. Kersten shifted and pulled her tight to her side.

"That is the land we will buy from you," Matias Koskinen announced. "He shouldn't be on that land."

Mundy snorted in disgust, but Brita considered Matias.

"You're right, Matias," she allowed. "Well, then, I suppose. Put him in the far side of the orchard."

"No!"

All eyes shot startled looks at Mundy.

"Mundy!"

"They can't buy it. That's our land." Mundy stepped towards the smirking Matias who tightened his gripped on the pick handle.

"Not now, Mundy," his mother scolded.

"But that's our land, and pa said—"

"I said not now! You go tend the cows."

Brita apologized for her son. She exhaled slowly, closing her eyes the way she did was tried to remember a recipe.

"No," she said. "I do want him buried back by that shed. That's final."

Mr. Engleman shrugged and drew out a spade from the wagon.

"And what of the minister for the service?" Mrs. Kersten asked. "I suppose you'll use Reverend Lorenson from town?"

"My sister's husband is a minister," Brita explained. "We will have a proper service someday. There is no hurry."

Mr. Engleman signaled for Kersten and Matias to follow him to the pasture.

"I hope she's not particular about the precise location," Mr. Kersten said.

"I don't think she minds," Engleman answered, straining with the first strikes of his shovel about ten feet from the shed, on the south side, which was furthest from the cabin. "So long as it is away from her."

Mundy did not help, and no one asked him to. He watched them with his arms crossed, still shaking with the anger that had spilled from him.

✳ ✳ ✳ ✳ ✳

The women in the cabin tightened stitches on the winding sheet of Lars Nelson while outside, the ground yielded a hard-won hole as the men wrestled rocks and roots. The men cooled themselves by dunking their heads in buckets of water, for it was hard work. They needed to dig deep enough so that foxes or raccoons wouldn't interfere with the body.

In the late afternoon, the men put on their black coats again. Mundy and Mr. Engleman carried the body out of the cabin, but Matias and the other two men guided it onto the wagon. Then Matias drove the wagon to the grave, slowly, followed by Mundy and Brita and the neighbors. Mrs. Kersten sang *There Is A Happy Land*, joined by Mrs. Engleman who hummed the melody but didn't know the lyrics. The men lowered the body first onto ropes laid next to the grave. Then, standing on either side of the opening, the men lowered the body into the grave. Mr. Engleman offered a prayer commending the soul of the departed to heaven. They all said amen, and the men filled the grave from the horseshoe of dirt, patting it flat with the backs of their shovels.

"That's about it," Mr. Kersten concluded.

"Our thoughts are with you, Mrs. Nelson." Mr. Engleman offered.

After another embrace, the neighbor women promised to call again soon, just as soon as they were able.

From the front of the cabin, they watched the neighbors leave. The sound of Mrs. Engleman teaching the hymn to Mrs. Kersten faded away into the evening. A sickle-shaped moon rose, wresting its life from the dying day in the faint violet tint of impending night. The sound of the day's last cicadas was replaced by an orchestra of croaking frogs and crickets.

Mundy asked his mother what they would use to mark the grave.

She wheeled on him and shook Mundy by the shoulders. "Let that damn shed be his headstone, for all I care!"

Mundy started crying, and he couldn't close his eyes, wondering if his mother was going to hit him, she was so angry. Instead, her eyes dropped to the ground, and she released her grip.

"We'll mark it at the service," she said. "Once your uncle arrives."

She drooped against one of the maple beams of the porch for the moment but with a sudden sharp breath, she marched to the woodpile, hefted the ax from the block. The hem of her dress kicked ahead of her rapid stride, met again by her next step, and her next, like balls on a string.

He called after her, but her attention was focused ahead of her. She cradled the ax against her chest. Mundy followed, running to catch up as she stepped over the fresh grave and beelined for the field shed. She landed her first blow with the momentum of her stride, notching a corner beam. She yanked the ax head out and steadied herself, striking the same beam and opening a vein of golden splinters.

Mundy pulled the ax from her before she could make a third chop, and she collapsed to the ground, her head bowed, arms limp, crying uncontrollably.

"I'll take it from here."

A voice behind him made Mundy whirl.

Koskinen's eyes glowed ice blue in the final glow of sunset.

"Leave us for a while, Mundy, so we can talk," he said. He helped Brita to her feet, and she fell into his chest. He put a hand on the back of her head.

"You let go of her!" Mundy brandished the ax, but Koskinen's hand shot out and grabbed the ax handle. He used it to shove Mundy across the chest, and Mundy stumbled backward, landing on the low mound of dirt covering his father's body.

Koskinen dropped the ax and knelt down to Brita, gathering her in his arms once more, their silhouette forming a ghostly triangle.

＊＊＊＊＊

Mundy shoveled manure in the muck yard the next day. Life went on whether he wanted it to or not. A calf began bellowing in a panic, and Mundy dropped the muck shovel and raced toward the sound. He leaped over the wooden stile fence and landed on the hard-packed ground under the barn awning. The heifer calf was trapped under hay bales that had fallen on her from where they'd been stacked along the wall. Mundy threw off the bales, one by one. The calf's mother trotted in from the pasture and nosed her calf as Mundy worked frantically to free her. Mundy pulled off the last bales, and the calf raised herself and wobbled out of the shadow of the barn followed closely by her mother.

"I thought that stack looked off balance."

A voice came from the corner of the barn. Matias leaned against a wall, holding the pitchfork. "I thought that, and then sure enough, it just toppled over at the lightest touch."

A rage filled Mundy's body. He dashed full speed toward Matias.

If Matias was afraid, he didn't show it. He simply planted the pitchfork handle into the ground and tipped the tines low toward Mundy. To avoid the sharp tines, Mundy dropped to the ground and pitched himself at Matias's feet, knocking the older boy down, the fork and the hook clattering off to the side. Mundy scrambled on top wedging his knees into the front of Matias's shoulders, pinning him down for however long it took for the bad-seed boy to buck him off. In those few moments he had, Mundy rained a series of punches down on the other boy's face.

Both boys were yelling and cursing. Matias freed one hand and then the other, reached one powerful jab under Mundy's chin that sent his head snapping back. Mundy's world exploded in pain, and Matias easily shoved him off. He stood over Mundy who crawled, trying to lift himself.

"You look just like that little calf!"

Matias delivered a hard kick that caught Mundy in the side, knocking the wind out of him. He kicked again, and Mundy gasped for breath. Mundy felt something sharp jabbing his knee, and his hand tightened along the smooth wooden handle of the baling hook. He would make one sudden upward punch with the hook resting against the back of his hand, and the hook would catch flesh, tearing open a line in Matias so his insides would spill out.

"What in heaven's name is happening here?"

Brita appeared from around the corner and rushed at the boys, putting herself between them. Mundy backed away, but he crouched low, still brandishing his weapon, his eyes burning with hatred. He wiped the back of his hand across his bleeding nose.

"Mundy! What are you doing with that hook? Put it down!"

"But he tried to kill the calf!" Mundy told her what happened, indicating the fallen hay.

"Accidents happen!" Matias smirked.

"I don't know what happened here," Brita said. "But neighbors fighting neighbors will not solve anything." She told Matias to go home, and he tried to strut away, but he limped with each step, and Mundy found that satisfying.

After Matias disappeared across the property line, Brita held Mundy's head in her hands, inspecting him for damage. He had a cut on his cheek, a bloody nose, his jaw throbbed, and the knuckles on both hands were purple raw.

"You'll live," she determined, tugging his ear lobes. "A strong, fighting man like you should be able to cut a lot of firewood."

"Can't we do something about Matias?"

"He lost his mother, just like you lost you father. Maybe you're both looking for a friend."

Mundy imagined his father storming off to confront Koskinen about keeping his boy off the Nelson farm with an "or else" thrown in as warning. Without his father, Mundy would find a way to deal with the Koskinens—and it wasn't through friendship.

* * * * *

The stifling summer heat rose to the rafters, making sleeping in the loft unbearable. Instead, he fidgeted on the floor downstairs trying to sleep. He pressed his foot against the woodstove, which was cooler than the air around him. The itchy blanket beneath him barely cushioned him from nail heads in the floorboards. He watched the Big Dipper through the open cabin door. Outside, an owl hooted, on the hunt for mice. His mother's breathing was slow and deep. At least one of them could sleep.

This was the time his father used to come in from one last check on the barn. He would climb the ladder to where Mundy slept. Standing on the ladder with the bottom of his beard pressed against the loft's floor, Lars whispered stories to his son, his head the only part of his body visible. If Brita fidgeted or called out for Lars before the story ended, he would stop his story in mid-sentence and say, we'll finish this another time, and climb down the ladder as quietly as he could.

He tried to remember his father's voice. That was the first thing to leave when his father died. His face and height and hands and putrid leg all had remained, but his voice had gone with his last breath. The voice, Mundy thought, must hold the soul of a man. He remembered the story his father had told him about the Nelson farm.

When your grandfather and grandmother came to this place, there were only trees. Big tall basswood and maple. They came here with another Norwegian named Petterson and his family: a wife and two young children. Between our two families we had only a crate of tools, the pair of oxen that pulled the wagon, and one milk cow.

My father—your grandfather—was called Dag. He and Jorgen Petterson spoke no English. Like now, there were no other Norwegians here.

There were three of us Nelson boys back then.

Jarl was the eldest, your uncle Trig was the youngest, but he died when he was young. He couldn't stop coughing. Our families helped one another dress timber and hoist logs into place, and soon enough, we had this cabin built, which we shared with the Pettersons until their own cabin was ready.

When your grandfather saw the tears of joy spill from Kjersten Petterson, the lovely young wife of Jorgen, he was as proud as a man could be. It was time to attend to his own farm. Winter was coming soon enough, and there was much to do.

That winter was bitter cold and long. A blizzard buried this cabin, and the snow drifted as deep as this loft. It snowed for three days, and the wind howled. After the storm passed, we could see the Petterson cabin was buried, too, but we didn't see smoke from their chimney. That was a bad sign, because smoke meant fire, and fire meant warmth.

My father and us three boys sloughed our way to the Petterson cabin. Even though it was close, it took us three hours to make our way through the drifts. We lit fires along the way to warm our fingers, because it was so cold. Even now on hot days, I think of walking through that snow, just to cool me down. When we finally arrived at their cabin, we called out to them, but there was no answer. There were no tracks around, and the snow was still piled high over the front door. That meant the Pettersons hadn't been outside, not even to empty their bed pots.

My father and us boys used our hands and shovels to dig out the hard snow ice that blocked the door. Trig and me stood shivering while Jarl and my father forced their way in. Well, they came tumbling back out within moments, and Jarl threw up in the snow as soon as feet were out of the door. The Petterson family was all dead, their throats slit. There was still a meal on the table.

It was trolls who did it. But no one else here knew about trolls, so the locals made up stories that my father had killed the Pettersons. They said he probably was in love with Petterson's wife, but this wasn't true. My father loved my mother. Then Indians stole a cow near here and everyone decided it was them who must have killed the Pettersons. They put a dollar bounty on every Indian scalp to be had.

And do you know what the meal was on the Petterson table? Boiled potatoes.

Trolls hate boiled potatoes!

The air in the cabin cooled enough that Mundy felt drowsy. As he fell into a deep sleep, the last thought on his mind was that the ocean was a barrier to the gods and heroes of the homeland, but it couldn't stop the monsters.

CHAPTER SIX

THE INGEGAARDS ARRIVE

A wall of thick fog filtered the early morning light. Mundy could see only a few feet ahead of him on the way to the barn. The dark green bunchgrass and nettles burst in contrast with the eerie, silver glow. He pushed open the big doors leading to the muck yard, but the herd stalled at the doorway, nosing the air, and only stepping into the damp, cool morning when Mundy reassured with calm words.

"Don't worry," he told them. "This fog will burn off soon."

Once they were out, Mundy swung the door shut again so they wouldn't be tempted to return to the barn. The cows needed to feed themselves during the summer when there was plenty for them to forage in the pasture and along all the fences. After all, only a few months more and autumn would slow growth and bring the first killing freezes.

A muffled ticking made his ears prick up, but from which direction, he couldn't tell. The fog cloaked its source. A few moments more, and the sound became clearer—a snapping, no! A creaking. Yes, wood creaking. He felt the earth beneath his feet rumble. That was the reverberation of a team pulling a wagon. Someone was coming.

Mundy followed the well-worn track toward the cabin when his mother appeared ahead of him from the fog, her bone-white dress radiant against the backdrop of swirling mist. She untied her blue gingham apron as she listened.

"Do you hear it?" Brita's breath caught as she strained to listen, and Mundy nodded. Singing trickled through the fog from the path leading to the Nelson farm, punctuated by snorts of large draft animals.

A girl sang, her voice piercing through the gray veil and sending a chill through Mundy.

Pass me not, O gentle Savior
Hear my humble cry
While on others Thou art calling
Do not pass me by

The speckled snouts of shaggy oxen broke into view, their nostrils flaring and flecked with beads of moisture. Koskinen walked alongside them gripping a tether to guide the team. On the buckboard sat three people, jostling side to side. The woman looked like Brita, except her eyes, which were rounder and her eyebrows were darker. Her eyes were half-closed, her expression drawn.

"Here we are!" Koskinen announced. "Look who I found wandering in the fog!"

Next to her, a young man slouched forward with his elbows resting on his knees. He was perhaps a year or two older than Mundy. The reins danced in his hands like they were made of smoke.

The singing continued even as Koskinen brought the team to a halt.

A man of about forty, tall and thin, with a clean-shaved face, swayed next to them with the motion of the wagon. No gray yet touched his chestnut hair, which was thick and pushed over the top of his head until it touched his shoulders. He wore a full black suit, now glistening with dew, but no hat. His nose was long and sharp hanging over his wide mouth that turned down at the corners. Startled by the man's gleaming brown eyes, rounded like marbles pressed into sockets, Mundy instinctively took a step back. Their reproving glare fixed on Mundy and found him wanting.

"It's your aunt and uncle!" Brita mussed Mundy's hair and laughed. Her eyes flooded with tears of joy. "Hello, Ingegaards!" Brita shouted. She threw her arms open as she ran to the wagon.

The woman on the cart shot awake and she gasped to see Brita running toward her. Koskinen guided her waist as she stiffly climbed down. The two women embraced, spinning in each other's arms. He'd never seen his mother so elated.

The young man yawned and stretched his arms before leaping down.

He was about six feet tall, but his shiny leather boots were too big for him. They weren't the kind of boots to be of much use on the farm.

"We're here," he announced to a fancy table, chairs, a wash tub, baskets, and the sealed wooden crates piled the back of the wagon. A girl appeared, her lips still shaping a song pleading not to be left behind. Her plaited honey-blonde hair radiated a gold halo against the surrounding gloom and the cream of her smooth skin. She looked like an angel floating in clouds—until she stopped singing and a look of disappointment marred the effect.

"Finally!" She scrunched her nose. "Is this it?"

Brita pulled away from her sister, Helga, but kept holding her hands. "But I can't believe you are here! We posted a letter only two days ago. Did you get it already?"

Helga shook her head. Like her daughter, her hair was plaited, but it was coarser with threads of white showing.

"Two days ago, we were in St. Peter being told the most horrible lies about tomatoes!"

Brita shook her head, sharing in her sister's disdain. "The things some people believe! But we won't eat them, will we Mundy?" She signaled for him to approach, for he was standing well back. "This is Mundy! He is thirteen."

Aunt Helga extended her hand, and Mundy shook it.

"Pleased to meet you," he said, uncertain if that was true.

"Mundy! Your aunt's hand is not an udder!"

Helga pried her hand free and held it in the air as if she were airing it out before returning it her side.

"Not to worry, Mundy," She said without a smile. "We have all the time in the world to teach you manners. We've come to stay for a while."

"But you don't know about Lars," Brita's lip trembled, and a wave of grief overcame her. "I can't tell you how marvelous it is that you are here."

"What about Lars?" Helga asked, but just then Koskinen slid next to them as if he belonged in the conversation.

"It was no trouble at all!" he declared. "These nice folks were lost in the fog, and I said I would be happy to help."

"Thank you, Mr. Koskinen." Brita sniffled and beamed a grateful smile. She placed her hand on Koskinen's forearm, and Mundy wasn't the only one to notice it. Helga's eyes locked on her sister's stray hand, which quickly glided back to Brita's side.

"Well, I best be off," Koskinen said. "Lots to do today!" He began to walk back into the fog and the sisters resumed their conversation, but then he stopped. "Oh! Come to think of it, Brita. Will you be bringing dinner later?"

Brita nodded and waved him off without answering.

"Now, what about Lars?"

Brita dabbed her eyes with the sleeve of her dress. "Later, but first who are these beautiful children?"

Aunt Helga introduced Tomas, the young man with the shiny boots, and Amanda, who curtsied, plucking the sides of her skirt as she bobbed down and up. Mundy never had seen anyone make a motion like that before, and he imagined it to be the start of an elaborate dance. She was about Mundy's age, maybe a year older. She was so clean and pretty that Mundy was afraid he might break her if he looked at her too long.

The man with the piercing gaze stood rigidly by the wagon wheel, and Amanda took his hand, guiding him to the group.

"And this is my father, the Reverend Halvar Ingegaard," she said. "Lately of Spring Grove, but suddenly cursed to wander in the wilderness and restore the tabernacle, like the Levites of old. Isn't that right, father?" She smiled up at him, but Uncle Halvar looked away.

"Stop that this instant," Aunt Helga warned.

"I'm sorry," Amanda demurred. "Perhaps I've gotten the story mixed up, mother? Perhaps it's more like Lot's family fleeing Sodom. I suppose that would make you Lot's wife?" She embraced her mother—an embrace Helga did not return. "Don't look back, mother!"

Tomas offered his hand to Mundy.

"Hello. I'm Tomas. I guess I'm your cousin."

"Hello," Mundy shook his hand, but only just long enough to say he'd done it.

"That's my sister. She's fourteen and about as dumb as a bag of rocks."

Amanda kicked at Tomas, but he jumped out of range.

"Don't you scuff these boots!" he yelled.

Uncle Halvar gripped Tomas hard at the shoulder, his eyes burning intensely.

"Turn your eyes away from worthless things!" The power of Halvar's voice jolted Mundy. "And preserve your life according to the word of the Lord!"

"Ow!" Tomas winced and wriggled away from his father's hold. "Of course, father! It's just that she almost scuffed my good boots!"

"Ignore him, please," Amanda told Mundy. "I caught him kissing a tree once."

"Keep quiet or I'll cut off your hair when you sleep!"

"Stop it!" Aunt Helga yelled. "What will my sister think of this? Me bringing two very rude children to her home?"

Tomas and Amanda apologized to their mother, but Amanda stuck out at her tongue at her brother. Brita explained to Helga and Halvar that Lars died, and she again said how happy she was that they had come when they did. Helga immediately drew Brita to her, and they wept together while Uncle Halvar placed his hands on them, announcing a prayer to the fog.

"The Lord will wipe away all tears from your eyes! There will be no more death! No more grief or crying or pain! The old things have disappeared. Amen."

"Amen."

Helga smiled at Brita.

While they all dawdled, no one minded the ox team, and that made Mundy nervous, but after the sisters finally broke from their embrace, Uncle Halvar commanded Tomas to unyoke the team. A man, he said, was coming to collect them.

"But he won't come in this fog," Tomas argued.

"Obey me at once!"

Tomas glanced down at his boots, sighed, and undid the laces before pulling them off. He pulled a silk handkerchief from his pocket and wiped the square toes.

"I don't suppose you know anything about oxen, do you?"

"Not particularly," Mundy admitted. "But I can help you unyoke them."

"That's good! I just don't want anything to happen to these boots. They cost four dollars, tailormade."

"But why do you have them?" Mundy whispered. He'd never seen boots with such a high gloss before—and with good reason. There was no need for them on a farm.

"I'm going into business soon, and I need to dress the part. How about you? What do you want to do?"

"What do you mean?" Mundy asked, baffled.

"Maybe he wants to farm," Amanda suggested.

"No!" Tomas declared but then saw Mundy's sheepish expression. "Really?"

"Yes, I want to run the farm."

"Not me!" Tomas shook his head. "As soon as I can, I'm off to a real city, like Minneapolis or Chicago."

"They look too big."

"I know that!" Tomas bristled. "I had them made extra big so I could grow into them.".

"You wouldn't believe how much he prizes those boots," Amanda told Mundy. "I swear he'd marry them, if he could."

Tomas took a swipe at his sister, but Uncle Halvar shot forward and grabbed his arm in a vice-like grip that made Tomas whimper.

"I'm sorry! I'm sorry! I'm sorry!"

Uncle Halvar let go of his son's arm.

"And you," he growled at Mundy. "I suppose you are a heathen like your father? If only we'd arrived before he died. We could have ministered to him and saved his soul."

Mundy was stunned.

"It would have been a great comfort to him," Brita managed after an awkward silence. "Why don't we go inside?"

The adults wandered off to the cabin, but the oxen were jangling their halters in agitation.

"We better tend to them," Mundy concluded. "Is your arm okay?"

Tomas held his arm out and pushed up the sleeve. "Probably get a bruise, but it'll be fine."

"You know better than to test father," Amanda cajoled. "He just isn't himself these days."

✳✳✳✳✳

For a strong, healthy boy, Tomas had no idea how to manage hitches. He nearly got crushed between the oxen, ducking between them to fiddle with the tug pole. Mundy yelled at him to move, which Tomas did, but slowly, reluctant to step in manure with his bare feet.

"But why?" Tomas asked, indignant. "They're, what'd you call it? Yoked."

"Their rears aren't yoked, and that's the part likely to flatten you if you pop up in between them, right where they can't see you."

Tomas shrugged. "Well, you do it then!"

Mundy pried out the lynch pin that connected the tow pole to the neck of the wagon, and then he slid the pole clean out of the tackle, leaving it on the ground. He brought the reins across the barrel bodies of the rust-colored oxen, whose hides twitched as biting flies landed on them. Without waiting for Tomas, Mundy led the team to the pond and let them drink their fill.

Lars Nelson would have been proud of Mundy, the way he could handle a team, and the way he showed up an older boy a whole head taller. That's my son, his father would have said. And then maybe he'd tell these people they could stay for a night or two, but then they'd have to clear off, unless they planned to work.

✳✳✳✳✳

Brita and Helga assembled a hasty lunch, and just as Mundy bit into a boiled egg, Uncle Halvar shot him a dirty look and began a long prayer. By then the fog had lifted revealing a beautiful clear sky. The air sprang to life in the calls of mourning doves and frogs. After lunch, Brita scolded Mundy for eating before the blessing, but he reminded her that he hadn't been aware of any such rule.

"Well, get used to it. Uncle Halvar will be doing a lot of praying out loud while the Ingegaards are staying with us," she explained. "You'll need to keep your mouth empty until you hear the amen."

She suggested that Mundy show his cousins around the farm, and he found Tomas and Amanda in the orchard throwing a black rubber ball, back and forth to one another, back and forth, like a couple of dawdlers.

"I'm supposed to show you around," he announced, but that didn't stop them from playing.

"Catch!" Amanda threw the ball to Mundy, but he dodged it. "You can't catch? Tomas, cousin Mundy can't catch a ball!" She laughed, and Mundy's face flushed with embarrassment. She apologized for teasing him, but the damage was done, his temper got the better of him. He picked up the ball and threw it as hard as he could. It bounced several times, leaping from waist-high grama grass where it hit uneven ground and veered toward the woods, where it disappeared.

"He can't catch, but he sure can throw!" Tomas marveled. "If you're going to show us around, might as well start by finding the ball."

Tomas loped forward to where they'd last seen the ball, and Mundy called for him to stop. He thought of the burial mound hidden in the trees. He didn't want Tomas and Amanda to know about it, not yet. They were strangers, even if they were family.

"I'll go," called. "You stay here. There are tree snakes in there," he lied. He pushed into the brush, stepping on young trees to fold them over for a better view of the ground. Tomas and Amanda chattered away to one another in the pasture where they waited for him.

"Do you see it?" Tomas called.

"Not yet!" Mundy called back. "Just stay there."

A fallen log, moss-covered and damp, lie further in. Perhaps the ball rolled up to it, but beyond the log was the mound. A chill ran through Mundy although the day was warm. Everything stopped—Amanda and Tomas's voices were silent, as were the birds, unseen in the boughs. The wind itself stilled. There was only the sound of his heart racing and the growing sense that something in the mound was trying to get out.

His attention was drawn to the cracking of a branch. His imagination leaped to the image of a hulking troll ready to strike him over the head with a club. Amanda peeked through a tangle of wild grape vines.

"There you are!" She grinned. "We didn't believe you about the snakes."

"Oh," he said, not arguing with her.

"Tomas is searching in the field," she explained. "He didn't want to scuff his boots on a stump. Can you believe that?"

"They are nice boots," Mundy offered as he tried to roll the log for a better view. Amanda approached to help but backed away in disgust.

"You smell bad, Tiddemund! Don't you bathe?"

"I swim sometimes. And sometimes it rains."

"I know it rains," Amanda's face scrunched with impatience. "I mean, how often do you get in a tub and wash yourself?"

"We heat water in the winter and fill a trough."

"Winter!" She stretched her hand to touch his sleeve with the tip of a finger. "Tiddemund, you need to bathe. Once a week at least."

She skipped away from him, but she probably didn't know how to avoid mink traps or itch weed. Mundy yelled for her to stop sharply enough to startle her.

"What is it?" She spun around to face him at the base of the burial mound.

"You just can't go walking off on your own, that's all."

"I've walked in the woods before, you know. We had trees in Spring Grove." She noticed the mound. "What's this hill doing here?"

"It might be a troll mound," he began, afraid she might scoff at him for talking about foolish superstitions, but her eyes widened. She looked impressed, so he continued. "But some people think it's a grave for Indians." He told her what the Mr. Lewis, the surveyor, had said, because he thought it sounded smart. "But no matter what it is, it's old."

"What do you think is in there?" asked Amanda.

Mundy shrugged. "Dirt and rocks, mostly. Maybe some arrowheads."

He didn't mention what he actually imagined buried there: a troll, bigger than three men, waiting under the dirt to jump out and eat them. He'd seen that in his nightmares.

"Well, I think it's full of songs," she announced. She pulled herself on top of the mound using the trunks of young trees to guide her. Mundy didn't follow. His heart raced, and he could feel his pulse pounding in his neck.

"Songs?"

"Yes, it's a grave of songs."

"What does that mean?"

"If you dug a hole, you'd hear the songs of the people buried here from hundreds of years ago."

"I don't think so."

"Why not?" she said, dismissing his doubts. "And the music will come pouring out, and we'll have to write it down as soon as we hear it, or else it will disappear into the air forever. Can you read music?"

Mundy thought that reading music sounded as impossible as the mound making music.

"Read music? You can't read music! You hear it!"

"Yes, you can!" She clapped her hands together. "Oh! You've got to learn, Tiddemund. Well, I can read music because I've taken piano lessons from a French lady who got stranded in Minnesota when her steamer boat sank in the river. She said I was good enough to give a recital, but then I guess I'm stuck here instead."

"There isn't a piano here," Mundy blurted. "You might have to go back home."

"Believe me, I tried to tell my parents that. They were the ones who made me take those piano lessons, after all! They think I should marry a minister and play for his church, that way the church wouldn't have to pay someone else. Speaking of church, does the church here have a piano or an organ?"

Mundy said he didn't remember, adding that they should find the ball and get back. It was almost time for afternoon milking.

"You know, I don't think I'll have a knack for farming," Amanda said, peering down at the mound. "I haven't ever had to do it before. Back in Spring Grove, I mostly did the mending, and playing the piano at church, but I better learn how to do something helpful or your family will trade me off to the Indians."

"We wouldn't do that!"

"It's happened before, you know. Not to me, of course, not yet. But some people have traded off their worthless daughters to the Indians. I heard about one girl who was traded for a leg of venison just before winter."

"There aren't any Indians here anymore," Mundy assured her. "It's the Finns that you got to watch out for."

She announced that she might like to become a teacher. "Could you imagine it? I could even teach you. Maybe I could teach you to read music! Besides, the church is bound to have a piano or an organ, otherwise I will be on the first train back to Spring Grove, no matter what my father says."

"The train doesn't go to Spring Grove from Annandale."

"I know that! Are you always going to be this stubborn?" She clambered to the top of the mound. "Here it is!" She held the ball in the air for him to see.

Mundy blinked.

"How did it get there?"

He couldn't understand how the ball could have passed through trees and brush to land on top of the mound in the woods. It didn't seem physically possible, and yet there Amanda stood, clutching the ball in her hand. Maybe it was some kind of troll magic.

Amanda closed her eyes and drew in a deep breath.

"I can hear the music now. Can you?"

Mundy listened. He even closed his eyes, but all he heard was the *whiit-whiit-whiit* of a bright red cardinal, flitting from branch to branch, looking for its mate, and a breeze stirring the tall poplars in whispers.

And then Amanda sang.

✻✻✻✻✻

"You found it!" Tomas exulted as Amanda and Mundy left the woods, Amanda waving the ball over her head in victory.

"We weren't going to find it out here," she quipped, tossing the ball to her brother.

"My boots are too nice to get scuffed in the woods."

"You could have taken them off!" she laughed.

"And get my feet dirty again?" Tomas made a face. "No, thank you."

Mundy, still puzzled about the ball, suggested they continue the tour so they could get to chores.

"We've done enough dawdling today," he grumbled. "Follow me."

This was the first time Mundy had an audience on the farm, and he felt important. He led them toward the barn, but Tomas asked about the turned dirt near the field shed.

"Is that where your father is buried?" Tomas asked, and Mundy said it was. "Why isn't there a headstone?"

Mundy's gaze fell to the ground. He didn't know anything about headstones or how some people had them while other people didn't. He knew where his father was buried.

"I'm sorry about your father," Amanda took Mundy's hand. "I wish I'd had a chance to meet him. What was he like?"

Mundy paused.

"He worked hard."

It was the first thing that came to mind, but it didn't convey the many things Mundy remembered about his father: the stories, the jokes, the moments in the barn when they saw new life being born, the final moments on the shed roof when Lars saved his son from falling. Maybe at the end of it all, words couldn't paint a full enough picture of a person to be worth trying, and so he said no more, even though his cousins waited patiently.

"I know this will be difficult for you," Tomas acknowledged. "I mean, with us being here. But it's difficult for us, too. I don't want to be here anymore than you want us here. I had to leave my friends behind to come here. I mean, there is nothing here!"

"There's plenty here!" Mundy retorted. He thought of the land and all the food it provided them. He thought of the myriad struggles and rituals of birds and mice and snakes and opossum. A cracked blue robin egg discarded after a hatch. The way nightcrawlers pressed against one another in the early morning until they felt a heavy footfall and slid back into the earth.

"That neighbor of yours—what's his name?"

"Koskinen."

"Yeah, Koskinen. He's not even Norwegian, is he? My mother said he's a Finn?"

"That's true," Mundy agreed.

"Well, that's just dandy! Finns for neighbors in the middle of nowhere. I'm surprised we didn't find you with your throat slit and your pants down."

"You don't even know them!" Amanda interjected. "He seemed perfectly nice! He helped get us here."

"Yeah, so he can come back later and rob us," Tomas asserted.

"They do!" Mundy's voice came to life. "They come here, the Finns, the dad and his son. They trespass. And they steal. And they tried to kill our cows."

"Well, of course they do!" Tomas fumed. "They're vermin. Is that what happened to your face?" Tomas pointed to Mundy's cheek which revealed purplish bruise tipped by a cut.

"How old is the son?"

"He's your age, maybe a year older. His name is Matias."

"How big is he?"

"Bigger than me, but," Mundy added. "Smaller than you."

Tomas puffed out his chest and flexed his arms. "In that case, you won't have to worry about him anymore. Since there's nothing to do here, I'll need a hobby."

Mundy was looking at the same barn, the same pasture, and the same weather as Tomas. He saw plenty to do.

"What's a hobby?" he asked.

"You see," Amanda touched the side of her face, brushing away a fly. "Not everyone is as lazy as you are, Tomas! Is this Matias handsome?"

"No, he is not!" Mundy thundered.

Amanda laughed.

"I'll be a better judge of that. By the way, Mundy," She stepped close to him and whispered in his ear. "I found the ball in the field—before I went into the woods." Then more loudly, she added, "You see? You boys don't know as much as you think you do!"

$$* * * * *$$

Mundy and Tomas unloaded the wagon, setting the crates and furniture on a canvas spread on the ground. Uncle Halvar stood in the doorway of the cabin, listening to the decisions being made by the women but keeping a careful eye on the boys. He called for them to come to the cabin, and Tomas dropped his half of the crate that he and Mundy were carrying. It was too heavy for Mundy alone to carry, and so he set down his end, too, and walked up to the cabin where they waited.

"I need you to remove the old table from inside." Uncle Halvar said. His voice was low, but thin, like the lowest note on a wood flute.

"But that's where we eat," Mundy countered.

Uncle Halvar's hand was quick, striking the soft part of Mundy's cheek so that his head snapped.

"You will address me as Reverend Ingegaard," his Uncle said calmly, even though he had just committed a violent act. "And you will do as you are told."

Mundy rubbed the spot. It wasn't that it hurt—the sting was already fading—it was the shock of it, being struck by a stranger in his own home. Wait until he told his mother about this.

"Now is the time for obedience to the Lord's will," Uncle Halvar emphasized, directing the way with the flat of his hand.

"Come on, Mundy," Tomas whispered, stepping inside. "We brought a perfectly good table. Better than yours. You'll still get to eat."

Mundy followed him inside, careful to duck under his Uncle's out-stretched hand. Brita and Aunt Helga were busy determining how to arrange the Nelson cabin to make room for the Ingegaards and their many furnishings. He shot a panicked look to his mother, but she was chatting to Aunt Helga in Norwegian, and Mundy thought how strange it was. His mother was another person just then: a girl happy to see her sister again.

"Ma! The table!"

Tomas was already lifting his end, ready to navigate the table out of the cabin.

"Oh, we have a very nice table," Aunt Helga patted her sister's arm. "It's big enough for all of us." Mundy's mother smiled and nodded, saying it would be nice that they all could eat together, but Mundy remained unconvinced.

"But my father made this table!" He said it first to Aunt Helga, who scowled at him, then to his mother, he said, "Remember?"

"Well, our table is from a proper store!" Aunt Helga answered. "You don't mind, do you, Brita?"

Mundy's mother said she didn't mind, and that, in fact, she always had hated the table her husband had made. "It was too small, and it wobbled," she declared. So it was that Mundy and Tomas dragged the Nelson's small table out of the cabin, relegated to the porch, where half of it stood unprotected by the awning.

When instructed by Uncle Halvar, the two boys struggled with the Ingegaard's longer table, its weight shifting too far left and then too far right, prompting Uncle Halvar to yell at them to be more careful.

Like his son, Uncle Halvar was tall—taller than Mundy's father. He stooped inside the cabin to avoid hitting his head on the crossbeams as he directed their activity. His frame lacked the sinew of muscles of Mundy's father, won by daily manual labor. Instead, his stomach rounded out like the sides of a pot stove. He seemed as if he might lend them a hand lifting and positioning things, but he was able to restrain the urge. The table, in its new place, nearly touched the far wall. The women polished it with beeswax until it shone.

The boys carried in chairs and a silver pot, which was only for decoration, according to Aunt Helga, swaddled in blankets. Soon the cabin was as full as a miser's gold sack with ornate and useless items that would have been better sold off or melted down.

Mundy cornered his mother in between loads. He asked how they all could sleep in the cabin.

"It will be crowded, sure," she agreed. "You'll share the loft with Tomas. Your cousin Amanda will sleep with me on the straw mattress over here." She indicated the floor space next to the fancy dining table. "And that leaves the bed free for your aunt and uncle."

"You're going to sleep on the floor?"

"Yes."

"Of your own home?"

"Yes, Mundy!" She was growing exasperated with him, her voice tense and breathy. "We are all making sacrifices. Unless you and Tomas want to sleep on the floor?"

Mundy looked around to make sure no one else was in earshot. The Ingegaards all seemed to be outside.

"Uncle Halvar struck me," he blurted.

"What did you do?"

"I didn't do anything!"

"Were you supposed to be doing something that you weren't doing?"

"No!" Mundy didn't even have to think about. He had done nothing at all wrong. "I only didn't call him Reverend, and he hit me!"

"Well, now you know," his mother shrugged. "He is a minister, and you will need to respect that." She was admiring a photograph of the Ingegaards. "Don't they look nice?" Mundy's mother said, flashing the portrait frame at him so the light from the cabin window illuminated a well-dressed, younger version of the Ingegaard family.

It was taken years before. The children were smaller, and Amanda was plumper in the face, but she had the same pretty eyes. She was the only Ingegaard in the photo not wearing black. Like her mother, she wore a high-neck blouse with white silk ruffles under her chin, but Amanda's blouse was striped. He couldn't tell which colors the stripes consisted of, because the entire photo was all black, white, and gray.

"We should have had our portrait taken," his mother sniffed as she set down the photo on a very polished round table jammed very near a green fabric chair. She touched the arm of the chair and tested the cushion with the palm of her hand, but she did not sit in it, and she told Mundy not to touch any of the Ingegaard's possessions without their permission. "Just do what your uncle asks," she said.

"I don't have to do what he says!"

"Yes, you do," his mother's voice was calm, but her eyes narrowed on Mundy so sharply that he had to look away.

"He's not my father!"

"Your father is dead. Uncle Halvar is the new head of this house."

Aunt Helga shadowed the doorway. Mundy noticed her hands were empty although there were items to carry in from the wagon. "We need to make room for Uncle Halvar's books. What's in that trunk there?" She pointed to the trunk that Grandfather Nelson had brought from Norway, filled with hand tools that Mundy's dad had cherished.

"Get your cousin and move that to the barn, Mundy."

Mundy couldn't believe what was happening. He stammered his reluctance.

"Don't make this more difficult than it needs to be. Be a good boy."

"Your boy needs to be taught manners, Brita." Aunt Helga looked at him like he was an Indian who had forced his way into the cabin on a war raid.

"He knows his manners, not to worry. It's just a difficult time for everyone."

"Of course," Aunt Helga allowed. "It's only that the boy should be grateful to have the influence of a good Christian like the Reverend Ingegaard."

CHAPTER SEVEN

THE PLAN

Like the day of the storm that had nearly knocked over the field shed, the Ingegaards came out of nowhere and darkened the skies.

About a week after the Ingegaards arrived, Mundy was scything in the orchard. His mother sang in Norwegian as she hung laundry on the line, a rare moment when she wasn't with her horrible sister. Mundy seized the opportunity, setting down his scythe and sharpening stone. His mind wasn't on field work or any of his other chores, anyway. Math was on his mind—the kind of math that his father used to talk about.

Soon he was helping her pin shirts and sheets so they wouldn't blow off in the hot, dry wind.

"Ma, there's four more mouths to feed now, aren't there?"

"Yes, that's true," she said, snapping one of Uncle Halvar's white shirts so the sleeves could wave in the wind. "But think about it a different way: there may be four more mouths, but that's eight more hands. Just a different way of thinking about the same thing."

"I suppose that's true," Mundy pretended to agree. "But that's eight hands that don't know much about farming."

"And you don't know about what they know: religion, and books, and music, and the like. We will learn from each other."

"But that'll cost us time away from chores we need to be doing."

"Have it your way, Mundy." She pulled another clothespin from her apron. "Think of it as an investment. We spend some time now to help them learn what needs doing, and then in a month or two, we'll all reap the rewards."

"But what chores will they do? Just so we know how to spend our time training them."

"I'll tell you what, since you seem to have a good head for farm business all of a sudden, why don't you tell me what you think makes sense."

"Well…"

His mother raised a finger to caution him. "Nothing in haste. Your father always used to sleep on important decisions."

That was true. And maybe this was an important decision, Mundy's very first one, that could affect the future of the farm.

"I'll sleep on it," he agreed.

✳ ✳ ✳ ✳ ✳

At supper, Uncle Halvar insisted the entire family kneel on the dirt floor, bow their heads, and pretend to think of their blessings. His prayer was interminable, padded with the same formality he demanded from Mundy.

Our heavenly king, the majesty of whose creating provides abundance to those unworthy prone before you…

Aunt Helga barely gave Mundy enough food for a single swallow. Mundy asked his mother for more parsnips, but instead of taking them from the pot, she gave them to him from her own plate. After clearing his plate, he stole peeks of Amanda, taking her face in parts. Her lips were full, but they turned up into a natural smile on each end. Her ears, although little more than lamb buds, tipped forward from the sides of her head so that, when she wore her honey hair braided, they showed prominently. Her eyes were round and large, helping to offset the finely shaped tip of her nose.

When she told stories, unrestrained by her father, her voice squeaked at the end of her sentences, which served as a natural bridge to her soft laughter. She provided her observations of the farm—or, rather, her wild misconceptions of it.

"But I swear that cow tried to stand up when I walked by," Amanda declared.

"The cow wasn't trying to stand," Mundy interjected. "It was mounting the other cow!"

His aunt and uncle reprimanded him simultaneously, but Mundy couldn't help himself: the laughter would not be constrained. A cow that could stand on two legs? Maybe if they stood on their front legs, upside-down, how much easier that would make milking! The image caused him to burst out again, and his mother dismissed him from the table.

✳✳✳✳✳

Sleeping in the loft with Tomas proved nearly impossible. The older boy stretched out his arms and legs when he slept, forcing Mundy into a cramped ball, teetering at the ledge, kept from falling to the plank floor below only by the top of the ladder. Mundy suffered through a long night, thinking of many things, including what he and his mother had discussed earlier. He dozed off just in time to awake for morning chores. He shook Tomas gently at first, trying to be polite, but Tomas fought against waking. Mundy shook him harder.

"Tomas! Tomas!"

"Let me sleep, will you?" Tomas whined like a baby. "I'm growing."

Then Tomas fell back asleep as if Mundy weren't even there. Mundy scrambled down the ladder to the main floor where his uncle prayed at the fancy table. His uncle, elbows on the table, did not look out the window as dawn broke the horizon. Instead, his eyes were closed, his hands clasped atop the table. His lips trembled, as if about to speak. Maybe he was thinking of the right words to say to God.

Mundy tried to sneak past his uncle, but the floorboard creaked and Uncle Halvar's eyes shot open blazing at him.

"Good morning, Reverend." Mundy said in a fearful half-whisper. He darted past like a startled mouse. It was time to milk the cows who would not stand on their back legs for him.

✳✳✳✳✳

Behind a shadowy mass of trees, the horizon glowed gold and pearl with the promise of sunrise. The trees were the only marker of the Petterson's homestead, the ones who'd been slaughtered during the blizzard. He couldn't imagine what that must have been like—finding them dead. They died together, at least. Maybe that was a blessing. A cool morning breeze greeted his grim thoughts, making him shiver.

The cows mooing became uproarious when Mundy heaved open the barn door to allow as much light in, but even in the semi-darkness, he could see well enough. Besides, with milking, seeing wasn't as important as feeling. His father once told him that watching your hands while milking was like watching your feet while dancing. Mundy didn't know anything about dancing, but he could milk with his eyes closed.

By the end of milking, Mundy had worked out a plan for the farm. In fact, that was most likely the last time he would do the milking on his own, because his plan involved sharing chores. Tomas would help with milking each morning and evening. After all, Tomas's legs weren't broken. His hands worked.

Tomas won't want to wear his fancy boots for milking, Mundy mused. Not only would they get scuffed (Tomas's worst fear), but because they were so big, they'd probably suck right into the barn muck. Tomas was liable to fall face first in manure. The thought made Mundy smile, but he also was buoyed by his new plan, which wasn't just for milking: Mundy had a plan for all the chores. He and Tomas would do the milking, mucking, town runs, and scything; Amanda would collect eggs, tend chickens, and wash clothes; Aunt Helga and ma would keep cooking and wash dishes. They all would help thresh grain and dig potatoes.

Except for Uncle Halvar. Mundy's plan didn't include anything for his uncle.

Once his mother heard the plan, she would agree that it made sense.

Mundy trotted back to the cabin for breakfast, excited to catch his mother alone and tell her about the plan. He was burning to talk to her. The silhouette of a man standing in the pasture forced Mundy to a dead stop. The tips of the man's hair glowed in the gold-orange dawn. It was Uncle Halvar, his arms extended straight over his head, and he was yelling at the sunrise.

"I beseech thee, Lord, make use of this worthless lump of clay!"

Mundy shook his head as he watched his uncle fall prostrate to the ground like a man begging for his life. His uncle was crazy, Mundy decided. It was up to Mundy to keep the farm going.

Aunt Helga and his mother were seated at the Ingegaard's boughten table. Brita was tightening the screws on the cheese press weight while Aunt Helga explained again how Uncle Halvar had very narrowly missed becoming the new minister in Spring Grove.

"He was doing very well, filling in on a temporary basis, because—"

"Because the other minister was thrown by a horse," Brita completed her sister's sentence. "I know. You mentioned it before."

"Did I?" Aunt Helga continued. "The town just wasn't ready for his message, and they picked a man name Hendrickson instead—a little mouse of a man who clearly doesn't have the calling like Halvar."

"Ma? Can I talk to you outside?" Mundy figured his mother would welcome the interruption. This was at least the third time Aunt Helga had told the exact same story, as if it were the only thing that had happened to the Ingegaard family: the Reverend Uncle Halvar Ingegaard's brush with being a real preacher.

Aunt Helga was not pleased. She muttered 'well' under her breath.

"Mundy!" Brita scowled at her son. "It's rude to interrupt adults when they're talking."

Mundy blinked and swallowed hard. "I'm sorry for interrupting, Aunt Helga."

Aunt Helga leaned back in her chair, her forearms sliding along the table as if she were too weak to lift them. "He thinks an apology will bring back the thread of our conversation, does he?"

"Oh, I think he's just excited to tell me about the farm work. Is that what it is, Mundy? Something wrong with the herd?"

Mundy nodded. "Yes, ma. Something wrong with the herd."

"I best go have a look," she said to her sister. "You just stay put, and I'll be right back."

She followed Mundy out to the yard, and he directed his mother to have a seat on the log bench he and his father had built.

"But I thought we were going out to the barn," she said, confused that they had stopped.

"I wanted to talk to you alone," Mundy admitted. "We still can increase the milk herd, like pa wanted to, and sell to the Buffalo creamery. Tomas and I deliver to the train depot. Amanda tends the chickens, and she can take the eggs to town with us if we ever have too many. But she can take over the churning all on her own, unless you or Aunt Helga want to do it."

She stopped him. "That all sounds sensible, Mundy. Except I know Helga's poor hands wouldn't be suited for churning or very much else."

"But there's more!" Mundy insisted. "I've got it all figured out."

Brita ignored his protests. "...and you can't just interrupt adults when we're talking. Your aunt was in the middle of a story when you came bursting in. Anything you say to me, you can say to your aunt and uncle."

Mundy couldn't help his reaction—a slight cock of the head, the rise of an eyebrow—enough to suggest there was some doubt about the matter.

"Do they know how you help Mr. Koskinen?" Mundy asked.

"Of course," she stammered. "Why shouldn't they? I'll tell your plan to Uncle Halvar and see what he decides.

"Uncle Halvar!" Mundy was shocked. "What does he know about farming?"

And then Brita Nelson said something to her son that made him feel like he'd been hit in the stomach.

"Uncle Halvar is in charge of the farm and of this family now, Mundy. You'll have to accept that. And anything you say to me, you can say to them."

But Mundy did not accept that. He pushed himself off the bench and looked her straight in the eye.

"No, I don't," he declared and walked away.

＊＊＊＊＊

Men from the neighboring farms appeared in the yard on foot that evening—Piers Kersten, Jonathon Engelman, the Englishman Lowell, Kauko Koskinen, and Matias, too—their work shirts stained with sweat.

Mr. Kersten, his gray hair flattened around his head by the hat he now clutched in front of him, stepped forward.

"We heard you had company," he said to Brita. "Thought we better come and make their acquaintance."

"I'm sure my sister's family would be happy to make your acquaintance."

"We heard the man is a minister," Mr. Lowell chimed in. "Is that true?"

Brita called for her sister, but it was Uncle Halvar who emerged from the cabin first, carrying his thick Bible, still opened to the page he'd been studying. Seeing the men, Uncle Halvar's demeanor changed. He called for his wife and children to come out in a commanding but warm tone.

"We have visitors," he boomed, smiling.

Aunt Helga and Amanda appeared and curtsied to the men. The Ingegaards were well practiced in the subtle art of smiles and pleasantries, and soon the neighbor men were invited to sit on log benches. Tomas brought the water pail and tin cups for them, while Helga offered the men the boiled potatoes and hunks of bread that were meant for supper.

Mundy sat on the ground, keeping his head between his knees, brushing his legs every minute or so to ward off the biting flies. He practiced his addition on the assembled farmers, figuring that collectively they owned more than two square miles of land in the county. Not all of the land was in production: there were plenty of sloughs and ponds and woods in the way of wheat fields and grazing. Then Mundy figured that in that two square miles, there were at least another dozen troll mounds, waiting for Lewis the surveyor to find them before they got leveled and the ancient songs were lost—if, as Amanda claimed, they were filled with music.

Piers Kersten asked where the Ingegaards had come from, how long their family had been in the country, and their views on religion, but he didn't allow Uncle Halvar to respond to the neighborly interrogation.

"Take our minister, Reverend Lorenson," Kersten said. "Fine man. Friendly."

"He'd give you the time of day whether he knew it or not," Lowell chimed in.

"…but he lacks passion."

"Hardly stirs the dust when he preaches," Lowell added.

Kersten shot Lowell a warning look before he continued. "I know Reverend Lorenson has been feeling poorly these past few months. That's what you said, didn't you, Lowell?"

"Yes," Lowell affirmed. "That's what I've heard. He has the gout, I believe, and it flares up enough that he can hardly stand, poor man. He has to lean heavy on the pulpit box we built for him. I keep waiting for him to come crashing into the congregation!"

Piers Kersten, exasperated, let out a sigh. "Let's not be unkind to Reverend Lorenson, now."

Undeterred, Mr. Lowell kept talking. "And he uses those fancy three-cent words—the kind of words you have to pretend to know until you do."

Uncle Halvar closed his eyes, knitting his eyebrows together, either listening intently or praying. The women fell quiet, expectant. Then after a few moments in this meditative state, Uncle Halvar opened his gleaming eyes.

"Gentlemen, I can help!" he declared. "I could do the ministry if Reverend Lorenson is not feeling up to it, on a temporary basis. That was precisely my role in Spring Grove."

Amanda's smile tightened. "Father, are you certain you're up for it? Remember the great strain that role placed upon you."

Uncle Halvar ignored Amanda's comment.

"I have many sermons at the ready," he explained. "And if it is dust that needs stirring, then a sandstorm you shall have!"

Aunt Helga, her hair tucked in her white bonnet, cocked her head in surprise. The movement reminded Mundy of a dandelion seed head in the breeze. She placed a hand on her husband's shoulder.

"But the congregation may not be accustomed to your point of view, husband," she offered.

"We're all Lutherans," he nodded to others until they were nodding too. "And that's a start."

"But, husband, I believe you had said it was important for you to remove yourself from ministry for the present for a life of contemplation."

"Yes, father," Amanda chirped. "The strain."

"Indeed, I did say that. But coming to this beautiful new place has stirred in me an awakening. Like a sunrise, I see all the flowers of the Lord's glorious creation. The night is over."

Aunt Helga removed her hand from his shoulder. It fell to her side like a baby bird blown from the nest, but then it became a fist, balling the cloth of her skirt.

Uncle Halvar continued, "Would you gentlemen introduce me to the Reverend Lorenson?"

"Of course! Of course. Happy to do it. I'm sure he would appreciate the help."

"Good. Mr. Kersten, let us travel tomorrow to meet with him, if you have the time to spare."

"Of course."

"Good! We'll all go!" He indicated his wife and children and in the same gesture rounded up Mundy and his mother.

"We have to drive the cows to the far pasture tomorrow," Mundy protested.

Uncle Halvar laughed. "Always thinking of yourself! That's the problem with the world today!" He closed his eyes and lifted his chin, reaching both hands to the sky. His voice boomed. "My people who are called by My name humble themselves and pray and seek My face, and turn from their wicked ways, then I will hear from heaven, forgive their sin, and heal their land."

The men were silent until Mr. Kersten spoke.

"Is that from the Book, Reverend?"

"Indeed! Indeed!" Uncle Halvar hoisted his battered old Bible into the air. "The second book of Chronicles."

If he's got the darned book memorized, why does he need to carry it around? Mundy wondered.

"You'll come with us tomorrow, Tiddemund, and when you return, you will find the farm very much as you left it. God's dumb animals have a way of fulfilling their earthly purposes, all on their own."

He may have been a minister of some kind, but Mundy knew his uncle didn't understand anything about tending to animals.

Uncle Halvar then introduced the topic of Roman Papism. He outdid himself with an impassioned exhortation to the Christian brotherhood assembled on the log benches to be tempered in the Lord's wisdom and united against the evils of the False Church. He steadied a gaze on Kauko Koskinen.

"And you! Are you a Catholic?"

Koskinen straightened himself under the steely stares of all present.

"Certainly not!" He sputtered. "I am a good Lutheran, like all of us!"

Uncle Halvar nodded. "Good! The Lord says, You shall have no other gods before me! You shall not make for yourself a carved image, or any likeness of anything that is in heaven above, or that is in the earth beneath, or that is in the water under the earth. You shall not bow down to them or serve them, for I the Lord your God am a jealous God."

The men received Uncle Halvar's message with hearty amens. They agreed that Catholicism was pretty bad, to be sure, but so was that wet spring weather they'd had and how it had given their fields a slow start into summer.

Bats swooped over the group in the gathering dusk. The neighbor men had stayed long enough to go from swatting flies to swatting mosquitoes as twilight progressed. They began their good-byes when Mundy noticed Amanda leaning against one of the apple trees his grandfather had planted, and Matias Koskinen resting one arm above her so he could lean in to tell her lies. With his other arm he fed himself an apple he'd taken from the tree without permission.

Amanda didn't know any better. She'd never encountered a Finn before. She laughed and was as warm and friendly with him as she had been with Mundy. He wanted to shout at Matias to get off their property, but not in front of company.

Just as Mundy had resigned himself to warning Amanda later in private, Tomas strode toward the orchard, his jaw clenched. He looked as angry as a mother bear separated from her cubs. Matias heard him coming and stood up straight, ready for a confrontation with Tomas who was taller and broader than Matias. Mundy hoped to see his cousin throttle the Finn, but, instead, Tomas grabbed his sister by the arm and dragged her off.

"Mother needs you now," he snapped.

Amanda wished Matias a rushed good night even as her feet scraped the ground.

Matias watched the brother and sister disappear into the cabin as the door shut hard against the cool evening air. Then he noticed Mundy watching him. He threw the half-eaten apple at Mundy.

Mundy leaped out of its path to avoid being hit in the face.

"What are you looking at?"

"A bad apple!" Mundy retorted.

It rained so hard the next day the pond looked like it might flood the woods. Would it reach the troll mound and shift the ancient structure of stones and roots? It hadn't yet, not in hundreds of years. The mound probably had lived through thousands of floods over the centuries. Mundy hoped another rainstorm wouldn't erase it.

He spent the day in the barn sharpening blades with a file, scythe blades and sawblades and even some field knives. They might come in handy if flood water seeped into the mound and brought the corpse of some evil troll back to life, and if one did claw its way out, seeking the flesh of a Norwegian boy, Mundy would be ready. Maybe he'd chase the troll over to the Koskinen farm.

By supper, Mundy was famished, but he had to kneel on the ground with the rest of the family as Uncle Halvar belabored his blessing. There were biscuits. He could smell them. Instead of praying, Mundy was calculating how to make sure he got the most food on his plate. He wanted at least a dozen of those biscuits smothered in butter. Then there were beans and potatoes. He'd eat them, too, but it was the biscuits that mattered.

The amen finally arrived and they all sat at the table with Mundy next to his mother. She served as a shield between her and Uncle Halvar, and no one seemed to mind the arrangement. Mundy's heart leapt to his throat when he noticed the plate of biscuits going the wrong way around the table. It started with Uncle Halvar who took four before passing the plate to Tomas who sat on his right. Tomas took four before passing the plate to Amanda, who took two. Aunt Helga at the other end of the table also took two, leaving only two biscuits on the plate. That number was far fewer than the dozen Mundy had hoped to eat.

"Ma, are there some more biscuits coming?" he asked before deciding whether he could take the last two for himself. His knew his mother needed to eat, too. She didn't answer but took hold of the plate from his grasp and tipped it so both biscuits landed on Mundy's plate.

"You can have mine, Mundy."

Brita scraped her food onto Mundy's plate.

"You spoil that boy, Brita," Aunt Helga was not pleased. "The boy who wants more for himself surely is stuffing his pockets full of the stones of inequity that will drown him in the fires of hell."

"Father," Amanda said. "Can a person drown in fire, as mother claims?"

Uncle Halvar cleared his throat as if about to speak but caught his wife's watchful eye, and he went back to the little boiled potatoes he was scooping on his plate.

"Well, it's just that your mother is simply painting a picture with words," Mundy's mother offered. "Her meaning is plain enough. There is no place for the greedy mouth in the Lord's house."

"Thank you, Aunt Brita," Amanda said hastily before returning her attention to her father. "May I ask another question?"

"Yes, I suppose so," Uncle Halvar hesitated. "If it has an answer."

"Is it sinful to ask for more than what you have?"

Amanda stared at her father, awaiting his response. He chewed his potatoes with a sideways grinding motion of his jaw, like one of the herd chewing oats.

"This is the Lord's creation. Anything that happens—anything that will happen—he had willed it in the beginning."

"So is it sinful..."

He cut her off: "It's wasteful. It demonstrates a faithlessness in the Almighty's omnipotence. So, yes, asking for more is sinful. It is! In fact, it's blasphemy!" His voice gathered power to near yelling, and he brought his fist down on the table causing their plates to clatter with the force of the blow.

Amanda seemed pleased with her father's reaction. She shot Mundy a glance as if to see if he'd noticed. Her mouth moved as if she were ready to pose another needling question to her father, but Amanda next directed her attention to her mother.

"Oh, mother, look! You've spoiled the beans again! Look, father, these are scorched. They must have stuck to the bottom of the pot. Poor thing, she can't get the hang of your stove, Aunt Brita."

Aunt Helga's eyes narrowed into slits and her mouth tightened, but she said nothing.

"You will eat everything on your plate, Amanda," her father warned. "And you will be grateful for it."

"Oh, I am quite grateful—especially that mother did not hurt herself! She surely is protected by the Lord's mercy! Remember when she nearly cut her fingers off peeling potatoes? But I guess when your hands get so arthritic, even the simple tasks become more difficult."

Aunt Helga slammed down her fork, fuming. Everyone froze, waiting to see what would happen next, and it was Tomas who broke the tension.

"I like them a little browned," he chirped. His plate was already licked clean. He reached across the table and took a biscuit from Mundy's plate, snatching it into his mouth in one bite.

"Tomas! Manners!" Aunt Helga reproved him.

Tomas, his mouth full of Mundy's biscuit, said, "I'm thaw-ry, Mundy" Crumbs sprayed out of his mouth as he spoke.

"You've got to keep your strength up, Tomas," Uncle Halvar declared. "You boys are making the delivery to the depot tomorrow, aren't you?"

"Yes, we are!" Tomas declared, as if he ever had lifted a finger around the place, other than separating Amanda from Matias.

"That's fine!" Uncle Halvar stared at his son with open pride, which made Mundy wish his father was there to give him a pat on the shoulder. "A young man showing enterprise! Eat up, son!"

Mundy seethed. Tomas was a worthless worker. What did he know about cream and cheese and railroad contracts? Nothing, that's what! Then for him to steal food from Mundy's plate—Mundy! Who was running the farm on his own while these Ingegaards sat around and talked, and yelled at him, and prayed, and generally frittered away their time! To top it all off, Tomas couldn't hitch a horse to his breeches, let alone to a wagon.

"Tomorrow is an important day for this family," Uncle Halvar raised his voice, as if he were winding up for another prayer. "I, too, have news!" He looked to his wife who watched him with a stark admiration that made Mundy's skin crawl. "The Lord has called me here, to this area, to shepherd the souls of this far-flung pasture, and tomorrow I shall find my flock."

How ridiculous, Mundy thought. It was the sheep that made a man a shepherd. No sheep, no shepherd. Without sheep, Uncle Halvar was only a man making Mundy's life hell, like winter or itch weed.

* * * * *

The morning came. Mundy jabbed Tomas in the ribs and dodged his cousin's wild swipe.

"It's too early," was all he said before collapsing back onto his mat, but Mundy threatened to pour hot grease on him if he didn't get up. After all, his father's plan to turn a real income from the herd was about to begin, but it took another half-hour before Tomas finally opened his eyes.

In the darkness outside, only the morning star gave any indication that the sun would soon paint the eastern horizon. The air held enough chill that Mundy wore one of his father's wool shirts over his own. The day would warm up, though, and fast.

Mundy did the milking on his own, and if he could have loaded the eight cans onto the wagon himself, he would have, but they were heavy. For lifting, Tomas's lanky frame came in handy.

Cloppie gave them some nonsense along the way to town, veering off toward any opening in the trail that she noticed, as if to say let's go anywhere but town. Mundy, already irritated, was no in no mood to deal with an old nag's faults.

"With the money we get from the creamery," Mundy said. "The first thing we should buy is a new horse."

"That's a good idea," Tomas agreed. "If we had a faster horse, the trip wouldn't take as long, and we wouldn't have to get up nearly so early."

"We'd get up as early, Tomas. You may as well face it. You live on a farm now."

"*Smuss*! Don't say that! As soon as I can raise enough money from this farming, I will leave it! That's what I'm doing with my share."

"What do you mean, your share?" Mundy had never heard of such a thing! "There are no shares! The money goes back to the farm. A new horse. Seed for spring sowing. Then more milk cans. Then more cows."

"Well, that's what you think," Tomas said looking off toward the lake as if the conversation bored him. "My father will tell you how the money is to be spent. And don't be surprised if you hear mention of his new church."

"What new church?"

"That's what my parents want," Tomas yawned. "They want their own church, even if they have to build it themselves, and that costs money."

"A church?" Mundy fumed. The idea was ridiculous. Turning the fruit of their labor over to Uncle Halvar for a church was as ridiculous as drilling a hole in one of the milk cans.

CHAPTER EIGHT

THE PRICE OF MILK

The agent wouldn't make the deal with them. Their eight cans stood in a row on the platform, but he waved for them to put them back on their trailer.

"It's not that I wouldn't like to proceed with our arrangement," the agent explained. He had breadcrumbs pressed into his cheek, suggesting he had fallen asleep at his desk. "But like I discussed with your father, to make this arrangement profitable for all parties, there has to be a volume of milk. Now your father had suggested there might be more than…" he counted the cans. "five hundred pounds of milk."

"That's six hundred and fifty!" Mundy corrected hotly.

"And how do I know you didn't water down the milk you do have?"

"You can check it for yourself!" Mundy went to pry open one of the lids so the agent could dip his finger in.

"No, no. The water issue is moot. My point is, I thought there would be more. Now if you had a thousand pounds! Do you think you could wring out a little more from each of your milkers, boys?"

Tomas shrugged. He was out of his depth entirely.

Mundy shook his head. "Too late in the season."

Tomas may not have much to say about milk or cows, but he did have his own interest in receiving payment.

"Mr. Stern, we have this milk here and now. It's got to be worth something."

"Look boys, I want to help you. I do. I know how tough it is to cut a living out of the land. Hell, I grew up slopping hogs and cutting firewood not fifteen miles from where we're standing! We fought off Indians during the uprising and mended our own broken bones back then. But this is business. You're what I would call an investment risk. What if my relationship with the creamery in Buffalo sours, pardon the pun? Yours isn't the only arrangement affected, you see? Maybe come back in the spring with more milk. And you," he nodded to Tomas. "Maybe have that pretty sister of yours come along with some eggs. Any time."

Tomas didn't like hearing anyone talk about his sister. He stood to his full height, and Mundy sensed that whatever happened next could permanently destroy their chances for a deal, so he gripped Tomas's arm.

"We'll take less," Mundy added quickly. "For this load."

"You'd have to do more than that, I'm afraid. I'm sorry to put you in such a tough spot, but that's just good business."

"Couldn't you help us out now, and we'll pay you later?"

"Is that how your father would do business, do you reckon? He struck me as a reasonable person, and I was sorry to hear about his passing. Look, I don't want to leave you stranded over a barrel. It's got to be fair, so I can get this load on the Buffalo train, but I'm going to have to increase my rates. You boys are a high-risk investment, like I said."

"But we'd barely break even," Tomas gasped.

"Break even or no deal, your choice. It's strictly commerce, son. Not to mention the way I need to inconvenience myself and others to make this arrangement work. Today, I'd have to bump this shipment off the freight run, for instance." The agent indicated four large crates on the edge of the platform. "From a good paying customer, too. Fella from the state geologist office."

"You mean Mr. Lewis?"

"Yeah, that's him. Said he dug up these trinkets not too far from your farm, there on the north shore of the big lake. Full of dead Indian trinkets, I reckon. Pow-wow pipes and what-not."

"Our milk will spoil, but dead Indian trinkets can wait for tomorrow's run, can't they?"

"I suppose so, but those crates would need to be pulled back under that awning. Know a couple of fellas who could manage it?" He put out his hand for Mundy to shake. Mundy shook. He had struck his first deal. He hoped, with practice, future deals turned more to his favor.

"I'll get your boys your money," the agent said.

The boys began dragging the surveyor's crates away from the platform, but there was one they couldn't budge. Mundy asked the agent if they could remove the lid and lighten the load.

"I don't suppose it'd hurt anything if you had a peek, so long as you put everything back." He disappeared into a little door that led to the office, thought better of it, and reappeared for a moment to add, "And don't bend those nails when you pry off the lid, or I'll charge you for new ones to tack it shut again."

"You know this Mr. Lewis?" Tomas asked Mundy. Mundy told him how Lewis had wanted to survey the Indian mound on the farm, but how his father had refused.

"How much would he pay us?" Tomas asked. Mundy had begun to suspect that money was too often on Tomas's mind.

"They aren't paying. Just something the government is doing."

Mundy slid the bar between the lid and worked his way around the top, prying only a little on each side until the lid was loose enough to lift off without damaging the nails. At first, all he could see was sawdust, but as he felt inside, he began to pick out objects. Broken pieces of pottery. Beads. More arrow points like the one Mr. Lewis had offered him earlier in the summer. But that wouldn't account for the crate's full weight.

"He told us that he didn't dig in those mounds," Mundy explained to his cousin. "He said he only measured them."

"This crate is heavy. There's got to be something else in here..." Mundy's hand, up to his elbow now in sawdust, felt to the bottom of the crate. His fingers touched a cool, metal surface. He directed Tomas to help, and together they found its edges and hoisted it from the crate in a shower of sawdust.

"What is that?" Tomas wondered, his eyes wide. It took both of them to lift it from the crate. Mundy brushed off the remaining sawdust to reveal what looked like an axe head, but bigger than any axe head they'd ever seen. It was as long as Mundy's arm from the butt to the blade. Although it was solid metal, it wasn't made from steel. They could tell that by the color: the surface gleamed ocher.

"That's fifty pounds, at least!" Mundy exclaimed. "No one man could swing something that heavy."

"Is it a two-man axe?" Tomas guessed. "Like those two-man saws."

"I can't see how two men could work on an axe together," Mundy answered. He pointed to etched symbols on the top edge: squares and circles connected by lines, straight and wavy. "What do you make of those?"

"Not English," Tomas answered. "Not Norwegian, either. Where'd you say it came from?"

"Mr. Lewis, the government surveyor. He's been working the north side of the big lake."

Mundy could almost hear his father say, this belonged to a troll. He wanted to explain about the trolls, but that could lead to problems with Uncle Halvar. The Ingegaards wouldn't believe Mundy about the trolls: they had their own monsters to fear.

The creaking of the office door and Mr. Stern's shuffling walk scraping the soles of his shoes against the planks of the depot platform interrupted their investigation of the artifact.

"Now, what did you boys go and uncover there?"

They held it up for him as if it were the rack of a trophy buck.

"What do you think it is?" Tomas asked.

"Look like a big axe to me," Mr. Stern replied. "And it looks like it's made from bronze. That's worth a pretty penny." He waved a paper note in his hand. "But pack it back up, boys! Let's conclude our business."

They reloaded the crate as best they could, but sawdust whirled off the platform in gusts of hot wind. The depot agent handed them one dollar and twenty-five cents.

"It's not enough," Mundy muttered as he tucked the money in his pocket.

Mr. Stern's expression landed somewhere between surprise and annoyance.

"What's that?"

"Knock it off, Tiddemund!" Tomas warned.

"He's robbing us," Mundy declared.

"Well, if it is robbery," Mr. Stern waved off the accusation. "At least you're being robbed on your own merits."

He walked off toward his office leaving them to ponder his meaning.

"We should take that axe," Mundy was angry. "We should take it and sell it."

"Are you crazy? For one thing, stealing is wrong."

"He is stealing from us! He just admitted it."

"For another thing, you wouldn't be stealing from him. You'd be stealing from the surveyor. Are you angry at him?"

"No, but maybe it doesn't really belong to anybody, anyway. He said he didn't dig up those mounds, so what's he doing with a crate full of treasure?"

Tomas shrugged, and added, "And for another thing, we'd be the first once caught out. You wouldn't want to be brought before my father as a thief, trust me."

"I guess so," Mundy agreed. "Still, we can't afford to make bad deals."

The boys left the depot and walked Cloppie back to where the main street began, Mundy held her lead tight so she wouldn't panic from the din of boots thudding on planks and the whirring of the mill and hammering from the smithy.

Tomas suddenly got as antsy as a trapped fox.

"I'll be right back."

"Where are you going?"

Tomas trotted down the boardwalk, leaving Mundy and Cloppie to watch him as he disappeared into the doorway of Mr. Buri's store. Minutes passed without sign of him. Soon enough, Cloppie had gone slack, like she was about to fall asleep or worse, so Mundy pulled her forward toward Buri's store, but he didn't want to get too close.

Tomas appeared from the doorway, smiling and looking as if he'd just gotten the last biscuit at dinner. He patted Mundy on the shoulder.

"Okay, let's go!"

"What'd you go in there for?"

"Looks like we need more money, doesn't it? We aren't going to get rich from dragging a ton of milk back and forth all the time, right?"

"What have we got to do with Mr. Buri?" Mundy didn't like the idea of a deal being made without being consulted.

"Don't worry!" Tomas's grin was infuriatingly smug. "Nothing to do with your precious cows! I'm taking a job with Mr. Buri as a shop apprentice!"

"What did he say?"

"He said I could work for him, and he'd pay me," Tomas laughed. "What else do you think it means to have a job?"

Mundy sputtered, "And you took it?" He was angry. After all, his plan for the farm didn't allow room for jobs in town.

"There was one condition—and this is where you get to help. We all have to go proper school."

Stunned didn't quite cover Mundy's reaction.

"We don't need no school!"

"Judging by your use of English, I'd say a little school will do you good. At any rate, it's not for you to say. It's for my father to decide."

"But the creamery deal…We have to deliver the milk. It's got to be done! That's what a farm is!"

Tomas shook his head, his lips pursed disdainfully. "You said it yourself. We're just losing money. All this farming is not for me. Look, Mundy, I don't plan to be around for long here. My plan is to apprentice with a slick merchant, like this Buri fellow. He doesn't do much business now, he says, but the town is growing, and then there's the summer visitors that'll come by the thousands. I'll get some good experience under my belt and then head into Minneapolis. See, it's all working indoors, people walking in the door to hand over their money, and money isn't as heavy to carry around as those milk cans. Speaking of money, how much did you say we got for that milk?"

"A dollar twenty-five."

"Are you sure? Show me."

As soon as Mundy opened his hand to take another look at the silver coins in his palm, Tomas snatched the money from him.

"Give it back!" Mundy clawed at his cousin, but the older boy easily pushed him away by the forehead.

"I don't trust you to give that to my father," his cousin declared.

Mundy rushed Tomas, shouldered into his midsection and they both hit the ground hard. Tomas soon rolled Mundy onto his back and pinned his shoulders down in a channel of horse muck.

"You better not scuff these boots," Tomas panted. "Or I will crush you! So, here's how it's got to be. I'll let you up, and you count to five to calm down."

"I ain't counting to five. I'm going to use those fingers to make a fist for your mouth!"

But Tomas was older and stronger. He knew where to tickle, where to prod, and how to make his younger cousin alternate between laughter and begging to be released.

$$*****$$

On the ride home, Mundy said nothing. He merely stewed, occasionally thwacking Cloppie with the reins to urge her onward. He wished a bear would have run out of the woods and attacked them and bit off Tomas's head.

He didn't even bother unharnessing Cloppie before he ran to the cabin—let Tomas earn his keep for once! He wanted to get there before his cousin to tell his mother about the money and Mr. Buri and the damn school and Tomas's job.

Yanking open the door, he called for his mother in a high-pitched voice although she was in plain sight, mending clothes with Aunt Helga next to the stove while Amanda sat at the table, braiding a wreath of wheat. Aunt Helga and Amanda were singing in Norwegian, a church song from what he could tell, about heaven and happiness, but his Norwegian wasn't very good.

"Tomas sneaked off and now Mr. Buri wants us schooled…"

Aunt Helga did not stop singing; in fact, she sang even louder, her smile contorting into a contemptuous sneer, each line of the song piercing his ears so that he needed to speak even louder.

Helvete vredes, himmelen gledes

Himmelen gledes med lovsang ny

"And the milk price is so low we need more cows and two horses… But if Tomas is a store clerk, we can't get the milk. It's bad enough he can't cut wood without nearly taking off his own head!"

Redningsmannen er oppstanden

Er oppstanden i morgen gry!

"Be calm, Mundy!" She cautioned. "You nearly made me poke myself with the needle."

"Hi, Tiddemund," Amanda smiled at him, ignoring his panicked intrusion. "Mother is teaching me the old hymns, because father said I can lead the choir at his church, once he has one. Too bad you can't carry a tune, mother. I'm sure there's something else you can you do to be useful. Or should I play the organ? Do you think I could do both? Lead the choir and play the organ?"

"That's good," Mundy replied hurriedly before recounting the trip to town as slowly as his pulse would allow. The second time around he made sure to point out how the farm would suffer with selling the milk, in case the point wasn't obvious enough.

"Wasting time in some shop in town and idling away in school while there's milking and chores to be done! It's all about as useful as Uncle Hal —" Mundy stopped himself.

His aunt lowered the britches she was mending, which probably belonged to Tomas. She peered at him with a smirk that said I caught you!

"Uncle Halvar's what?" she sneered.

His mother interceded. "Never mind. He's just upset. Now, Mundy, I know how stubborn your father was on the subject, but your cousin is right, and your uncle may see some good in the arrangement."

"But it doesn't make sense!"

Aunt Helga rose and abruptly struck Mundy across the face. "It makes sense if your uncle says it makes sense, because he is the head of this family now! Who do you think you are?"

Amanda suddenly stood up and stalked after her mother, spinning her around by the wrist. Then Amanda slapped her mother. Everyone froze, including Aunt Helga who was shocked by the assault.

"You must learn to control yourself, mother," Amanda said calmly. "We wouldn't want a recurrence of your illness, now would we?" To Mundy and Brita, Amanda explained, "Mother suffers from bouts of hysteria, you see. Common for women of her age. Although, Aunt Brita doesn't seem to suffer from it, do you?"

Brita tightened her lips but didn't answer. She placed a comforting hand on her sister's shoulder. Aunt Helga's eyes burned with fury as she shrugged off her sister's hand and returned to her mending. Suddenly she dropped her knitting to the floor and wheeled on Mundy before they could restrain her. She peppered Mundy with blows, one after the other, as he cowered against one leg of the dining table. Brita shouted for her sister to stop, and Amanda tried to hold her mother's wrists. Mundy scrambled out from under the table and ran blindly out of the cabin toward the woods, hot tears streaming down his cheeks, but a voice shouting at him from near the barn made him stop.

"Hey, your cows got loose!"

Tomas spoke with Matias by the cart. They leaned against the box frame watching him in wonder as they chatted. Cloppie stood in harness, waiting impatiently to be let into the pasture. Why wouldn't Tomas un-harness her and let her into the pasture? Why did Mundy have to think of everything? There was so much to do. But Mundy was still angry and in shock from his aunt's attack. He was shaking and couldn't think straight. He could feel his Aunt's blows on his head and on his back and on his arms after he'd raised them to defend himself. Now there were the cows and Cloppie, and the Finn was here, too.

His feet carried him only as far as his father's grave, already obscured by tall clumps of weeds. All strength left his body, and his legs quiv-ered before he collapsed on the ground and sobbed. His body matted down lamb's-quarter and milkweed whose little white flowers practi-cally glowed with their own light. A breeze swept through the tall grass around him, carrying to him the chatter of sparrows, the long vibrating call of the cicada, the faraway call of the crow, the lowing of the herd: a river of sound that put his sobbing to shame until it was lost.

He fell asleep.

He was on the farm, only there were no buildings. That's how dreams are: enough was the same as in real life, but enough was different to get your attention. From the trees, a giant staring out at him. It had human features, but something was odd about its eyes. The pupils were side-ways, like goats' eyes. When Mundy moved, the giant moved, tracking him from behind the trees. Mundy wanted to run, but he sensed that if he tried to flee, the giant would break cover and chase Mundy down.

Why are you hiding? Mundy called. Why don't you come out?

Then an arrow landed at Mundy's feet. And then another.

He realized that the giant was hiding from a band of Indian warriors there on the farm, but not only there. This was a big war, all over the land for miles, a roving battle—a race of giant trolls wielding huge stone ax heads mounted on tree branches, surrounded by Sioux warriors with their flint arrows and stone knives. Mundy was in the midst of the bat-tle, and he didn't know which side he was fighting for. Something struck him in the face. An arrow? Blood splatter?

He shook himself awake, wiping at his cheek where a fly had landed. The overcast sky diffused the sun so that it was difficult to tell how much time had passed. He jerked himself upright when he suddenly noticed Amanda standing over him, tugging a clump of brown seed head from a tall burdock plant. She tossed it at Mundy.

"Stop it!" he snarled, turning away from her, but he didn't leave. He fell back to the ground and hid his head between his knees. "What am I supposed to do?"

Amanda shrugged. "I suppose you'll do like everyone else. You'll become a man and then you'll just know what to do."

"But the farm will be ruined soon, well before I become a man."

She reached her arm around his waist, and he didn't pull away.

"Don't worry. You'll figure something out. Until then, I would avoid my mother. And you might want to steer clear of father, too. Shall I sing for you?"

"Yes," he said.

*****

As much as Mundy wished he could avoid contact with his aunt and uncle, he couldn't miss supper. These days, he was hungry more often than not, and hunger made him willing to risk even a beating.

Aunt Helga's eyes flashed at Mundy when she looked at him at dinner with dark, narrow contempt, her tightened jaw set to spring like a trap on him. He endured the prayer, willing his mind back to the train platform and that giant axe. When his uncle's voice finally insisted on an amen, Mundy gladly spoke it. Then he swallowed his food in whole bites like a starving wolf before excusing himself for chores.

It was getting dark, so he lit two lamps and hung them on long iron hooks that hung from the rafters. He spent longer than usual in the barn before bed, mucking out a stall that his favorite milker liked. He moved slowly, hoping everyone in the cabin would be in bed before he went back. Finally, when exhaustion began to overtake him, Mundy blew out the lamps and wished his little herd a good night. On the way out of the barn, he heard grass rustling nearby, and he had the impression someone (or something) was quite near, but he couldn't tell for certain where, and, more importantly, what it was. It could be a bear or worse. He bolted for the cabin with a final push of his remaining energy. There was something out there, but he was tired, too tired to deal with it—and he certainly wasn't going to trouble his uncle who already was snoring in broken snorts. Mundy climbed quietly to the loft and shoved his cousin's gangly legs out of the way. He fell asleep in his little corner of the loft, wedged against the wall, trying to avoid Tomas's sprawling body.

✳ ✳ ✳ ✳ ✳

The Ingegaard's wagon was gone. On his way to the barn the next morning, Mundy noticed ruts and a trail of matted grass where the wagon had been led off. Mundy had heard something the night before, and whoever it was managed to take the cart.

When theft was at hand, a Finn was always within reach—that's what his father used to say. Mundy marched into the cabin, nostrils flaring with righteous indignation. Uncle Halvar sat at the fancy table, his head bowed on his folded hands, his elbows resting on his thick, black Bible. He exhaled a frustrated breath, peeved to have his morning contemplation interrupted.

"What is it, boy?"

As much as Mundy didn't want to risk saying or doing the wrong thing, his outrage couldn't contain itself.

"Your wagon is gone! Stolen!"

Uncle Halvar glowered at Mundy.

"Well? I'm waiting?"

Mundy blinked rapidly, his mind racing with how to respond, when he remembered how he was supposed to address his uncle.

"Reverend Ingegaard!" Mundy managed to stammer. "And I know who took it, sir."

"Oh? And who might that be?"

"Those Finns, the Koskinens!" Mundy couldn't help himself now, the words just spilled out. "I reckon if we follow the track, it'll lead right down the road to their farm." He tacked on a quick, "Reverend Ingegaard" at the end. It was an afterthought, but it seemed to keep his uncle placated.

"Sit down, boy," Uncle Halvar opened his Bible and slowly flicked through pages until his thumb thudded a verse. "Read that aloud."

Mundy's lower lip trembled. His reading wasn't strong, and the fear of his uncle's disapproval only made his nervousness worse. His stomach felt like it was turning inside-out, but he took a deep breath before he began, reading each word slowly, careful to say it correctly.

"Thou…shall…not…bear…false…witness…against…thy…neighbor."

Uncle Halvar jabbed the page with his index finger to emphasize each of his words.

"And what does this mean?"

False witness. The words meant something, but exactly what, Mundy couldn't comprehend.

"It means that we should fear and love the Lord, so that we do not lie about, betray or slander our neighbor, but excuse him, speak well of him, and put the best construction on everything."

"Yes, Reverend Ingegaard."

"That's the Eighth Commandment!" Uncle Halvar slammed closed the Bible, the corner grazed Mundy's nose.

"But, Reverend Ingegaard, I'm sure that the Koskinens did steal the wagon."

His uncle backhanded Mundy across the jaw, snapping his head to one side.

"You're certain, are you?" Uncle Halvar was fuming mad. "And are you certain that Mr. Koskinen, in fact, didn't come here to ask to borrow the wagon—my wagon—from me?"

"No, sir," Mundy was on the verge of tears. Part of him only wanted at that moment to get away from his uncle, but part of him—the stubborn part—wanted to stay and prove that he was right. "I was here with you the last time Mr. Koskinen was here, Reverend, and he never mentioned borrowing the wagon."

Uncle Halvar raised his hand to strike Mundy again, but the boy shot out of his chair and rounded the corner of the table to put space between himself and his uncle.

"They stole it! I'm sure of it! Why would they take it in the middle of the night? I'm going over there," Mundy declared. "They can't come to this farm and take what they want."

"The Lord is not with you," Uncle Halvar grumbled.

"But I am," chimed a soft voice behind them. Amanda, her face set hard without her usual smile. "He's right. They took it, and it's ours, and they have no right to it. Come on, Tiddemund!"

Amanda led the way out of the cabin and up the drive at a trot.

"Amanda! Wait!" He caught up with her, breathless.

"What is it?" Her eyes twinkled, and her lips curled in a slight smile that she tried to hide. Mundy realized then she didn't care about the wagon one way or the other. She wanted to see Matias Koskinen under any pretense.

"I just wanted to ask," Mundy's jaw still ached, and his cheek felt swollen where Uncle Halvar had struck him. "Does your father...does he ever hit you?"

Amanda snorted with disdain.

"No, of course not! I know too much about him and mother. Besides, I'm a good girl." She curtsied and laughed. "But you, on the other hand, don't know anything about my parents. They'll keep you weak and half-starved just to keep you in line, Mundy. Don't you let them! I'll do what I can to help."

Her comment stung him like a fresh blow. He was concerned about her welfare. He didn't want protection from a girl: he was supposed to be the protector.

"And poor Aunt Brita just seems so lost in all of this," Amanda continued. "I suppose she has to walk on eggshells, so mother and father don't find out about her and Mr. Koskinen."

Mundy grabbed her arm and spun her around.

"What do you mean by that?" he shouted.

She wrinkled her nose at him and stepped back.

"I don't like that, Tiddemund. Don't ever do that."

"I'm sorry."

His question hung unanswered between them as they reached the Koskinen property line. Biting flies besieged them making them swat their necks and wrists as they hustled through the tall grass flattened only by a track of wheels. The Koskinen cabin came into view from behind an alder thicket. The structure was made of good timber—undoubtedly stolen from Koskinen's logging company—but they were not put together well. Gaps between them were filled thick with gobs of chinking. A corner leaned, too, causing the south and east walls to dip. A half-dozen dirty hogs pressed hard against the planks of a small shed, bulging the wall inward as they rubbed their black-bristled hides against the wood. The wood was gray and splattered with manure, and the rank air was filled with their stench, for the Koskinens did not muck their hog yard.

Mundy spotted the wagon, jutting from around the corner of the hog shed, and he clapped a fist into the palm of his hand.

"I knew it! They're trying to hide it!"

"It doesn't prove they stole it, though," Amanda cautioned.

"I'll check for damage," he told her. "See if there's anything of theirs that needs to come out. I don't want them to accuse us of stealing. Then I'll round up Cloppie and haul it home."

Amanda pulled herself on top of the wheel to peer over the top board and into the wagon bed. She screeched. Matias Koskinen sat up, right in front of her, holding a rifle across his chest.

"What are you two doing here, besides trespassing?"

"Why were you in the wagon?" Amanda asked. "Did you sleep there all night?"

Matias stood up and drew his suspenders over his thin bare shoulders in one motion. He leveled the gun at Mundy's chest.

"He must have slept in the wagon to protect it from its rightful owners," Mundy snapped. He knew better than to make a move toward Matias. Like it or not, a gun is a fearful thing when you're on the wrong side of it.

"I could shoot you," he grinned. "Legally, I mean."

"Oh, put that down!" Amanda smiled. "No one is shooting anyone! Now, did you steal our wagon or not?"

"Steal?" Matias lowered the rifle. "No."

"Yes, you did!" Mundy countered "Admit it!"

Amanda's attention was drawn to a faint but persistent mewling. She cocked her head to better locate the sound.

"Is that a cat?" Amanda asked, starting off for the side of the Koskinen cabin.

Mundy followed her, and there mounted to the long plank wall of the house was a wire cage. Inside was a single kitten, long gray fur, mewling in an unbroken strain of fear. It wobbled, barely able to stand on the thin wire beneath its paws.

Matias appeared behind them, as curious as Mundy was about what would happen next.

"Why is that kitten in a cage?"

She fumbled at the latch, but it was corroded and hard for her to work. Matias grabbed her wrist and forced her away.

"Leave that alone! I saved that pest from a litter we drowned. I'm going to trap a squirrel and watch them fight."

Amanda's face bunched into a look of open disgust.

"Fight a squirrel? Are you crazy?"

"Knock it off!" Matias gripped Amanda's wrist to keep her from prying open the cage. "No one has any use for cats."

"He's trying to live like everything else!" Amanda said. She was a head shorter than Matias, but she squared up to him as if size didn't matter. "Besides, don't cats hunt mice? That's useful. Now give me the kitten," she demanded.

"Another mouth to feed," Mundy cautioned her.

"I think we have enough milk for a kitten, Tiddemund, don't you?" Her rebuke was sharp, and he thought he better get on her side and quick.

"Tiddemund," Matias laughed. "What a stupid name."

A sly look taking over his face, and he leaned against the corner of the cage.

"Well, that cat is worth something to me, so I reckon I'll need a square deal."

"What do you want?"

Matias's lips lengthened into a smile like a fox about to snatch a hen.

"I want twenty kisses," he said.

Amanda blinked.

"No one in their right mind would ever kiss you!"

"Well, that's my offer."

Amanda peered into the cage again and wriggled a finger through the wire. The kitten stumbled up to it, yowling, and pressed its wet nose against her. She stepped toward Matias intent on discharging the kissing debt then and there.

"Oh, not now. And not all at once. Just whenever I say. Twenty kisses. Or I swear I will find that kitten and wrench its neck right in front of you."

He took one kiss then, right in front of Mundy who yelled at him to stop and shoved at the Finn's shoulders, but to no avail. Matias held Amanda, locked her in his arms and gave her a long, slow kiss, and she didn't fight back.

"One," he counted after he let her go. He opened the cage, scooped out the kitten and gave it to Amanda. "Only nineteen to go."

"I'll be right back," Mundy stated. He ran the entire distance that separated the Koskinen homestead from the Nelsons. He found Cloppie, but she only wanted to graze, and she kept pulling away from him. Mundy was in no mood for negotiation. He found a coil of rope hanging on a nearby fence post, and he tied off a loop, got it over Cloppie's head, and dragged her to the barn. There he got her into harness and jumped on her back without a saddle and, through the force of his will and some very unkind words, he convinced Cloppie to nose out toward the Koskinen farm.

When he returned, Amanda was holding the shivering kitten, puss running out of its eyes, but Mundy could hear it purring from ten feet away. Matias was standing by her, pretending that he cared about the cat. He was talking in a sickeningly sweet voice, but it was a ploy to get his body into contact with Amanda, and he sidled up to her, their shoulders touching.

Mundy hitched Cloppie to the wagon in a flash, and he commanded Amanda to climb up on the buckboard. She handed him the kitten so she could climb up, and as he looked down at it, its pink nose flecked with dirt, its big runny eyes filled with confusion and fear, Mundy figured that was the most pitiful thing he'd ever seen.

"Look, it's sick," Mundy told Amanda as he handed her the kitten, but she ignored him.

"I'll call him Stump, because he's so small."

"You know it's just going to die."

She scowled at him. "Well, if he does die, at least he'll die in a nice warm pile of rags and not in a cage!" She ignored Mundy, pouring her attention and affectionate phrases on the little lump of fur clinging to her arm.

Matias set a hand on the side of the wagon.

"You're wasting your time on this wagon," he said. He had the rifle, but it was at his side, the muzzle nearly touching the ground. "We'll get this wagon back—and soon. Going to need it."

"What are you talking about?" Mundy glared at him. "What could you possibly need this wagon for?"

Matias shrugged. "We've got a lot of tools and such to haul over to that field you're going to sell us."

Mundy laughed. He was about to say there was no way that the Nelsons would sell any of their land to the Koskinens, but that was what his father would have said—if he were alive—but he wasn't. His future wasn't any more certain than that sick kitten's fate. The creamery deal wasn't what he'd hoped. He didn't know what his mother was up to. He had no control over his uncle's decisions, and his aunt hated him.

Mundy got angry. Very angry. He jumped off the wagon and rounded the corner as if he were going to tackle Matias, but the rifle came up, pointed a little higher than Mundy's head, and BANG! An explosion tore the air around Mundy. He flinched and instinctively dropped to the ground. Matias put a boot on the back of Mundy's neck, pinning his face in the dirt. Matias pressed the muzzle to the back of Mundy's head.

"You don't think I'd do it?" Matias said. His voice was quiet and tense, not filled with his usual cocksure bravado. "I'd be doing your family a favor. You're a big pain in the ass for everyone, and the world would be better off without you."

Mundy didn't dare move. He could feel the round cold muzzle, but he wasn't afraid of that rifle. He wasn't even afraid of Matias. He was afraid of the bullet. He held still and let Matias say whatever he wanted to say until Amanda interceded for him. She didn't get down from the wagon, but she didn't need to.

"You leave him alone," she screamed. "Or I will never speak to you again!"

Matias laughed at her, but he swung the rifle up so that it rested against his shoulder.

"Yes, you will," he grinned. "You like me. Besides, you owe me."

Mundy scrambled to his feet and returned to the wagon. He kept his head low, and he didn't say a word to Amanda on the way home even as she asked him if he was alright. She kept asking and asking until she got mad at him for not answering.

"Fine!" she said. "Maybe Matias is right! Maybe I should have let him shoot you!" She slumped back into her seat and stroked the kitten.

If Amanda thought Tomas was going to back her choice to rescue the kitten, she was disappointed. He reminded her that cats were immoral, and that their father would make them kill it. She stormed off, but she must have taken Tomas' words to heart, because instead of heading to the cabin to show the kitten to her parents, she took it to the barn. Meanwhile Mundy explained how Amanda had come to be the kitten's newest protector and how she'd bargained for it. Tomas was incensed, just as Mundy had hoped he would be.

"She let him kiss her?" He muttered. Then he added something about going over to the Koskinen farm to settle this, but Mundy tackled him and held his legs. The two boys tumbled to the ground.

"He's got a rifle, Tomas, and he's dumb enough to use it."

They lay panting on the ground, but the wheels were spinning in Tomas's brain. Mundy noticed that Tomas had Aunt Helga's eyes, and they couldn't hide the anger brewing there. This wasn't over.

CHAPTER NINE

THE KITTEN

To Mundy, who was swinging the curved blade of the scythe in full torso-bending twists, the wheat standing in front of him was about as far away from bread as he could imagine.

Scything would be easier if he were taller, or if the scythe handle was a little shorter. His father used to scythe huge swathes of wheat into tidy windrows, which Mundy collected and bundled before piling the sheaves in neat stacks, the way his father had taught him. His own windrows didn't make clean, straight lines. They were heaped in jagged rows in the lane behind him. Maybe he would get the hang of it by the third acre.

This was the job for a team of men or a machine, but at least he wasn't all alone. Amanda bundled the fallen wheat, but she was far behind him, and he would need to help her tie them up and load them on the wagon. They weren't speaking to one another, but, at least for Mundy, she was in his thoughts.

As much as he hated to admit it, Tomas might have done a better job scything, after a little practice, anyway. But Tomas was gone to town for his job at Mr. Buri's store, dressed in a suit. He left early with his boots strung over his shoulders so they wouldn't get scuffed on the path to town.

The only sounds were the whoosh of Mundy's blade and the snapping of stalks as a little ripple of wind rustled the standing wheat heads, making them bob, awaiting the blade. They parted, and Amanda stood, looking at him. Her hair hung at the sides of her face in loose curls. She gazed at him for a moment before walking over the swathed wheat toward him. When she got near, she reached for the scythe.

"Let me try," she said.

"What?" He pulled the scythe out of her hand.

"Let me try scything."

He stepped away from her. "What? Girls don't scythe."

"That's nonsense. In Spring Grove, the women scythe even better than men. It comes natural to us. Here."

She tried to grab the handle again, but Mundy slid it further away. She dashed to one side, and to the other as he tried to keep the handle away from her. To and fro she raced, until they were both laughing. Soon she had her hands on the scythe, Mundy was too winded from laughter to stop her, and soon enough she was dropping wheat into tidy windrows that were even cleaner and tighter than what Mundy had done.

Watching her swing the scythe with more and more confidence, Mundy knew she was right. He would have to bundle the wheat. But he figured that Tomas still would have been better at scything than either of them, but they'd never know because of Tomas's town job.

✳✳✳✳✳

At supper, Tomas hadn't yet returned, so the rest of them knelt on the floor to endure the evening prayer. Mundy's mind drifted back to the wheat field, to the laughter, to Amanda. When he sneaked a look, she was there on the floor across from him, hidden in flickering shadows, her father booming on about grace and blessing.

Make us worthy, oh Lord. Amen.

Amen.

Soon Mundy had downed his first plate. Amanda nearly kept pace with him, but Mundy noticed she was tearing off about every third helping and putting it in her lap. Her father asked her about the field, but her mouth was filled with bread, and she could only smile at him in response.

Aunt Helga was particularly sullen, and her plate remained empty. She had said nothing until Mundy reached for another potato. Then her face came alive like a writhing coil of snakes and she slapped his hand away so that the potato dropped back in the bowl.

"That's for Tomas!" she hissed.

His mother touched his shoulder. "Aunt Helga's tooth is hurting," she said in a low, warning voice. "Try to be good."

"Well, even though Tomas is only exploring the world of commerce and not breaking his back in the dirt, he will certainly be hungry after a long day of exercising his mind," Uncle Halvar said as he dropped another potato on his plate. No one smacked his hand.

Mundy dropped his fork and let it clatter to the floor. Amanda, next to him at the table, gripped his leg, momentarily anchoring him, but he pulled free from Amanda's grasp and rushed at his uncle, his arms flailing, and his fists clenched. His uncle rose quick, full of lightning, and struck Mundy hard against the head, and then again. Uncle Halvar pinned Mundy to the floor with a hand on his throat and yelled at Tomas to fetch the shaving strop. He whipped Mundy around the face and shoulders, the leather welting his skin.

Powerless to resist the beating, Mundy tried not to cry out, but in spite of himself, the pain took control of his breath, giving voice in the staccato of hissing blows rained down on him. Finally, his mother insisted that it was enough, and she stopped Uncle Halvar's arm.

"A minister must temper justice with mercy," she cautioned urgently, her chest heaving.

Amanda began to cry and left the cabin. Mundy rolled free of his uncle's grip and stumbled out of the cabin after her, toward the barn where she had beelined.

Her eyes were wet and looked at him in anger.

"You can't be like that with father," she insisted. "He will only hurt you, more and more."

"It's not so bad," Mundy shrugged. The truth was his jaw hurt, but otherwise, he felt exhilarated. He had been on the other side, the one to dole out punishment for once. For one brief moment, he had been brave—foolish, yes, but brave.

Amanda revealed food she saved from her plate. She crumbled bread into smaller pieces and was reaching into a crate she'd lined with rags for the kitten.

"You can't feed that kitten solid food yet," he told her. "It's too young."

"Well, it's got to eat, Tiddemund!"

"You're in luck then. We've got about a ton of milk."

"Good," she said flatly, wiping her nose with the back of her hand. "Go get some."

A few minutes later, Mundy brought her a cup filled with fresh milk, blobs of cream dotted the surface. She was holding the kitten. It was quiet.

"He's dead," she gasped. "The poor little fellow!"

The gray fur of its little body was matted with its own waste, but Amanda held it to her chest anyway, her eyes moist with tears.

"There's no one to watch over the innocent, Mundy."

"There's you," he offered.

"I don't know anything about kittens or cows, or how to help them."

All Mundy knew was that he wanted to make her happy. More than anything, that's what he wanted. If he could have brought the kitten back to life, he would have, even though cats were a curse. He would gladly suffer a curse for his cousin.

"Maybe..." he began. "Maybe you could give it a burial. A good one. With a song."

She sniffled, but she smiled. "I like that idea. "You'll be there, too?"

He nodded.

Amanda took the kitten outside, grabbing a short-handled shovel on her way out of the barn. Mundy returned to milking but nearly jumped out of his own skin. Tomas squatted in one of the stalls, leaning against a rail. His face was swollen and his lip split.

"What happened?"

Tomas' voice came from far away, as if it were difficult for him to speak.

"I ran into Matias Koskinen on the way home from town. He said some foul things."

"Did you hit him?"

"I had to hit him!"

"What did he say?"

"You won't want to know, Mundy. All I know is that we need to get revenge."

"Revenge? How? Tell me what he said?"

"I want to be left alone now. If you want to help, tell my parents that you heard from one of the neighbors that I stayed over in town."

Mundy dipped a rag in the water trough and handed it to Tomas.

"Here. Please, tell me what he said."

"Okay. You asked for it," Tomas' steady gaze was only a warning volley. "He said your mother is a whore. She sleeps with Mr. Koskinen for food. He said when we eat, we're eating his food."

"That's a lie!"

"He said we all should come over to his farm and help with the harvest, because we owe him."

If Matias Koskinen had said that to Mundy, he would be the one crouching in pain instead of Tomas or maybe this time that bullet would have found him. The kitten's burial and Amanda's song would have to wait.

Tomas pulled his pair of shiny boots from behind him. "Look! Didn't even scuff them!"

Mundy knelt down next to Tomas in the straw.

"What did you mean about getting revenge?"

*****

For the first time, it was Tomas who shook Mundy awake in the pitch black. His hand had slipped out from under the covers, and it was icy. He tried to retract it so he could fall back to sleep, drawing himself into a ball under the covers, just like Tomas liked to do.

"Wake up," Tomas urged. "It's time."

Tomas was already dressed, and maybe he hadn't slept at all. It was strange, this reversal. Usually it was Mundy doing the waking. It only took a minute for Mundy to get dressed, and they slipped out of the cabin close to one another, so they might seem as one person, in case Aunt Helga was having one of her restless nights. One boy leaving the cabin could mean chores. Two boys leaving meant trouble.

Tomas led the way to the Koskinen farm. In silhouette, the Finn's outbuildings looked like a series of packing crates lined next to one another, which wasn't far from the truth. Mr. Koskinen had salvaged various outbuildings on his farm and from surrounding farms, sledging them over, pulled by his borrowed workhorses, and connecting one after the other through rough framing: a granary, an abandoned schoolhouse, the old Finnish church.

Tomas nosed the air.

"God, that smells awful!"

"It's them hogs," Mundy explained.

"I know," Tomas smirked. "Follow me."

At the hog pen, Tomas revealed his plan, and Mundy balked.

"You think we should go splashing around in pig muck in the middle of the night?"

"I never said we. You're the little farmer boy. I'm not a farmer. If I had my way, we'd sell the farm and open a textile shop in Minneapolis, and to talk to rich women all day long. No, between the two of us, I'd say you're better suited to work with these animals."

"Well, you may not be a farmer, but you are the son of a minister, so I expect you're going to have to shovel shit one way or another."

"Don't you fret. I'll be doing my part." Tomas directed Mundy to several buckets that lay scattered around the low rail fence.

Soon enough, Mundy found himself ankle deep in hog muck, collecting the putrid waste into buckets that he carried to Tomas at the front of the Koskinen house. Tomas scooped it out by the handful to smear across the clapboards until the house, whose whitewashed boards had glowed faintly under a half moon, now were muted pig manure as high as the roof peak, where Tomas could reach.

Load after load, Mundy carried buckets to set at Tomas' feet, collecting the empty ones to be refilled in the hog pen. On one of his return trips, Mundy heard rustling from inside the house, the scraping of wood on wood—or was it a boot step? He dropped the buckets and ran to Tomas, tapping him urgently on the shoulder, and the boys tore back to their farm. Mundy felt the delicious combination of fear and excitement that adventure sprang. They ran straight for the pond, diving into the cold water with their clothes on.

"We're going to be in so much trouble!" Mundy laughed in spite of his concern.

"Don't you worry," Tomas stood in waist-deep water, rubbing his sopping wet shirt with the palms of both hands. "What we did was right. It was justice. Justice always prevails."

"But Koskinen will tell your father—you think your father will see it your way?"

Tomas shrugged. "It will work out."

*****

The next day, Mundy was the one in harness behind Cloppie. He was struggling to keep the curved plowshare blade from sinking too deep in the soil or turning off course, because whenever the blade snared, Cloppie stopped, and when Cloppie stopped, she took a long time to get moving again. Mundy's shoulders and legs ached with the effort. He was plowing only a half-acre, but it was a half-acre that his father had said would be a good spot for pasture, the spot where Mundy had pulled blackberry canes only weeks before. He hoped the plow would give their roots a run for their money.

Uncle Halvar appeared, walking with his hands folded behind him. His brown hair was thick and wild, sprouting from all sides of his head. Only his thick beard betrayed any hint of age, gray hairs salted in here and there that could easily be mistaken for a trick of the light. Darker than his hair, his eyes were clear and piercing. His face clouded, and Mundy sensed that he was about to get a stern lecture on the best methods of plowing, from the Christian perspective.

"You! Boy!" Uncle Halvar pointed to the ground in front of him. "Come here. Now."

Mundy wriggled free of the straps and patted Cloppie on the haunches.

"I'll be back, Cloppie," he whispered, adding, "I hope."

"I had a most unpleasant visit from Mr. Koskinen," his uncle's tone was almost matter of fact, as if relaying some unimportant detail for conversation's sake, but Mundy knew better than to be lulled in complacency.

"Now, I know you and your father have had your petty problems with the Koskinens, but your father is gone. What you did last night was reprehensible and suggests a deeply rooted evil in you. That you dragged my son into your malicious act is beyond reprehensible, and I am going to teach you a lesson you won't soon forget."

His uncle hooked his hand around the back of Mundy's neck. Mundy thought about revealing that it had been Tomas's idea in the first place, but he realized Uncle Halvar wouldn't believe him. He was to be beaten regardless of anything he said, so there was no point bringing Tomas into it.

"I can see that you're frightened, Tiddemund, and I would have to say that you should be. In fact, if I were in your position, I would be grateful for these last few moments before the pain commences."

Mundy could feel the tension in the small muscles, as if his uncle were holding back his impulse to throttle him out in the open. Uncle Halvar steered Mundy to the woods. For an instant, a figure, impossibly tall, towered by the line of woods that hid the final burial mound. After he blinked, it was gone. Uncle Halvar shoved Mundy toward the trees.

"Bring me a dozen branches, about this wide and this long," his uncle made chopping motions in the air to indicate the sizes that he wanted. "And fetch some of those nettles, too."

Mundy did as he was told, wading among the understory of grasses and burdock on the outer edge of the woods. He snapped off twelve branches and nettles that were taller than he was. His uncle gripped each branch and whipped it through the air. He discarded several until only five remained. These he bound with the nettles, twisting them together to form a singular rod.

"Now, take down your drawers."

There was no way out of this, Mundy knew. He was helpless against the punishment. He lowered the braces off his shoulders and began wriggling out of his breeches.

His uncle's mouth hung open as he raised the whipping bundle in the air. Mundy's painful lesson was about to begin. Suddenly the air filled with a high hum and there was a quick snapping sound coming from all around and a white-hot burst of light exploded the air.

Uncle Halvar crumpled where he stood. He landed face-first in a furrow, his face pressing against a carpet of vetch and plantain, smoke coming from his torso. It took a moment for Mundy to piece together that his uncle had been struck by lightning. Once he comprehended it, Mundy had the very un-Christian hope that Uncle Halvar was dead, and that hope thrilled him as much as any electrical charge. He looked dead with his lips curled back. The smell of burning hair and sulfur filled the air.

Cloppie had seen it, too, and she tried to bolt off, but the plow anchored her in place.

Mundy pulled his braces back over his shoulder as Uncle Halvar groaned, spittle trickled from his mouth, and his arms and legs flailed like he was dreaming of falling from the sky.

"Reverend Ingegaard! Are you alright?" Mundy called to him from several feet away, not wanting to risk being burned by any stray lightning that might have been hiding in his uncle's body.

Uncle Halvar's eyelids flickered open.

"I can't move my arms! My legs! Help me!"

Mundy hesitated.

"You got struck by lightning." Mundy looked up. "Not a cloud in the sky!"

"Help me up! Now!"

Mundy did as he was told, and soon the Reverend Halvar Ingegaard was on shaky legs under Mundy's assistance.

"Hallelujah!" he shouted to the sky in his deep and reverent tone. He looked positively unholy, his hair standing straight out, his face covered in fresh-turned dirt, and the front of his trousers damp from where his bladder had loosed itself. "The Lord has indwelt his powers within me! I have walked through his purging flames and arisen pure!"

CHAPTER TEN

SIGNS AND MIRACLES

When Uncle Halvar recounted his experience to the family, he left out the part where he pissed himself, preferring to emphasize the purity and indwelling parts of the story. Aunt Helga looked happier than Mundy had ever seen her.

"It's a powerful sign!" She exuded a level of awe appropriate for the presence of the Anointed of the Lord. "He has called you, Halvar Ingegaard!"

"Hallelujah!" Uncle Halvar shouted as loud as when he had yelled it in the field, part joy, part triumph.

"Hallelujah," Mundy's mother added.

Supper prayers took longer than usual. The Reverend Uncle had a lot to trumpet about before they could pass around the parsnip mash. If he had died from the lightning bolt, they'd probably all be eating by now.

When they finally could be alone, Mundy recounted to Tomas the events leading up to the lightning strike and how he had narrowly escaped a whipping.

Tomas nodded and then unceremoniously shoved Mundy. "I told you! Didn't I tell you it would work out? God was on our side."

Mundy supposed God could have played a part. Maybe He hated Finns as much as Mundy did.

*****

In the morning, Uncle Halvar awoke every soul in the cabin with a steady, low bellow. It had started softly, and then increased in volume and intensity. The nearest sound Mundy could think of to describe it was the grunting of a heifer in heat, only Uncle Halvar's voice was long and unbroken—in spite of Aunt Helga urging him to wake up.

Mundy and Tomas gave each other wide-eyed looks, the color drained from their faces, before clambering down from the loft. Mundy's mother and his aunt both leaned over Uncle Halvar, shaking him by the shoulders. His eyes were open wide, his expression joyous, and yet the sound came.

Two minutes, maybe three, passed without a break in his voice, but it was more than his voice alone, Mundy would swear it. A note on a bugle. A wind. The roar of a bear. And then his uncle gasped for air and began the sound again. This went on for nearly half of an hour as the family variously hovered about his bed, stepped outside, and yelled at one another in confusion about how to help him, but at last the sound dissipated, returning Uncle Halvar's voice to a raspy trickle until he had no more breath in his lungs. He panted heavily, his forehead glistening with sweat.

"God has given me a vision! He has vanquished the winter so that we can do His work! It will be a season for sowing his Word!"

"Lie back," his wife insisted, and she and her sister forced him down.

"You will expect the killing frost! The first snow! But it will not come! Nay, neither will the gray deep chill descend to freeze the earth!"

Aunt Helga roared at everyone to leave the cabin at once, but Mundy, Amanda, and Tomas could hear the strange prophesy through the closed cabin door.

"And the howl of the frosty wind will pass this place so that we might redeem ourselves in the warmth of His salvation!"

Mundy wondered what his father would have made of all this noise. Going on about winter not coming. He might say something like, "More time for mending fences. Thank your god for me."

Amanda and Tomas consulted one another in low tones. Mundy scanned their faces, trying to discern their thoughts, but maybe they were as confused as he was.

"Do you think your father was called by God?"

"Certainly!" Amanda said, startled that he'd asked. Even though direct questions weren't polite, sometimes there was no other way.

"Long before any silly lightning bolt hit him!" she added. "He was called from birth."

Mundy laughed to imagine it. God or an angel standing by bed of a woman straining with birthing pains.

"I need another minister, little Halvar. Come on out of there!"

He tried to convey the image to Amanda and Tomas, but they did not laugh.

*****

The next day, a bony man from town rode his horse up to the door of the cabin, screeching for Uncle Halvar to come out. Aunt Helga was the first to meet him, followed by Mundy. She explained to the rider that the Reverend Ingegaard wasn't feeling himself at the moment and that she was happy to convey any messages to him.

The rider grunted his disapproval.

"Well, I hope it's nothing serious and that he gets better right quick. Congregation could use him about now. Here." He handed her a folded piece of paper into her hand, clicked his tongue at his horse, and then rode off.

Aunt Helga unfolded the note, read it to herself with trembling lips. One of her hands covered her mouth, and she gasped. Even though her hand hid her mouth, Mundy could tell she was smiling and that she had wanted to hide her reaction from Mundy.

"Oh! That is too bad," she said, casting a furtive look to Mundy. She folded the letter neatly and dropped it in the front of her apron. "Since your mother has disappeared yet again, you will drive me to town. We will make a visit to the Reverend Lorenson today. He is ill, so you will keep very quiet. In fact, you will keep out of sight."

Reverend Lorenson was the town's Lutheran minister. He was a serious man who concluded his homilies with a few quiet coughs into his hand. Not more than two hours later, Mundy found himself riding the buckboard next to his aunt, with Cloppie pulling particularly slow in the heat. In spite of the weather, Aunt Helga wore her best dress and a lilac shawl. There was only the sound of the old wagon creaking intermingling with the rattle of cicadas and Mundy urging Cloppie on.

Aunt Helga hadn't said anything the entire ride into town, which was fine with him. She seemed preoccupied and very pleased with herself. That made Mundy nervous. She was up to no good. Maybe she was about to turn him in as a ward of the church and get rid of him from the farm. After all, just as Amanda had heard stories about worthless girls being traded to Indians, Mundy had heard that churches loved to snatch up all the orphan boys they could and put them to work on vegetable farms and building gangs. He had no intention of working on someone else's farm or building roads for Lutherans, even if being Lutheran for a Norwegian was like swimming in water for a fish, as his uncle said. Plenty of other kinds of people were Lutheran, too, and they didn't like Norwegians—Lutheran or not.

They arrived in town and pulled up in front of the small, white parish house next to the church where the Reverend and Mrs. Lorenson lived, and Aunt Helga instructed Mundy to pull up his braces over his undershirt and to put on the black coat she had brought. The cloth was hot from sitting in the sun, and it was too long on him by an inch all the way around.

"Oh, my," she said disapprovingly. "You're very small for your age, aren't you?"

He was about to answer that he didn't feel small, but then he thought better of it. He was learning to hold his tongue around her and her crazy husband.

Aunt Helga knocked lightly on the door. She noticed Mundy was wearing his hat, and she smacked him on the back of the head.

"Be polite," she growled through a smile that she had plastered on in hopes someone would come to the door the quickly before it melted.

Holding his hat in hand, Mundy looked around, planning the best avenue of escape should the need arise. The door opened and a wispy old lady answered, hunched from the burden of her years, which, as far as Mundy could tell, was at least seventy, but she could have been a hundred for all he knew. Aunt Helga explained who they were, and that they had received the note regarding Reverend Lorenson's illness.

"I'm sorry dear," Mrs. Lorenson replied, shaking her head. "I can't understand you. Do you speak English?"

Mundy swallowed the chuckle that tickled his throat. Aunt Helga repeated her explanation, speaking slowly and loudly. Mrs. Lorenson stood aside to let them in, seemingly relieved.

"But where is your husband, dear?" the old woman asked.

"He is busy," Aunt Helga was practically shouting. "Doing the Lord's work."

"Whose work?"

"THE LORD'S."

"Well, it's a shame he couldn't make it here himself. This is very important, but it is nice that he is willing to help. The Reverend Lorenson can't seem to keep any food down, you see. And if only he were able to sleep, that would be such a blessing."

Mundy heard the slow ticking of a grandfather clock coming from one corner of the otherwise uninteresting front room. He'd never seen one in person, but his father had described it to him. Unlike the plain wooden chairs lined along the chalk-colored plaster walls, which were the only other furnishings, a clock—as tall as a man—fascinated Mundy. Its oak body, heavy and dark, had grape vines carved along its length. The clock's face had ornate numbers trimmed in gold, fringed by a gold halo of stars and other celestial bodies. The hands, probably brass, shone with a light of their own as they stretched toward their encompassing heaven. Best of all, the body of the clock—the workings of pendulum, gears, and weights—were revealed by a pane of beveled glass. He longed to sidle toward it, move into arm's length, and open the oaken door to understand how the machinery worked. But Mundy knew he was expected to stand still and await his aunt's direction. It seemed like the kind of fancy but impractical item that the Ingegaards would have brought with them.

"May I see your husband, Mrs. Lorenson?"

"Oh, I don't know, dear."

"It's only that I cared for my own father when he had a similar complaint."

"Oh? Did he recover?"

"I should say so! Why, with but a little care, do you know, my father is still with us at the great age of eighty-five."

Mundy, who had been mesmerized by the swinging pendulum, snapped to attention. Aunt Helga's father was his own mother's father, Grandfather Lund. And he was dead. He'd been dead for years. Why would Aunt Helga lie? But the lie did the trick. It gave Mrs. Lorenson confidence that Aunt Helga would know how to treat her husband and, perhaps, even help in his recovery.

They entered the Lorenson bedroom, which happened to be on the side of the house taking a merciless beating from the early afternoon sun. Stifling though the air was, the Reverend Lorenson was covered to his chin in bed sheets.

Aunt Helga rushed to his side and placed a hand to his forehead.

"The poor man is burning up. Mundy! Fetch a pail of water from the pump."

Soon enough, Mundy pumped water, fetched dishes from the cupboard in the Lorenson's kitchen, dug carrots and potatoes from their garden, and chopped vegetables. Was this Aunt Helga's plan? To turn Mundy into a slave to the Lutherans?

Mundy started a fire outside, it being too hot inside to use the cooking stove. He set up the three-legged spider to hang a cast iron pot over the flames. He added water while Aunt Helga added the chopped vegetables and various herbs that she had scavenged from the garden next to the parish house.

While the kettle simmered, Mundy tended to Cloppie, giving her water and two of the carrots he had hidden in his large coat. She munched them, one by one, favoring one side of her mouth. Sure enough, her gums were swollen on one side. Another bad tooth was going to have to come out one way or another.

When he returned to the house, Aunt Helga insisted that Mrs. Lorenson rest, her vigil could resume in the morning. It wasn't until that moment that Mundy realized that they were staying for the night, which meant the milking would go undone, which meant the cows would be restless and harder to manage in the morning. But what could he say? He was at his aunt's mercy. Maybe he would try to explain.

If he were a man, like his father, he would have insisted on finding Tomas and dragging him here to sit in idleness watching people sleep. That was a task to which Tomas would be well suited. Mundy held his tongue and the long hours became night. He slept on the floor of the front room using his forearm as a cushion.

Before dawn, Aunt Helga appeared at the door. Mundy heard Mrs. Lorenson sobbing from their bedroom.

"Come along," she stated flatly. "Nothing more we can do here."

Mundy knew that wasn't true. There were a hundred tasks that needed doing when someone died.

144

✳ ✳ ✳ ✳ ✳

While the widow Lorenson grieved alone, Aunt Helga led Mundy toward the church. They passed graves in the side-yard—a handful of settlers who had died over the past few years. They were buried under a canopy of elms whose leaves were tinged brown in the summer heat. Mundy slowed his pace. This was the place they would bury Reverend Lorenson he supposed. This where they would bury his father if the land deal with the Finns ever happened. They'd have to dig up his father, lay him out on tarp in the wagon, and drive him into town. And it would probably have to be Mundy who did it. Mundy wouldn't let that happen.

He ran his hand over one of the stones. *Joseph Marbury*, it read in raised letters. *5 Mo.s*

"What does this mean?" He said it aloud, not expecting a response. He was startled when his aunt was next to him. She gripped his shoulder.

"That means that little boy was only five months old when he died," she jeered at Mundy like he was a slug, inching along in her path. "Some families are more fortunate than others. Now stop your dawdling! Come on."

Dragging him in tow, she pushed open the door to the church hard enough that it hit the wall with a thud. There was a gleam in his aunt's eyes, a crazy gleam that made Mundy nervous. At first Mundy had thought she was angry, but he recognized this mood—not from any adult in his life—but from Amanda. This was how Amanda acted when something made her happy.

Her hands went to her mouth. Then, slowly, she spun around in the aisle, her hands brushing the tops of the polished wooden pews, drinking in the tin-paneled ceiling, the dark maple wainscoting below the bone-gray walls, the white box where the minister stood. Her fingers glided over the polished backs of pews as she sauntered down the aisle, even though she told him not to touch anything.

"Oh, yes," she said. "This will do!"

Mundy's eye fell on the altar. It was a simple shelf painted white like the pulpit box. On it stood a cross. It looked like gold glowing pink in the rays of morning sun that streamed through the three stained-glass windows on the eastern wall, but it couldn't be gold. It was probably brass, the same alloy they made fancy spittoons out of, the same as the giant axe at the depot. The letters HIS were inscribed on it.

"Take the wagon back to the farm and fetch your uncle," she instructed him. "Tell him to wear his burying suit and to bring his book!"

Mundy took one last look at the cross, disappointed that he couldn't touch its smooth, cool surface. He was more than happy to have an excuse to leave his aunt, however, so he returned to the Lorenson's yard where Cloppie was tethered, and off they went, Mundy in no particular hurry, in spite of the urgency expressed by his aunt. Let her stew in her own juice for a while. The dead minister wasn't going anywhere, and Cloppie was in no mood to hurry, either.

As the wagon neared the farm, Cloppie straining with the burden of the cart, Mundy met his mother crossing the road from the Finns' farm. Her hair was disheveled, and she didn't raise her head to meet his eyes. Koskinen watched them from the property line like a fox waiting for sunset.

✳ ✳ ✳ ✳ ✳

The Reverend Lorenson was buried with the service officiated by Reverend Halvar Ingegaard, recently of Annandale by way of Spring Grove. Brita forced Mundy forced to attend the funeral, in spite of his protests about chores. If nothing else, the service gave Mundy an opportunity to see how different his uncle behaved around the church members than when he was on the farm. He seemed like a different person: warm and respectable. Even Aunt Helga was all soft smiles and kind words, guiding the widow Lorenson to her seat, but Mundy knew better.

The person you were in your own home is who you were. Everything else was just an act.

It wasn't long after the funeral that the church elders visited the farm and asked Uncle Halvar to serve as the temporary minister, which meant they would move to town. The announcement pleased Uncle Halvar and his wife, of course—and Tomas, too, who hated farm life. He welcomed a move into town, which was a minute's walk to Mr. Buri's store. Amanda was thrilled, too: a member of the church was donating a piano that his young wife used to play before she died giving birth. Mundy was happy, too. No more being hit, no more insults, no more lengthy prayers: just him and his mother at their plain, old supper table that his father made.

There was the small problem that the parish house was still occupied, and so the widow Lorenson was shunted off on a train to her remaining family in Bismarck, North Dakota.

Mundy was glad to help the Ingegaards move. He and Tomas unloaded the Ingegaard's possessions from the wagon into the parish house, even the fancy dinner table. Mundy recognized the part of the table where he'd sat, which was across a surface nick caused by Tomas who dropped his plate while getting seconds.

Several men from the congregation arrived too late to help with the wagon. Uncle Halvar greeted them with a warmth seldom exhibited except during a lightning strike. They cautiously accepted his hand and asked where they were needed.

They winced when he shook each of their hands.

"My, Reverend! That's quite a grip you got on you!" said the first.

"I surrender!" the other joked.

"The Lord has imbued me with a great strength!" Uncle Halvar announced, but the strength was not applied to the mundane task of unloading furniture. "Let me consult with Mrs. Ingegaard as to how you men can help her." Uncle Halvar disappeared into the house.

To the men, a boy like Mundy didn't exist. He was a fence post, a stalk of corn, a wagon wheel. They filled their pipes and spoke to one another in the breath of purple pipe smoke.

"All I'm saying is I wouldn't want her nursing me."

"No, sir. Me neither."

"If you ever take ill, best to go without eating than to eat anything she makes."

"Agreed."

Uncle Halvar returned with instructions from his wife. "Gentlemen, if you'll come with me?" He led the men inside, but within a few moments, Aunt Helga shooed them to the threshold.

"No pipes in our house," she warned, and they submitted, tapping the bowls of their pipes, sending ash into the air. "Have you had your lunch yet?"

They said they had already eaten, but they thanked her for the kindness.

*****

After Sunday lunch at the parish house with the Ingegaards, Mundy and Amanda strolled the path leading to the lake shore. They found a spot where the tall grass had been flattened by deer where they could hear the waves lapping the shore. Wood ducks bobbed past the reeds over the deeper water, and a redwing blackbird twitched at them from the low branch of a nearby tree.

Amanda seemed quieter than usual.

"Are you sad?"

"A little," she admitted. "Worried more, I suppose."

Mundy paused before he added, "Is it because you don't see Matias anymore?"

"No, I see Matias plenty. He comes into town just to see me."

"Oh," Mundy said.

"So, that's not it. It's just that I'm worried father has let his new position go to his head. He's going to ruin everything," she lamented. "This is how it started in Spring Grove. I'd hoped he'd changed. If things go as they did there, mother will fall apart, father will take things too far with his ministry, and we'll have to move again."

"Back to the farm?" Mundy was startled to think it. He had enjoyed having the farm back to himself and his mother.

"I doubt that," she murmured. "More likely we'd have to go somewhere new, like the Dakota Territory. I don't want to move again. The church is getting a piano. A piano, Tiddemund! Can you believe it? But father is quite right."

She explained that even though her father's role was meant to be temporary, he already had begun dictating plans for the future, which included building a larger church.

"Do you remember his second sermon?"

"Not really," he admitted. Mundy let his mind wander whenever he was confined in church.

"Well, in his second sermon," she continued. "He insisted that the Lord wanted the congregation to increase the rate of their tithing by ten percent to feed the new building fund. When the elders reminded him that he might not be around to see its completion, father told them he was chosen, not by flesh-and-blood men, but by the hand of God. That didn't win him any friends, I can tell you."

Mundy shrugged. "They probably want a bigger church, too. That's not so bad."

"But then he laid hands on Mrs. Kerkhoven, right in Mr. Wells's store."

"What? Why did he do that?"

"She mentioned that her rheumatism ached, so father laid hands on her and prayed one of his loud prayers—you know the type—and asked the Lord to heal the woman. People around here just don't do that sort of thing."

Mundy thought for a moment.

"But what about your mother? She has arthritis that pains her. Why doesn't your father heal her?"

Amanda's face softened to its usual mirth. "Can I tell you a little secret? There is nothing wrong with mother! She uses the arthritis excuse when it pleases her."

"But her hands get all gnarled," Mundy countered. "They look useless. Even I've seen that."

Amanda lifted her hand and curled her fingertips at the middle joints until they resembled talons.

"I've watched her do this very thing when she thought I wasn't looking," Amanda explained. She straightened her fingers and flitted them about like butterfly wings. "I couldn't imagine not being able to play the piano!" She touched his shoulder, her usual enthusiasm now restored. "Did I tell you the church is getting a piano?"

"Yes," Mundy laughed. "You've mentioned it just a few times already."

"And do you know what else? Matias has promised to buy me a piano of my very own."

The smile drained from Mundy's face when she said it, but she didn't seem to notice.

"How is a Finn going to afford a piano?" Mundy shook his head. "More likely he'll steal one, if he even knows what a piano is."

"Do you even know what a piano is?" Amanda asked. "I don't know why you don't like Matias. He's very kind, once you get to know him."

"I know him as much as I care to!"

"Well, from what Matias and your mother say, you soon may have to get along very well. And believe me, he's no happier about it than you are."

"What's that supposed to mean?"

She shrugged, and instead of answering, she pointed at a muskrat gliding through the lily pads.

"Isn't that adorable? Matias says it looks like a big swimming rat."

Mundy couldn't let her cryptic statement go.

"What did you mean, about Matias and me having to get along soon?"

She pursed her lip and made a locking motion with the tips of her fingers.

"I've already said too much," she replied. "He told me in secret."

"I suppose Matias tells you secrets while you watch the swimming rats here?"

"Sometimes," She admitted, but noticing his angry look, Amanda gently touched his forearm.

"We are all God's creatures! Even Matias."

She pushed him playfully so that he rocked to one side. Her bemused expression vanished, replaced by a sudden, startled look. "We should get back," she declared, smoothing her skirt. "Father will be angry, and mother may need help. You know, because of her arthritis."

✳✳✳✳✳

Mundy and Amanda walked hurriedly along on the planks laid along Annandale's main street in hopes of returning to the parish house without incident. Their hopes were dashed, however, when they saw Uncle Halvar, and his eyes narrowed on them. He must have been out looking for them and likely would have dragged Mundy off by the ear if no one had been around. Lucky for Mundy, Uncle Halvar was forced to control his temper, because he was talking with Jere Larken, a second-generation farmer with a section of land south of town. Uncle Halvar stood stock straight, towering over Larken, who was explaining something nervously as Amanda and Mundy approached.

"So, you see, Reverend," Larken said. "Last couple of days have been good drying conditions in the field, and the moon was up, so we just worked through the night. We were just too bone-tired to attend the service this morning."

Uncle Halvar shook his head and smiled his pulpit-bursting smile.

"Mr. Larken, I don't know how Reverend Lorenson instructed you on the commandments, but I adhere to the ten as listed in the Holy Bible. Are you familiar with those?"

"Yes, Reverend." Larken shifted his weight to his other leg, his head lowered.

"Then I'm certain you will recognize the third commandment, Remember the Sabbath day and keep it holy."

"Yes, Reverend, I understand that, but—"

"What does this commandment mean?"

"I know what it means, Reverend, it's just that—"

"It means that we should fear and love the Lord and not despise the teaching of His Holy Word and hold it sacred and gladly hear it."

"Well, I'm certainly getting an earful of preaching now," Larken shot a baleful look at Mundy and Amanda. "Doesn't this count?"

"And gladly hear it!" Uncle Halvar shouted. "Now why did you forego the Lord's third commandment, Brother Larken, on this day, the Sabbath?"

"To provide for my family during the winter!" Larken declared, his eyes fired.

"I have good news, Brother Larken!" Uncle Halvar clapped his hand on Larken's shoulder, an act that made Larken stand upright, his eyes wide. He looked like he was about to say something, his lips trembled. "The Lord has passed His mighty hand over this land to hold back the winter. You'll be gathering your wheat in short sleeves for the new year!"

"Father!" Amanda pulled away from Mundy and took her father's hand. "We should go home now." She yanked him away from Larken and led her father down the street.

Mundy and Larken watched them for a minute, bickering at one another. Amanda stopped and yelled something at her father, stamping her foot, but Mundy couldn't hear it. She was telling him not to spoil things in town. She really wanted to play the piano in church.

"Did you hear that?" Larken looked down at Mundy. "Harvesting in January? I reckon the Reverend doesn't know much about farming wheat. Wonder what the town council will make of that."

*****

While it was true that Mundy was troubled by his circumstances, but he also noticed his mother carried herself with the forlorn countenance of a condemned criminal. She put on a false smile in the presence of her sister, who now had become insufferably happy, pleased with the Ingegaards' new position.

At first, Mundy supposed she was sad that her sister had moved further away. Or maybe she was envious that her sister's husband was finding his way while her own husband was dead. Whatever was bothering her, it definitely made Mundy feel a distance between them. They typically exchanged only the barest of conversation, relying on the routine of the farm to keep their days together moving forward into the unknown future.

One evening, however, he found his mother sobbing as she shelled beans. He rushed up to her and took her hand.

"What's wrong, ma?"

She smiled, one of those tight-lipped, meaningless gestures adults made when they didn't want to talk about something.

"Nothing at all." She wiped tears from her eyes as she spoke. "Why do you ask?"

"Maybe because you're not happy."

A genuine smile softened her face, her eyes still glossy with tears. She started laughing—just a little at first. Mundy laughed with her, like a contagion, thinking he had inadvertently said something funny, that had worked to lift her spirits, and he thought, *Good! Now we can get back to normal*, but then her laughing came in fits until a new wave of tears spilled from her eyes, and she returned to sobbing and shelling beans, as if he weren't there.

Mundy watched her for a minute and then bowed his head. A change of subject, he decided, might break the spell.

"Ma," Mundy patted her hand to get her attention. "What do the letters mean on the cross in church?"

She inhaled sharply.

"What are you talking about?"

"The three letters on the cross in church," he explained. "IHS. What do they mean?"

"Ask your uncle. Your uncle knows."

Maybe she didn't know the answer, or maybe it was another secret. Mundy knew one thing for certain: his mother was more than just sad. She was exhausted. Even knowing that couldn't stop Mundy's frustration spill out.

"To hell with my uncle!"

He sounded sharper than he meant to. Her eyes searched his expression, trying to fathom his intention or maybe his state of mind. Mundy swallowed hard, trying not to give anything away. Finally, the chirping crickets and the coo of a mourning dove calmed the room.

"Think of it, Mundy," Brita half-whispered. "We can't survive on our own."

Now they were talking about something bigger than the letters on the cross or how Mundy cursed his uncle. They were talking about the future of the farm, but not out in the open. It was if they were speaking to each other with a layer of turf between them, one of them in the light of knowing, the other trapped in the dark, unable to move.

"But we have everything we need," he raised his voice again. "More than enough!"

"But you're only a boy! There's too much to do."

"I won't be a boy for long. I'm strong."

"…and the winter will come."

"But Uncle Halvar said…"

"I know what he said, Mundy. Winter will come, no matter what he says. One lightning strike can't stave off the north wind." She wiped the empty bean pods into a basket on the floor. "Look Mundy. This is serious. We have to sell this place or at least join forces.

"That's why I had the plan, so that everyone would pitch in."

Brita shook her to cut off any further progress of that idea.

"It's too late for that," she said. "Mr. Koskinen has offered to take care of us like his own family."

"You mean, we would live with those people?"

"Yes, he's actually a very gentle man. He needs a wife, and I need a husband, and you, well, you're just a sweet boy! You still need a father..."

Mundy didn't hear the rest. He stormed out, but the slamming cabin door did nothing to silence his wild thoughts. He couldn't live with the Finns. Matias would murder him in his sleep. Maybe he would be shunted off to live with Uncle Halvar and Aunt Helga in town? There he would die, beaten and starved, but even death seemed preferable to losing the farm.

If he died, would he see his father?

CHAPTER ELEVEN

POWERLESS

Sundays belonged to God, even after Uncle Halvar assumed his new life in town. Mundy, sullen, wore a clean shirt that made him itch, guiding the wagon along the bumpy lake road. He said nothing to his mother, and she didn't try to speak to him. Their thoughts were heavy, like stone piers on opposite sides of a cavern, with no bridge to connect them.

He looked forward only to seeing Amanda and the brass cross with its mysterious inscription. Today, he determined, he would find a way to touch it, maybe after the service, to confirm his suspicions that it was solid and not a trick of the light. Of course, that meant pretending to pray and to sing at the right times and to stay awake.

A Sunday service delivered by Reverend Halvar Ingegaard was a test of endurance.

Stiff from sitting in the wood pew, Mundy wished the singing would stop. A cacophony of misguided voices drowned out the sound he wished to hear: the lovely fingertip touches of his cousin playing the piano. After two hymns—each with a galling number of verses—Reverend Halvar Ingegaard ascended the three steps to the altar, a far-away, misty look in his eye. His demeanor suggested that he expected God to set a crown on his forehead, but even God had to know better than to put that man in charge of anything.

"Let us pray," Revered Ingegaard boomed.

The air changed next to him, a small rustle of fabric as Mundy's mother joined her hands in the shape of prayer. Her expression melted into piety, a look he has not seen on her face. She was a stranger to him.

Mundy prayed too, but not in the words recited by the mindless drones around him. Straining to connect with whatever primal creative force that hid itself beyond a thin veneer of civility and social order, Mundy shut his eyes tighter and gripped his own fingers until they swelled purple like dusk. He called on the spark that fueled animal shapes and that burned in the face of hope and hopelessness. Ancient, deeper, and more powerful than the gods of men, beyond the reach of their feeble struggles. He heard no voice, had no vision, but he was filled with the desolate realization of how puny he was in the scheme of all things. He could melt or he could break.

✳ ✳ ✳ ✳ ✳

Reverend Ingegaard's sermon finally concluded with a frenetic, arm-warming, and very un-Lutheran exhortation to avoid the sin of Pride. His brash staccato voice rose to fevered pitch, waking up the old men in the sweltering church just in time for the final hymn.

Afterwards the Nelsons and the Ingegaards gathered at the parish house for dinner, which at least was a chance to see Amanda, even if he needed to put up with Tomas' new self-important interjections about local gossip and how very well he was getting along in Mr. Buri's store.

Uncle Halvar, still buoyant from his shift in the pulpit, announced that he was negotiating with Kauko Koskinen to sell off the Nelson's farm.

Mundy nearly choked on his food.

"I have made up my mind about this," Uncle Halvar declared, shooting a hot glance at Mundy as if expecting trouble.

"It's for the best," Brita agreed, her head bowed. She'd warned Mundy that this was coming, but it was still a shock to hear it.

"Good for you, sister," Aunt Helga said. "You'll be much happier living with us."

Brita opened her lips, about to respond, but then thought better of it. Mundy knew she had her own plans with Koskinen, but Mundy's only plan had been to keep the farm and sell milk just like his father had wanted.

"I'll handle the sale of the property, of course," Uncle Halvar continued. "We'll set aside some of the money for you and the boy."

Brita snapped to attention.

"What do you mean you'll set aside some of the money? That's my money! All of it!"

"Now, now." He raised his hands, shields against her outrage. "As head of this family, I must think for the good of each one of us, and the Lord has spoken to me."

Amanda's chair nearly tipped over as she bolted to her feet.

"Our Lord would not have you take money from a widow and her child!"

"Shush, Amanda!" Aunt Helga was appalled at her daughter's outburst. She, too, arose and attempted to make Amanda sit down, but Amanda wriggled away from her.

"And you!" She hissed at her mother. "You would turn against your own sister?"

"There's no use arguing about it. My mind is made up." Uncle Halvar returned his attention to his meal, but Amanda stormed out. "Frankly, I'm surprised at this unwarranted attack on our generosity, after all we've done for you both."

Brita reflexively gripped Mundy's wrist to keep him from leaping up and yelling. Her expression implored him to remain quiet. She was right. No good would come from more shouting at Uncle Halvar. He'd tried it before and been rewarded only with beatings.

"The Koskinens are willing to buy, but only if we tear down that old building and remove Mr. Nelson's body."

"Which old building?" Mundy blurted.

"Don't speak, boy!" Aunt Helga hissed at him.

"The one your father fell through. It is a hazard, and we must move your father's body. We will give him a plot in the church yard as if he were a good Christian."

Mundy kept his mouth shut, but his mind raced with a thousand thoughts at once. Tomas tried to break the tension with small talk.

"I haven't seen you come in while I'm working, Mundy," Tomas said. "You should come in. I can keep Mr. Buri from tanning your hide long enough for you to get an eyeful at some plowpoints."

"I'm never going in there again," Mundy responded. "Not without a rifle, anyway."

The Ingegaards were outraged, the chatter that erupted around the fancy table reminded him of his chicken flock when a raccoon got in the coop.

Brita scolded him and told him to go to the wagon for the basket of turnips and potatoes they'd harvested. He was happy for an excuse to go outside. Outside in the summer was where farmers belonged, even on these cursed Sundays. Mundy toted the basket to the kitchen at a most opportune moment: Aunt Helga was removing a pan of biscuits from the oven box. She shoved a plate of biscuits at Mundy.

"Take these out to the men. And don't even think about eating any of them. I've counted them, and I will check with my husband to see how many you carried in!"

He delivered the biscuits as fast as a quarter horse and was about to sit at the table to slather butter on his lone, steaming biscuit, but his mother shooed him outside, afraid he might say some other rude thing, so he sat on the stump under the awning, where he could hear the family chatting at dinner, and then the plates being cleared. He wondered if anyone would even notice he was gone. Through the open window, he eventually heard his mother and Aunt Helga talking above the clatter of plates and fancy cutlery in the kitchen.

"...but it is for the best," Aunt Helga said. "Besides, I miss being with you like when we were girls, do you remember?"

"Yes," Brita's voice came softly.

"It will be just like old times, you and me in town, only now I am a minister's wife. Could you lift that pan for me? My rheumatism is acting up."

"Of course, you poor thing." There was a pause before Brita spoke again. "There's something I need to talk to you about."

"Yes?"

"Well, it's just that..." Brita stammered. Mundy pricked up his ears. He suspected is mother was about to reveal her relationship with Kauko Koskinen, but instead Brita's secret remained cloaked. "I just want to be happy," she concluded.

"I know! I couldn't agree more. I just want us all to be happy. Just to enjoy this parish. Minister to the sick and the dying. Maybe someday a Sunday service in Norwegian. But, to be honest, Brita, I fear that Halvar is coming on too strong lately. Now he even wants to have calling cards printed."

"What would he need calling cards for?"

"For calling on people! Calling cards that say that he is Reverend Halvar Ingegaard, Minister and Magnetic Healer. It's vanity, foolish vanity, that's all that is."

"He is a man of God," Brita assured her sister.

"I know, but the Lord's calling is a double-edged sword at times. Calling cards, of all things!"

Mundy didn't know anything about calling cards, but he did know that he'd ferreted two extra biscuits into his pocket. He took those out and ate them.

CHAPTER TWELVE

THE SURVEYOR

Mundy slept in his clothes under a light blanket, not in the loft, but on the floor of the kitchen. He rolled himself onto his elbows and got his feet under him and crept to the door of the cabin. He applied upward pressure so that the door wouldn't squeak on its hinges and wake his mother, but in the gray morning light that sneaked through the open door, he could see she wasn't in her bed anyway.

Soon his trouser legs were drenched with dew from the yard to the orchard where he picked three apples, still mostly green and tart. Two he gave to Cloppie, patting her wet snout, as he told her they needed to make a trip. The third apple he bit into as they rode through an early morning fog, and it made his lips pucker.

From the farm to the north shore of Clearwater Lake (which people called "the big lake") was about five miles. It would take them an hour or more to reach it across the rutted trail. He'd never been to the shore of the big lake before, but he'd seen it plenty through the trees on the way to other places.

The trail forked, and Cloppie had to push hard through overgrown thistles and grasping fox grape vines. The morning revealed itself first on the lake, a thin, gray tissue of clouds that made the calm surface look like silver. Another hour passed with Mundy struggling in the underbrush. Soon he saw a small rise in the ground. And then another. In all, six rounded mounds surrounded him, as tall he was.

He tied up Cloppie and then followed the sounds of clanging metal and the crackle of burning wood toward the center of the mounds. Mr. Lewis stared into a cast iron pot on the tripod over the fire. Mundy called out to him, and the man's head swiveled, sharp eyes pinpointing the voice. His face relaxed when he recognized Mundy.

"Didn't your father teach you to avoid the likes of me?" He laughed, wiping his face with the back of his glove, streaking his cheek with black ash like accidental war paint. "Or did your father change his mind about the survey?"

Mundy sat on log across the fire from Lewis without being asked.

"My father is dead."

"Oh! Was it quick?"

"No."

"Terrible shame. I'm sorry to hear that. I always say, if you have to die, it should be quick. One last surprise moment." He snapped his fingers. "Like that."

"He had blood poisoning."

"Not a good way to go," Mr. Lewis stirred the iron pot. "Good news is I got enough beans for two hungry men here. Want some?" Mundy nodded. Lewis handed him a flat wedge of firewood. "Don't have out the fancy China dishes for guests."

He ladled steaming hot beans from the pot onto the wedge as he spoke.

"I had a cousin who died the same way in the war between the States," he explained. "He got shot—a tiny scratch—but it turned his forearm purple," the surveyor ran a finger up his arm. "Like a corrupting spider web stretching all the way to his shoulder. He refused to let anyone amputate it. Vanity, that's all that was. He ran away from the army and ended up dying in the backwoods of Kentucky."

Lewis scooped beans for himself on another wood wedge.

"I always say, if you have to die slow, at least die surrounded by people. That mad bastard died all alone, no doubt with terrible suffering. They finally found his body and buried him there because he was already half-eaten by foxes and what-not."

"My uncle died in the war. He was at Antietam."

Mr. Lewis nodded. "If you have to die, die fighting. No sense going to battle and getting wounded and then getting eaten by foxes in the backwoods of Kentucky. What brings you out here?"

Mundy explained about his uncle's plans to sell the farm, and how his father and grandfather had built it out of the earth with their own hands. It was the only home Mundy had ever known.

"And you see it as your birthright, is that it?"

"Birthright?"

"Yes, your inheritance. Something that should belong to you."

"I suppose so," Mundy said slowly, adding in a more confident tone, "Yes, my birthright."

"Are you sure that's what you want? A farm is a big commitment that doesn't go anywhere but down. It's stubborn and needy."

"It's what I know. It's mine."

"You've never been anywhere except into town. If you could see some of the places out there, wild places, let me tell you, you'd think twice about putting roots down in one place. I've seen waterfalls bigger than this county. I've seen elephants! You ever seen an elephant?"

"No sir."

"Taller than all your cows standing on each other's backs! And trees, all types of trees, and places where absolutely nothing but prickly cactus will grow. You've never even heard of a cactus, have you? It's like a tree with porcupine quills all over it, and it grows in the desert, just sand and rocks and heat. Damnedest thing. Holds water when there isn't any water for hundreds of miles."

"What about trolls?"

"What's that?"

"Trolls," Mundy repeated. "The evil giants that eat people."

Mr. Lewis looked troubled and was about to say something but stopped himself. A black fly, flying too slow near his head, was dispatched in a sudden clap of the man's palm and flicked into the fire.

"What did your pa tell you about giants?"

"He said they followed us from Norway, the trolls. They turn into stone in the sunlight. They're buried in the little hills, like these."

"Did he ever dig up one of those little hills on your land?"

"Yes, sir."

"Did he tell you what he found in that little hill?"

"Yes, sir."

"Did he ever show you what he found?"

"No, sir."

Lewis slid beans into his mouth and stared hard at Mundy.

"Did he mention finding bones? Big bones?"

163

"Yes, sir! That's exactly what he mentioned."

"What happened to those bones?"

"They're still there, in the ground, except the field shed is over the top of them, and now my uncle wants to sell land to the Finns, and they want us to tear that building down first."

Mundy couldn't make out what Lewis murmured to himself as he withdrew a small leather-bound journal and a pencil from the inside of his vest. He jotted notes for a moment, winced, and then shook his wrist before returning his attention to Mundy.

"Have you ever seen giant bones, Mr. Lewis?" Mundy asked.

The man laughed, but it seemed to Mundy to be a nervous sort of laugh. "Oh, no. I'm a surveyor, not a digger. You need to stay put too long to be a digger."

Mundy wanted to ask him about the crate at the station, the one with the huge axe head, but maybe Lewis would lie about it. Mundy didn't want to meet anymore liars.

"But I sure have met a lot of people saying they saw some," Mr. Lewis continued. "And who knows? Maybe they have. The trouble is, they're not supposed to see any, because giants—or trolls, whatever you want to call them—they aren't supposed to exist. So maybe people are crazy or lying, or maybe they're telling the truth. In any case, there are some very real men who take an interest in all those claims—lies or not. And those men are diggers. Any man who makes his living digging is capable of any sort of evil."

"Like planting potatoes?"

"No, not that kind of digging. That's just planting. I'm talking about grave robbers with fancy titles. Half the reason I'm running all over this state in such a panic is to stay ahead of those diggers! They dig up secrets, and then they bury the truth. Mark my words: stay away from diggers."

They sat around the fire eating beans until the pot was empty. Mundy thanked Mr. Lewis for sharing his lunch.

"But there's something on your mind besides beans, isn't there?" Mr. Lewis asked.

"Yes, sir," Mundy admitted, although he wasn't sure how to ask for help. It certainly wasn't something his father had done. "I thought, because we had that one mound under the shed, and the mound there in the woods, maybe you could help stop the sale."

Lewis nodded. His face tightened in contemplation. Finally, he asked, "Now that your father has passed on, do you reckon your mother would let us come over to the farm and get some surveys of the property? Heck, surveys are good for more than recording Indian burials. You can see low points where it's too wet to plant and you can see places likely to have gold..."

"Gold?"

"Certainly! Likely as not to have a big field of gold right under your feet!"

"We don't have any gold!" Mundy laughed, because the idea was ridiculous. He'd seen enough rocks out of the field to know none of them had any gold in them.

"And how do you know for sure? Are you a trained geologist?"

"No, but I've never seen any gold, and no one has gold around here!"

"But you don't know for sure, do you? And neither does your mother, right? Or that Finn or your uncle?" He dropped his chin so that when he looked at Mundy, his glance came from beneath his bushy eyebrows. It dawned on Mundy what Mr. Lewis was saying. They could play a trick on Koskinen and Uncle Halvar.

"There could be anything on that land!" Mundy laughed.

"Now you're getting it! And you know what gold prospectors do before they stake a claim? They hire a survey team. Yes sir, you can tell a lot about a place by taking a survey. Just good land management."

"You think we might have gold on our farm?"

"Not on your life!" Lewis slapped another fly on his leg. "Not unless your people brought it with them from Norway. I was trying to show you how important a survey could be. You are a sharp boy after all, aren't you? You remind me of my boy. Daniel, his name was. He was your age when he died. His hair was lighter, but your eyes, the way you look around you and ask questions, it reminds me of him and makes me miss him very much."

"How did he die?"

"He caught the croup, had a real bad fever. Coughed his way into the Kingdom." Lewis licked the wedge and tossed it into the fire. "The moment I regret most was that I wasn't with him and his mother when it happened."

"Why weren't you there?"

"Mine is a traveling occupation, son. Like a glacier! You know what a glacier is, boy?"

Mundy shook his head.

"Well, a long time ago this whole area, for a thousand miles, was all ice bound. Ice maybe a mile thick! Can you imagine?

"My dad told me a story about an ice giant. His name was Buri, like the name of the mayor in town."

"I never heard that one. That's a good one. Reminds me of the Ojibwa tribe. They have a story about an ice giant. They called him Mesabi, and he was so big no one could walk around him." Lewis used a twig to light his pipe, chewing on the stem as he spoke. "And they have other stories about giants that would turn your hair white. Cannibal giants called Wendigos."

Mr. Lewis was a good storyteller, and Mundy was enthralled. Only his father had ever told him stories like these, and, somehow, it was if his father was there with them, listening in. Maybe stories are like souls that go on living in tall tales, passed on from life to life.

"...and all that glacier ice, the Mesabi, kept a-moving around, like me, only real slow, and it pushed rocks and dirt under it. Rearranged the whole land, you could say. It ebbed and flowed two or three different times, like a slow powerful ocean of ice, scouring out holes all over the place. Those holes became water impoundments. You know what a water impoundment is, son?"

"No, sir. What's a water impoundment?"

"You're looking at one right there." Lewis pointed to the lake. "This lake and all the others over this territory—thousands of them—are what's left from that glacier thousands of years ago."

Lewis fumbled in a worn leather case. Again, he winced from the motion and used his other hand in place of the first one.

"Now that your father is gone, I guess there's no reason why you shouldn't have this."

He handed Mundy the arrowhead that his father had made him give back.

"I reckon it doesn't matter much," Mundy replied softly, pocketing the arrowhead.

"You know, I had a thought. This is my last stop in the north before winter. Heading south after this. Maybe you could come work with me.

Learn the trade. I can't pay you much, but you'd always have something to eat. Beans mostly, I guess. It's not an easy life, but neither is farming those milk cows. You'd get to see more of these..." The surveyor indicated the mounds around them with the stem of his pipe. "Yes sir, get a good look at them now. These mounds will be gone, either by the plow or from those diggers from Washington."

Mundy didn't answer, but his mind raced. Uncovering buried treasure and gold deposits and the bones of trolls: that was exciting.

Lewis puffed on his pipe and stared intently at Mundy. Maybe he knew Mundy's answer already.

"You know something about land deals, like the one with your uncle and that Finn? They have to be very official-like. They need a good, legal survey. Yes sir, depending on how a survey turns out, some deals have been known to sour."

✳ ✳ ✳ ✳ ✳

After meeting with Mr. Lewis, Mundy felt one step ahead of Uncle Halvar and Koskinen, and that made the next week a little more bearable. Finally, Mundy had a secret, and it was one that might help him keep the farm.

Acting upon Mr. Lewis's advice, Mundy waited for the right moment to set the bait. That moment finally arrived the next Sunday at family dinner after another unusual service.

Although no one spoke for minutes on end, the table was hardly quiet. Uncle Halvar's humming was one force keeping silence at bay. His humming wasn't musical, rather, it was simply a quieter form of the bellowing he had undergone after the lightning strike. Otherwise there came the usual sorts of sounds one expects at dinner: chewing, slicing, and the clinks of fancy silverware tapping fancy ceramic plates with the blue flower border.

And then there was Aunt Helga's high-pitched, short bursts of laughter. Undoubtedly, she worried after Uncle Halvar had just laid his "hands of healing" on any parishioner brave enough to waggle a finger in the air when he asked if anyone ailed in body or spirit. Several people had raised their hands, and Reverend Halvar Ingegaard, Minister and Magnetic Healer, had pounced on them with the Holy Spirit flowing through him.

Tomas made a sudden addition to the dinner sounds when he accidentally bumped the salt pot and scattered grains on the fancy table. Aunt Helga tittered, and Tomas apologized, and Aunt Helga tittered again, this time shaking her head.

Amanda's eyebrows furrowed, "Mother, perhaps you need to lie down. You know, to calm yourself."

Aunt Helga waved off the suggestion but couldn't contain yet another nervous laugh.

Uncle Halvar stopped humming and looked questioningly at his wife. He scooped a serving of squash into his mouth, and then the humming resumed even as he chewed.

"Reverend Halvar," Mundy began. "May I speak?"

"Only if you have something sensible to say."

"Yes, sir. I'd like to apologize to you for my disrespectful behavior at this table last week, and to everyone here. I'm sorry."

"Well!" Uncle Halvar's face brightened and he raised his hand in the air to salute the ceiling. "We have one returning to the fold of the righteous, O Lord!" Then he recited: "All Scripture is breathed by God and profitable for teaching, for reproof, for correction so that the man may be equipped for every good work."

"And you won't oppose the sale of the farm? Not going to give me any problems?"

"Oh, no sir!" Mundy should have had his fingers crossed. "In fact, I only want to help."

Amanda looked at him, shocked at what he was saying.

Uncle Halvar further extolled the virtues of disciplining children and how the rod made straight the road to virtue, but Mundy interrupted him as gently as he could.

"Excuse me, Reverend Ingegaard, but I heard Mayor Buri tell my dad once that when someone wants to sell a plot of land, there needs to be a land survey to make it legal."

"Mayor Buri said that?"

Mundy nodded. He had never heard any such advice from the Mayor, but it sounded like the kind of thing Mr. Buri would say.

"That's an expense," his uncle grumbled. "I hadn't accounted for any expenses. Perhaps Koskinen will pay for it."

"Who would know the difference?" Aunt Helga retorted. "Sell this place and let's be well shot of it."

"Oh no! I'll not run afoul of the law! The tyrant is ever waiting to strangle the righteous through his barbed trickery!"

"I wonder..." Mundy pretended to concentrate, but he really was only staring at the cheese and wondering how much of it he could fit in his mouth.

"Yes?" Uncle Halvar leaned forward. "What do you wonder?"

"Wasn't the man who came here...oh, what was his name? Lewis?"

"Yes, Lewis. So?"

"Wasn't he a surveyor?"

"Yes, I suppose he was!"

"Didn't he offer to survey our land at no cost?"

"Did he? No cost?" Uncle Halvar's face fell. "Well, a load of good that does us. I would have no idea how to find the man now."

Mundy had to remind himself not to pull the noose on his uncle too soon. He let a few moments lapse before he presented his final bait.

"Come to think of it," Mundy began slowly. "I spoke to this Mr. Lewis in town just a few days ago. He mentioned that he's surveying along the big lake. He even offered to take me on as an apprentice."

"He did?"

"Yes."

"And why are you here? A vocation like that would give you a future once this farm is gone."

"I don't mind inquiring after him about the survey and the apprenticeship," Mundy offered.

"The Lord's word is a lamp unto my feet, and a light unto my path!" Uncle Halvar declared. "The farm will be sold! The boy will learn a trade! And we have our parish! Hallelujah!"

"No! I want him with me!" Mundy's mother interjected. "And I want him to finish his schooling."

"A life of service to others affords the finest lessons!" Aunt Helga retorted. "Besides, he's just another mouth to feed."

Mundy didn't mind her saying that. He didn't mind at all. The trap was sprung.

He barely finished eating his cherry crumble when he excused himself.

"I'll go see Mr. Lewis now and see if he can help you." Mundy sounded as genuine as a gold liberty coin, and Uncle Halvar said that sounded like a fine idea.

He saddled Cloppie, but just as he was about to mount and ride off to the big lake, Amanda called to him, waving frantically.

"Let me ride with you a-ways," she spoke insistently.

"What's wrong?"

"Oh, I just told mother and father about Matias, and they are forbidding me to see him. Do you think that's right?"

"Yes, actually," Mundy said thoughtfully. "I think that's about the only thing I'd agree with them on."

She ignored him. "I'm just so upset, and I thought a little ride might help clear my head." She pouted. "Can't I come with you, please?"

Mundy agreed, and he got in saddle first and pulled Amanda up behind him. Cloppie was none too pleased with the arrangement, shifting side to side to show her displeasure. They rode off toward the lake, and Mundy was feeling good. Not only had the first step gone according to plan, but Amanda was holding him as the trotted along the path. It was a lovely evening, and he could smell clover in the air.

As they passed the Koskinen farm, Amanda let go of him and slid off of Cloppie, narrowly missing being trampled.

Mundy circled Cloppie but then realized Amanda hadn't slipped. She had jumped down to meet Matias who was waiting for her near a mulberry tree.

"Thank you for the ride!" Amanda waved to him and then ran to Matias. Matias also waved, but he was sneering.

Mundy shook his head and continued on his journey to the big lake alone, finding Mr. Lewis sharpening his straight-edge razor.

"Thinking about shaving," Lewis quipped. "Want to be ready if the feeling overtakes me."

Mundy told him that his uncle had taken the bait.

"Well, I'm not surprised!" Lewis said. "Most people already have saddles on their backs and bits in their mouths before they realize they're already being ridden and getting their flanks spurred."

Mundy relished the thought of Mr. Lewis astride Uncle Halvar, spurring him on, shouting giddy-up, little Halvar!

"Like I said, you're a sharp boy. I hope you'll still at least consider apprenticing with me. I sure could use the help. And the companionship would be good, too."

"Thank you, Mr. Lewis. I've been considering it."

"I'll be at your farm tomorrow morning, first thing. Let me do the talking. Can you remember that?"

*****

Mundy did remember. The next morning when Mr. Lewis rode up, his uncle, aunt, mother, and Mr. Koskinen lined the drive to watch the surveyor dismount. Koskinen stood so the side of his body surreptitiously brushed against his mother's body, but she seemed half-dazed, not having slept.

Uncle Halvar shook the surveyor's hand and then immediately gripped his forearm, drawing Lewis into him. He told Lewis how their meeting was all part of the Lord's plan.

"Let us pray," Uncle Halvar intoned.

"Hold on now," Lewis tried to pull free but gave up, searching Mundy's face for guidance. Mundy shrugged.

"Gracious heavenly Father, let the dealings between men be honest. Give us Your wisdom, O Mighty Lord, to mark the limits of this bounteous land You have given a poor, struggling family—"

Lewis yelped and pulled his arm free, rubbing his wrist.

"My arm feels like it's on fire!"

Uncle Halvar first looked peeved at the disruption, but then his stern countenance melted. "Were you ailing before you arrived here, Brother Lewis?"

"I'll admit, I sprained this arm." He shook his right arm so that his flopped like a fish splashing for mayflies. "But, by God, if it doesn't feel better!"

"Amen!" Uncle Halvar slapped the surveyor on the back.

Mr. Lewis scanned the ground and, noticing a chunk of field stone, he lifted it shoulder high. "I mean it, too! Why before I came here, I had the greatest of difficulty saddling Isabel, the pain was so sharp." He threw the stone with apparent ease. "Would you look at that? Like a brand-new arm!"

Uncle Halvar seemed very pleased. "The Lord is powerful, and I am but a vessel." Mundy could see that acting humble and being humble were two different things, and his uncle could be only one.

"For that miraculous healing, Reverend, I intend not to charge you a thin dime for this survey! No sir, I wouldn't accept your money!"

"That's how I understood the arrangement, Mr. Lewis." Uncle Halvar looked with suspicious eyes at Mundy. "According to the boy, anyway. When can you start?"

"Oh, I can get started on some preliminary work right now."

"Don't you normally have another man and those chains?"

"Indeed, indeed. That is the preferred method of our forefathers, but thanks to advances in modern cadastralmancy, that is to say, the measurement of geospatial locales..."

"Plain speaking, Mr. Lewis, is the foundation of civil discourse. You mean land surveying."

"As you say, Reverend. In land surveying, the use of chains is entirely superfluous. Give me only the sun, a compass, and a sure monument, and I can triangulate the entire Northwest passage. If I were forced to work with limited manpower, that is, but I find that able-bodied young men like these two here..." He indicated Mundy and Tomas who both stood by watching this energetic exchange. "They are very apt pupils, and if you are willing to supply one or two, it reduces the time of surveying greatly."

"That one needs to learn something useful," Aunt Helga indicated Mundy with a nod of her head. "He eats like a horse."

Mundy didn't eat half as much as Tomas, so what did that make her own son?

"You said it's a quarter-section we'll be dealing with?"

"That's right," Uncle Halvar said, pointing into the distance. "From that fence, to those trees..."

"Reverend, I must ask you to refrain from influencing this survey."

"But I was only pointing out the rough boundaries..."

"It is my lawful duty as a licensed surveyor in the employ of the State of Minnesota's Geological Society that my work be objective, impartial, and free from parties with commercial interests trying to assert undue influence. Now, triangulating a quarter section that's fairly cleared of cover isn't much of a job. Two weeks, depending on weather."

"Two weeks?" Uncle Halvar leaned toward Mr. Lewis and lowered his voice. "But Koskinen has good money in hand right now, and I don't know how long he can keep it in his pocket. I had hoped to be clear of this deal sooner."

"Maybe a week-and-a-half, if the boys can assist me."

"By all means," Uncle Halvar agreed.

"I insist," Aunt Helga added.

Uncle Halvar was satisfied and said now was as good as time as any to begin the survey, but once the other adults were out of earshot, Lewis's face squeezed into a tight ball of wrinkled pain.

"Does your arm hurt?" Mundy asked. "I thought Uncle Halvar healed it."

Lewis rubbed his forearm. "There wasn't anything wrong with that arm to begin with, but, boy! Did he squeeze it fierce! But he thinks he healed it, and that's what is important."

Mundy and Tomas began immediately. Mundy unloaded gear, and Tomas followed Mr. Lewis around the survey site. Mr. Lewis explained their duties.

"It's not hard work for strong boys like you: hauling gear, holding the sighting rod straight, and watching for my signals. I might point left or right, so you'd move where I need you to be. It's going to be hot, and those flies are going to near drive you insane, but I need you to keep that rod straight no matter what."

"Yes, sir," Tomas agreed. "I'll help out as much as I can, but I do have a job in town, so I won't be able to help out tomorrow or the day after."

"How about you, Mundy? Do you have someplace else you'd rather be?"

"No, sir," Mundy answered, and he meant it on more than one level.

After an hour, Tomas called for Mr. Lewis from across the field hoping this voice would carry in the breeze. Lewis looked up but only to signal that Tomas should move the sighting rod south several paces. Tomas swatted the air around him to discourage the horde of gnats circling him.

"Did you need something?" Mundy asked. "I can tell him."

"Yes, tell him I don't want to be his dressmaker's mannequin anymore. I'm getting eaten alive out here!"

"Give it another hour," Mundy suggested.

"What will change in an hour? Only that it will be hotter, and even more pests will try to kill me." Tomas lowered the rod and began walking towards Mr. Lewis who waved him to go back to his position so he could get his measurements.

When Mr. Lewis was in earshot, Tomas told the surveyor that he should consider Matias Koskinen as an assistant.

"He's the person you'd want for this type of work," Tomas concluded. "My vocation leans more toward interior duties." He walked away to the cabin where, presumably, his calling leaned.

"Hmm," Lewis consulted his notes. "It sure would make this easier with another set of hands. Where'd you say those Koskinens live?"

"They're Finns, Mr. Lewis," Mundy sputtered. "Liars and thieves!"

"Still, it wouldn't hurt to meet the boy. What's his name? Matias? Hard work might be just the experience for a young man who's a little rough around the edges."

"You'd have to pay him!" Mundy declared. "He's not going to work for free, and since you're not getting paid."

"It just so happens I'm willing to pay out of my own pocket, if it helps me find a good worker."

"Please, Mr. Lewis, no. He's a bad seed."

"Look, Mundy, I honestly need someone to help me over the winter in the south. That's why I'd like to try out a few of you strapping farm lads to see if I can pan out a gold nugget among you—especially considering you haven't changed your mind about farming." He looked hard at Mundy. "You haven't changed your mind, have you?"

"No," Mundy admitted. "I want to save the farm. He set a different tack. "But it isn't right, having Matias or any of them here. My father would never allow a Finn to work on the property."

Lewis put a firm hand on Mundy's shoulder.

"But, boy, I'm sorry to say, your father isn't here anymore. All his thoughts, all the rules he imposed, none of it matters a whit anymore. Like the arrowhead you took from me. It didn't matter that your father said you shouldn't have it. You can see that. This hatred of your neighbors, that isn't very Christian, is it?"

"No, I suppose not," Mundy agreed. "But we aren't Christian."

Lewis smiled as he released his grip on Mundy.

"Well, that's just…Aren't a Christian, eh? What are you then? What kind of wild heathen am I dealing with?"

Mundy shrugged. He didn't know what kind of heathen he was yet.

"Besides," Lewis added. "Do you remember why we're doing this? To help save your farm, right?" Mundy nodded reluctantly. "Well, how sweet will the victory taste knowing that your enemies helped you win it?"

Mundy couldn't let it go. His stubborn streak was growing stronger. He explained that it was too dangerous to go to the Koskinen farm. He recounted to Mr. Lewis the previous occasion when Matias aimed a rifle aimed at him.

"Well, aiming and shooting are two different things," Mr. Lewis said. "Tell you what, I'll go over there myself. That way I can explain the situation to the father," Lewis shook Mundy's shoulder and laughed. "Cheer up! This is what we need for our plan to bear fruit!"

✳ ✳ ✳ ✳ ✳

Mr. Koskinen agreed to allow Matias to join the survey crew. It didn't take much persuading, because there was mention of thirty cents per day, and possibly more if he showed a knack for the job. Mundy watched from the road as the two men shook hands. Mr. Koskinen fairly shoved Matias out the door.

Once at the Nelson farm, Matias soon began harassing Mundy: shoving him whenever he had the opportunity, name calling, knocking his hat from his head. No amount of warning from Lewis would make him stop, and the work was frequently interrupted by a frustrated Mr. Lewis. Matias yelled his apologies but would still take swipes at Mundy.

At the end of the first day, they all were worn out from the heat and the plodding pace of things. Mr. Lewis told them to get a good night's sleep and rode off on Isabel.

"You going to try to outwork me tomorrow?" Matias smirked.

"I don't have to try," Mundy replied. "Because you're worthless."

Mundy knew he worked harder than any boy his age, every day. He would have been the easy choice for Lewis, if Mundy were interested in traveling the country and seeing all the troll mounds, but there was too much to do on the farm.

Suddenly, Mundy realized that if Mr. Lewis did take Matias as assistant, Matias wouldn't bother him or Amanda anymore. That sounded like a good thing, so why was Mundy still feeling jealous?

✶✶✶✶✶

That evening, Mundy rode Cloppie to town for supper at the parish house by order of his mother. She claimed she had plans and told Mundy to send her regrets. Mundy knew her plans were with Kauko Koskinen. Her last words to him were that he should behave and not do anything to upset anyone.

Mundy was too tired to argue. He even fell asleep as he rode, a light rain drenching his clothes, but he didn't care. He shivered at the dinner table and was allowed about half the portion that Tomas received—the reason being that Tomas was a working man. As Mundy knelt on the floor with the others, the food taunted him as Uncle Halvar recited a lengthy prayer. Even after the amen, they waited to begin eating, sitting at an uncomfortable attention, because Uncle Halvar announced that he had bad news.

"Mr. Koskinen will not proceed with the farm purchase—survey or not—until the field shed comes down. So, tomorrow you boys will tear that moldering heap down and burn it," Uncle Halvar concluded.

"Is that the building where your father got hurt?" Amanda asked Mundy. "I'm sure you'll be glad to tear it down and burn it for nails."

Mundy didn't want any part of tearing down the shed, but he said nothing. Tomas grumbled that he was supposed to work at Mr. Buri's shop, and besides, he didn't like working out-of-doors, but his father offered him some stern warnings about idleness. Aunt Helga took a softer approach with him.

"Don't worry Tomas," she cooed as she stroked his cheek. "Your papa will smooth things over with Mr. Buri. He's the minister, after all!"

"Well, mother, he is only one of the ministers in town," Amanda countered. "And as I'm given to understand, the position is only temporary!"

Uncle Halvar raised his voice to return to his main point. "Tomas and Mundy, you know what must happen, and it must be tomorrow." He pounded the table with both fists. "That shed will come down."

Neither Lars Nelson's death, nor the ax his mother wielded, nor year after year of north winds or summer storms had wiped that field shed from the land. His grandfather had built it, and his father had died because of it, and something was buried beneath it: that's what his father had said.

"Reverend Ingegaard," Mundy kept his voice soft and his head low. "What about the survey? Mr. Lewis will be there again."

"Yes, yes," Uncle Halvar waved off this concern. "Is it not possible that both events could happen in the same day? For remember, to Him —" Uncle Halvar pointed a finger to the ceiling of the dining room. "One day is as a thousand years, and a thousand years as one day."

"If we have to do this tomorrow, father, then I do hope it will go more quickly than a thousand years," Tomas said. "I am needed at the store. We are moving some of the stock into storage now, and..."

"Make your point, boy!"

"I was about to say that maybe Mr. Koskinen will bring over that big horse of his to pull at the corners. I don't think Mundy's old horse is going to be of much help! She's as rickety as that shed!"

Everyone except Mundy laughed, and emotion bubbled up inside of him: words, dangerous and angry, were forming from a pit in his stomach, coursing up his throat, and shooting out of his mouth.

"Cloppie has done more to help the farm than you ever could," Mundy blurted.

"Tiddemund!" Amanda sat upright. She looked first at him and then immediately looked to Uncle Halvar, and Mundy's eyes followed hers. Would Uncle Halvar punish him again for his outburst? Mundy prepared himself. If his uncle made a move toward him, he would shove back his chair from the table and dash for the door and ride off on Cloppie back to the farm, but Uncle Halvar merely shook his head and gave him a most disapproving stare.

"The Lord says if a man has a stubborn and rebellious son who will not obey, then his father and his mother shall take hold of him and bring him out to the city gate and all the men of the city shall stone him to death."

"Amen!" Aunt Helga agreed.

"Is that what you want?" Tomas added. "You want people to throw rocks at you until you're dead?"

Mundy looked down at his lap and shook his head.

"No, I don't want people to throw rocks at me." He had sneaked another biscuit from the plate and was trying to decide how to hide it in his pocket. He excused himself from the table. Now that the church was unattended, he was going to steal the brass cross from the altar.

CHAPTER THIRTEEN
FIRE AND BONES

The Ingegaards were at the farm early the next day, both to help the packing process along and to demolish the shed. At some point, Brita Nelson would have to tell her sister that she wasn't moving to the parish house, but she apparently hadn't yet worked up the courage.

While in the cabin, Brita, Amanda, and Aunt Helga filled crates and wrapped fragile items in rags. Outside at the field shed, Uncle Halvar bossed Mundy and Tomas with directions that, to Mundy, seemed unnecessary, like telling them to swing their hammers hard when already they swung as hard as they could. Then Uncle Halvar would complain that the women were probably getting nothing done, and he would wander off to offer them guidance. Mundy bet his uncle's inside guidance was as helpful as his outside guidance.

He understood that the shed coming down was inevitable. Another strong storm might have done it anyway, but he couldn't help but imagine his father and uncle, about the same ages as he and Tomas, nailing the same wood in place a score of years before. Mundy was destroying what they had built. At least whatever was underneath the shed, whatever had been in the first burial mound, was still safely buried.

Mr. Lewis arrived when the sun was well up. He found Mundy and Tomas already hammering loose wood planks on the shed. Tomas explained they needed to knock down the shed to move the farm sale forward, but he was welcome to help, if he cared to. Mr. Lewis remembered that he needed to go to town for some supplies anyway, not the least of which was tobacco to refill his pouch. He looked at Mundy, checking for indications that all was well, and Mundy gave him a little smile.

As Mr. Lewis was leaving, he saluted Mr. Koskinen and Matias, who were coming over with the big Friesian. He cautioned Matias not to tire himself out.

"There'll be plenty of survey work after this shed nonsense concludes."

Mr. Koskinen said something rude in Finnish that made both Matias and his father laugh.

"Fires make their own time!" Koskinen called after Lewis. "Who knows? Maybe by the time you come back, nothing will be left of this place!"

Mr. Lewis shrugged and rode off, muttering about immigrants.

Amanda waited outside when the Koskinens appeared, wearing her nicest dress, the same one she wore to play the church piano. Matias called her over and told her to take the stallion's tether from him. She ran like a little girl, too eager for the first cake out of the oven, and she pulled the tether too tight. The stallion towered over her, and anytime he wanted to, he could crush her with a simple turn of his flanks. He pulled against the tether, jerking her arm up and to the side.

Even as Matias laughed at her, Mundy charged the horse and grabbed the tether from her, pulling firm and yelling commands at the horse to move it toward the shed.

Amanda, annoyed, yelled at Mundy that she didn't need his help. "I was getting a feel for him, that's all."

"You were about to get your neck broken, is what it was!" Mundy shot back.

Tomas and Mundy had notched an opening in the shed wall, and they lashed the Friesian to one corner using lengths of thick rope that Mr. Koskinen had undoubtedly stolen from his logging job. Then Mr. Koskinen yelled for them to stand back and took control of the stallion, guiding him to pull away until the thick rope grew taut and the shed creaked and cracked. More pulling, more creaking, and then one post snapped, and the entire shed tilted and then collapsed in a great heap. The shed's roof—the same roof that had caused his father's death—fell to the ground and unsettled a cloud of dust.

They built a fire using kindling, twigs, and sawdust, adding branches and broken slats of weathered wood, and soon the field shed caught easily and burned. Mundy couldn't stop watching it. The smoke rolled over him until his eyes were red. At their peak, the flames reached thirty, forty feet high, and they took on form: skating women born of blue flames, gliding along the ridge of charred, fallen beams, their snow the sparks and ash, rising into the low clouds of billowing smoke, the sails of a smoldering shipwreck.

"Quite a fire," Mr. Lewis' voice startled Mundy. "I could see it all the way from Buri's store." He ignited a twig in the conflagration to light his pipe, which was plugged with fresh tobacco. "I'm ready to start surveying around the pond, if you boys can tear yourselves away from firebugging."

"We better make sure this doesn't spread," Mundy suggested. "We need to be ready to beat it down if it catches in a breeze."

Lewis watched the fire in a slight daze.

"You ever notice how wood holds its shape, even after it's burned up?" He jabbed the air with his pipe indicating the burning beams and posts. "Burn a log. Still looks like a log until you go poking at it with a fire hook. Then it all falls apart. Makes a man wonder, doesn't it? That moment?"

"What moment is that, Mr. Lewis?"

"Well, the best I can figure it, there's got to be one precise moment when the log ceases to be a log at all, and it becomes ash. Plenty of folks have rescued a postal card, a teacup, a book or what have you, and the item is burned but it's still what they intended to keep—but only because they got to it before that moment of ash. Touch it and..." He blew a puff of smoke at the fire. "It's powder."

Mundy responded only with a slight nod, too lost in the fire's display to swim out and wrestle words from the deep. Tomas, too, was sitting cross-legged on the perimeter, hypnotized. Lewis announced there wasn't much hope getting any work done that day after all.

"You boys look run down. I'll be back tomorrow," Lewis promised. "Keep an eye on those two." He winked at Mundy as he pointed his chin toward Matias and Amanda, who were surreptitiously touching hands just out of sight of Uncle Halvar.

Mundy remembered that tomorrow would be his day to hold the sighting rod and for Matias to do the running. He hoped Matias got cramps in both legs and fell down crying like a baby. But the thought of what Mr. Lewis had said about the fire stayed with him. That moment. His father. A spark in the sky, drifting, weightless, gone.

The fire took a full day to turn every bit of wood black and then gray and then they turned any remnant of solidity in the remaining rubble, rekindling the blaze so that, at the end, even the thick crossbeam, rumored to have been red oak, was a bar of ash.

Now his father's grave had only mounds of white ash and rusted nails as a headstone—but only for a little longer. Mundy had stowed the brass cross from the church in the barn. Soon his father's grave would be marked better than any grave in the county.

***** *

Another light rain late in the afternoon put an end to the fire, but it didn't stop evening milking. Mundy left the barn with a pail of warm milk and saw Amanda and the Koskinens and Uncle Halvar, who appeared to be practicing his next sermon right there in front of the cabin. Meanwhile, Tomas had found a way to make himself useful by collecting iron: nails, hooks, braces—whatever they might reuse or sell—the only solid remains of the field shed. He'd encased his boots in wet burlap sacks to keep them from getting scorched, and he wore a kerchief over his face to keep out the smoke, but Mundy saw him just as he nearly fell face-first into the pile. Tomas quickly used the long-handled fire hook to prop himself upright. As he did so, he kicked up a cloud of ash in the effort.

"Hey!" Tomas called. "What's this?" He stooped over the area he had kicked free of ash and soil. "Father! Come and see!"

Uncle Halvar, the Koskinens, and Amanda came to see what Tomas was making such a fuss over. Mundy's heart sank. Had Tomas uncovered what Mundy's father and uncle had left buried under the shed?

Tomas and Matias started shoveling ash into a handcart to clear the spot before Mundy could think of a way to stop them. He rushed to where they were, hoping to think of a good reason why they needed to be anywhere else on the farm at that moment.

"What is that?" Tomas poked the ground with a shovel. Uncle Halvar peered down and yelled out a hallelujah!

The top of a skull gleamed white and hard in the late afternoon sun, peeking out from the scorched ground. Uncle Halvar, on his hands and knees, loosened the ground around the skull when, like all Great Secrets, the skull would not come loose on the first pull. He shouted confused directions, at once demanding that no one touch anything, driving away his own children with the edge of a spade, and then in another turn cursing them for their idleness. Spotting Mundy, he bellowed for him.

"Where have you been? Wasting your time staring at your cows, no doubt. Get over here and help with this!"

The group dug a perimeter around the skull until it was loose enough to remove from the ground. Tomas hoisted it out with some difficulty. It was heavy. Everyone watched in amazement, stunned at the size of the skull—eyeholes large enough for a man's fist to fit into. The open jaw could easily fit over Tomas's entire head. This discovery only spurred them to work harder in the dying light. They retrieved an assortment of other bones that they laid out on a canvas: two long bones, a ribcage, and the gleaming tops of more skulls—skulls that were the same shape as any man's skull, but much larger.

"Look at the size of this!" Uncle Halvar was as wild-eyed as he had been after the lightning strike, and Mundy was afraid his uncle would revert to his steady stream of yelling, but, instead, he mumbled beneath earshot, until Mundy figured out he was babbling a continuous prayer of thanksgiving, punctuated by a strange word Mundy had never heard before: Nephilim.

As the sun set, it was as if Uncle Halvar suddenly had awakened from a fever dream. His treatment of the Koskinens changed abruptly.

"You need to leave the property now," Uncle Halvar said, guiding Kauko Koskinen and son by the elbows away from site. "And don't sneak over here in the night, Koskinen!" Uncle Halvar raged.

Koskinen shot back that anything of value that they found should be shared equally as part of the land sale, but Uncle Halvar said the land was still theirs.

It was getting too dark to work anymore, but they'd revealed a half dozen giant skeletons.

"Cover them up in case it rains again," Uncle Halvar instructed. "You boys will sleep here tonight. I don't want any marauders, human or otherwise, to make off with this...this...message!"

That night the boys camped beside the hole and the covered bones, shivering and sleepless in the pre-dawn chill. After sunrise, they kept digging as Uncle Halvar prayed loudly over them. Milking had to wait. Everything had to wait.

As much as he'd hoped to keep the farm as it used to be, Mundy, too, was caught up in the excitement of discovery of these giants. The hard earth yielded more bones the deeper they dug, and Mundy felt his breath coming in short bursts as he strained each spade of dirt into a pile. It was

183

hard work, but he didn't feel tired, and neither did Tomas. They worked side by side, one occasionally rushing over to help the other pry up a field stone that impeded the digging.

Soon one canvas was not enough to protect their discovery, and Uncle Halvar roared for Brita to bring out her bedsheets, which did not please her in the least, but she did as she was told. By noon, seven giant skeletons were outlined on the sleeping sheets, more or less complete, but with some missing bits or tips shattered in hasty digging. As a joke, Tomas lay down on the canvas in the midst of them until his father yelled himself hoarse for him to get away. The contrast between Tomas, who was a tall young man, with the bones of these monsters was striking. Each one of them must have been at least eight feet tall.

The grave yielded more than skeletons. Tomas and Mundy also nearly filled a nail keg with clay beads, flecks of blue and red paint visible beneath the coating of soil. They found small metal spheres, rounder and smoother than the beads, bigger than buckshot, with an orange tone shining through corrosion in spots. Copper, Uncle Halvar claimed. Mixed in were also the bones of what might have been a large dog, but with a longer jaw and more incisors than Mundy would imagine a normal dog to have.

"Maybe a wolf?" Tomas wondered.

"A very big wolf!" Mundy answered as the tip of his spade had struck something solid, not bone, and he felt around with the spade to find its edges, thinking it was yet another rock. Soon he had it outlined and then pried it loose: an ax head nearly a foot long on the cutting end. It weighed about twenty pounds, as Mundy quickly found out as he and Tomas wrenched it free.

"This is like the one at the train station," Tomas exclaimed.

"Except this one is stone," Mundy added.

"No man among us could wield such a terrible implement," Uncle Halvar said, his voice a half-whisper. "No mere mortal man, anyway." He hefted the axe head in both hands skyward like Moses with the Commandments. "Only a mighty man of old could! Hallelujah!"

"They are trolls," Mundy added quietly, which was a fact so patently clear that it needed no elaboration. Uncle Halvar dropped the axe head and slapped Mundy hard across the side of his head so that Mundy's ears buzzed even after the pain subsided.

"Your superstitions will land you in hell, boy! There aren't trolls! These are the bones of the Nephilim! Half man, half angel!" Uncle Halvar fell to his knees, sending up a cloud of ash from the dead fire, his arms outstretched, his face to the sun. "They were on the earth in those days, when the daughters of men bore children to the sons of God. These were the heroes of old, the unconquered warriors. Genesis, chapter six! Do you not see?"

✻✻✻✻✻

Mr. Lewis had barely made the turn onto the Nelson drive when Mundy urged him to leave.

"My uncle is crazy right now," he explained in a rush. "He might try to kill you to protect what we dug up."

Lewis, rather than being cautioned, strained forward to see what was happening where the shed once stood. "Something you dug up, you say?"

He dismounted and didn't even bother tying up Isabel. He left her standing right where she was, and he strode past Mundy toward where Reverend Ingegaard was delivering a boisterous sermon to no one in particular at the edge of the pit they'd dug in the middle of an ash heap.

"Good morning, Reverend!" Lewis announced himself.

"Get away!" Uncle Halvar's shovel was in easy reach, and he soon had it in hand, swinging it at waist level.

Lewis leapt back a few paces, safely out of range. "The boy says you dug up something, and I'm guessing it wasn't turnips."

"Not turnips, but the proof of things unseen! The cure for the faithless! The truth for non-believers!"

"You've got my full attention, Reverend. Do tell what it is you have found."

Uncle Halvar muttered to himself—or prayed, it was hard to tell the difference anymore—and then determined that he would share the wondrous discovery with the surveyor. He was about to unfurl the sheet covering their find, but he stopped.

"On one condition," he said. "You must pledge yourself before our Heavenly Father not to pillage, plunder, or otherwise rob this trove of sacred relics."

"I'm used to offering my word as a man of honor," Lewis said with a bemused expression. "But I can see that my word alone is woefully ill-fit to this purpose. I so pledge."

Uncle Halvar shivered as if the lightning still flowed through his body as he uncovered the skeletons. Lewis rushed forward again to be nearer the discovery, but in a flash the shovel again was raised like the angel's flaming sword in the Garden of Eden.

Lewis eyed the pit then examined the skeletons and the ax head on the sheets.

"Tell me everything." He lowered himself to the ground, his legs crossed, a willing congregant to the Reverend Uncle's onrush of confusing Bible verses. Finally, Uncle Halvar collapsed in tearful prayer.

Mundy leaned close to Mr. Lewis and, pointing to the giant skeletons, he whispered, "That's why my grandfather built the field shed. And that's why my father died trying to repair it."

That was only partially true. His father had died trying to protect Mundy from falling off the roof.

Nodding, Mr. Lewis said it was the most remarkable discovery he'd seen that year.

"I will say this, Reverend. What you've got here, you're going to want to keep it to yourself."

"To myself?" Uncle Halvar was not a man known to laugh, but here did the unthinkable, laughing at Lewis until he was crying again. "This is a revelation from the Lord!"

"Yes, it is certainly remarkable and, to be fair, I don't think I've ever seen its equal. All the same, it's for that very same reason you'd be well compensated by peace of mind to keep this under your hat."

Seeing the perplexed looks on both the minister's and Mundy's faces, Lewis continued. "It's like this, if I may speak plainly? There are certain people with a very specific viewpoint about the present based on their understanding of the past. For example, yourself. You see these fine dead gentlemen and, possibly, ladies, and you think of them a certain way. To you, they signify a specific fact based on your own viewpoint."

"My viewpoint is God's Holy Word! This is proof!" Uncle Halvar was back on his feet, pointing at the skeletons. "Proof of the Bible's veracity in a sinful age where doubt and indifference have replaced obedience!"

Lewis cleared his throat. "Again, I can appreciate your position, but, for a moment, let's consider a less theological perspective. You know there's more than a few native legends about the tribes having to fight off big men like these. Tribes had to join forces and fight back, and it was brutal."

"That is foolish superstition!" Uncle Halvar muttered.

"Maybe, but in my line of work, I've met a few people—good husbands and fathers, like you. They'd get excited about some wild discovery they made when they tore into one these little mounds while they were leveling off a field. Only thing is, some of what they found sort of challenged what most folks believe to be true. Well, like you, they were enthusiastic, got to drawing attention to themselves, and they talked about them, and then..."

"And then what?" Uncle Halvar scoffed.

"Well, and then they all disappeared: bones, weapons, pottery, and the farmers, too. Just vanished."

"Liar!" Uncle Halvar raged.

"Is that true?" Mundy asked.

"It's not a lie," Lewis responded. "And it's not an exaggeration. There are those who will come after me whose saddles I personally would rather not be slung over, dead or alive."

"I will not tolerate threats!" Uncle Halvar's eyes fired with righteous anger, and the muscles of his forearms corded as his palm disappeared into fists. "The Lord has made clear my path, and the Lord is my strength! For the path of the righteous shall not be lost even in the darkness. The Lord's truth lights my way!"

Lewis shook his head calmly and turned to go back to Isabel.

"I can see you're adamant about this, so there's nothing to be done when a man has his mind made up." Lewis didn't look back, but added, "But Reverend, keep those men in mind. Government men with a different outlook on the world. They will come."

CHAPTER FOURTEEN
MIGHTY MEN OF OLD

The next day, Uncle Halvar woke up singing. He sang hymns, and he sang them loudly.

Where are our fathers gone?
Whither gone the mighty men of old?
The patriarchs, prophets, princes, kings
In sacred books enrolled.

He stopped singing only to tell Mundy to hitch Cloppie to the wagon, and then he kept singing.

Gone to the resting place of man,
His long, his silent home;
Where ages past have gone before,
Where future ages come.

Uncle Halvar even sang at the top of his lungs the entire way to town without flagging, which was unnerving to a boy who was used to the obdurate silence of his parents, but at least Uncle Halvar wasn't paying any attention to Mundy. If Uncle Halvar wanted to embarrass himself in town, that was up to him.

When they reached Annandale, Uncle Halvar told Mundy to wait with the wagon.

"Don't bother even tying her up! Stay right there!" He was smiling—smiling at Mundy like an excited boy who got his first kiss. Uncle Halvar ran into Buri's store, then to the smithy, then over to Dunton the casket-makers shop. Up and down the street he ran, darting into each doorway, grabbing people by the arm right on the street, shouting at men on horseback, until a crowd of townspeople gathered in the street asking one another what the commotion was all about. The wild gleam in Uncle Halvar's eye was enough to tempt people back to minding their own business and quick.

"You must come see the Nephilim!" he shouted. "We have found a race of ancient giants!"

A few men—parishioners at the church, mostly—felt obliged to follow him back to the wagon, and once a group of five or so upstanding citizens were gathered there, another five decided they better find out what was going on. At the entrance to his shop, Mr. Buri kept his arms folded across his chest, trying to look uninterested, but he too really leaned in for a good look.

And then Mundy understood why his uncle had wanted to take the wagon to town. Uncle Halvar climbed on the back and now towered over the crowd of onlookers. He had a ready-made stage. Mundy knew better than to leave his position on the buckboard, but a hot shame reddened his face.

His uncle told the crowd about what they had dug up at the Nelson farm. He explained the story from Genesis and how the angels mated with the daughters of men to create the mighty men of old, and now he had proof that the story was true. Some of their eyes widened, unsure of the minister's mental state. Others listened placidly, as if he were listing off the prices for butter and wheat bushels. He told them how the discovery was proof that the Bible was literally true, proof that it indeed was the divine Word of God, and how they needed to attend his sermon that coming Sunday.

"Spread the word!" He told them all. "You will never hear the like of this message again!"

Whether they believed his claims or not, the townspeople must have spread the word. That next Sunday, horses and carts lined the street in front of the white clapboard church. People from Maple Lake and South Haven and even a big landowner from Kimball were pressed hip to hip on the wooden pews. The aisles were clogged with half-shined boots and dusty parasols. The young people—including Mundy and Amanda—were made to stand along the back wall so there were enough seats for the adults. Except for Tomas who sat in the front row of pews with his mother, and Amanda was angry about that. She and Mundy had to squeeze together so that their shoulders touched. She whispered to him that she did not appreciate being treated like any other child in the town, forced to give up her seat, as if he could do anything about it.

Mundy was glad to be well back from where his uncle stood behind the pulpit, because, at any moment, someone—it could be a parishioner, it could be his aunt, or it could be the good reverend himself—was going to notice the cross missing from the altar. Of course, no one would know it was him who taken it, except maybe God.

After the preliminary invocation, Tomas read a verse from the big Bible on the pulpit.

"This morning's reading is from Genesis, chapter six, verse four," Tomas said. He was shaking and his voice sounded tinny. "There were giants in the earth in those days; and also after that, when the sons of God came in unto the daughters of men, and they bore children to them, the same became mighty men which were of old, men of renown. Amen."

"Amen," the congregation responded.

Then the congregation let their voices fight over which key the opening hymn should be sung in, and then Reverend Ingegaard rose to begin his sermon. The room was silent except for the creaking of wooden pews, wriggling behinds seeking a comfortable position for the duration of the service. In a shot, he was off in his maniacal style, telling of the giant skeletons, of the massive ax, and the Truth of Salvation apparent all around us. He spoke quickly then slowly, but always loud, loud, loud, thumping the pulpit, his blows deadened by the weight of the Bible beneath his fists. This went on for ten minutes, then twenty minutes, a torrent of bold claims woven together with snippets of scripture until finally some heathen farmer from French Lake or thereabouts yelled out, "Prove it!"

Reverend Ingegaard stopped in mid-sentence. His head snapped toward the man, and Mundy recognized that look. If his uncle could have reached from where he stood, he might have slapped the man across the face.

"The Apostle Paul wrote, Faith is the evidence of things unseen. But for those of you with less faith than that..." A smile slowly developed on his lips. He nodded to Tomas who smiled to the congregation as his shiny black boots flapped on the steps leading to the dais. He knelt next to a crate and removed the lid, and then Uncle Halvar reached down and lifted a giant skull over his head.

"Here's your proof, brother!" He shook the giant skull, turning it so its eye sockets, the size of each as a big as two men's fists, could be seen by all. "Here's your proof, sister!"

The church filled with gasps. Children in the back recoiled in horror, and the smallest among them began wailing. Amanda gripped Mundy's hand, until she thought better of it, and left the impression of her fingers mingled with his only a warm memory. Old Joe Garret, the oldest parishioner, asked what all the fuss was about, because his sight wasn't as sharp as it used to be.

"The heroes of old!" Reverend Ingegaard shouted to Old Joe. "The unconquered warriors! Genesis Six!"

Aunt Helga lifted her hands to shoulder height and offered a quiet hallelujah.

The offering came next. Tomas stood in the aisle to track the movement of the plate as is passed from hand to hand, the sound of coins being added on top of more coins. The congregation was in a generous mood after the thrill of seeing the skull. All that money, Mundy thought, probably enough to buy another cow—maybe even enough for a decent horse.

During the closing hymn, A Mighty Fortress, Aunt Helga swiveled in her pew, looking around the sanctuary in a panic and then back to the altar. She finally had noticed the missing cross. Her eyes scanned the pews full of strangers, and her lips tightened holding back the word thief!

Mundy rushed out of the church as soon at the final amen to avoid having to shuffle through the receiving line where parishioners shook hands with the minister and his family and told them how wonderful his sermon was. The air was cool and fresh, a welcome relief from the stifling air inside the church, degraded by the stench of manure, pine pitch, and ladies' toilet water.

Amanda, in her high-collar dress, lined up with her family on the steps leading down from the church door. They were shaking hands and smiling, and soon Amanda was pretending to be nice to Old Joe Garret, who only had his left hand to shake, because he lost the other one in Texas during the Mexican-American War back in '46. She was smiling at the man, but her smile was a lie, not a song for the lips.

*****

One evening later in the week, the hens in the coop squawked in a panic. Mundy dropped the pail he was carrying and rushed toward them in time to see a cloud of feathers. Upon closer inspection, he found that something had burrowed under the coop frame. He counted the flock: one big hen was missing. He heard clucking and a scuffle near the trees and spotted a lean fox that had paused to look at him, its auburn maw soaked in blood, gripping the struggling hen like a dare.

Come and take it from me, if you can, it seemed to say before it disappeared into the dark underbrush next to the final troll mound.

"*Jævla fitte*," he cursed in Norwegian the way his father did, but he didn't know what it meant. But he was too tired to deal with it, and so he took one of the field stones lying next to the skeleton pit and blocked the hole leading to the coop for the night.

✳ ✳ ✳ ✳ ✳

Before the sun had raised its head above the edge of the earth, the eastern horizon was canvas tinted purple and pink. The growing light of the day's new sun chased off the last fading stars. Only the setting moon watched Mundy as he entered the woods to track the fox.

Mundy knew that in the woods he would find a circle of feathers, white but painted in blood and muck, and then he would look for tracks leading him to the fox den, but he froze as he neared the mound, and a chill passed through his body. Maybe there would be even more of those giant skeletons or maybe even ancient songs, like Amanda claimed, but whatever was buried there was secret and unknown. What if he and Uncle Halvar and Tomas had made the spirits of these mighty men of old angry by digging up the other skeletons? Would they carry Mundy off into the grave like a fox carrying off a hen?

He heard a wagon approaching: a breeze of voices in idle conversation capping the sound of the wheels grinding their axles, the creaking of the cart, the sputter of the draw horses. He came running back out of the woods, his feet moving faster to put distance between himself and the lurking evil troll spirits.

A group of twenty or more people bobbed along on the backs of the wagon, seated on bales of hay, comprised mostly of men, but a handful of them seemed to be accompanied by their wives. Most of them were strangers to Mundy, except for the wagon drivers, men whom he recognized from town, and the strangers were dressed as if they were going to church.

The first driver announced, "Here it is!"

All conversation ceased, and their sudden silence contrasted with the creaking of the wagons that continued as the horses turned off the path toward the cabin.

"I don't see them, do you?" One of the strangers said breaking the silence. They scanned the yard, and Uncle Halvar came riding up on the deceased minister's mare.

"Yes, yes! This is the place," he said, bringing his horse to the front of them and then, spotting Mundy, he added, "Tell your mother to make coffee. A lot of coffee." But Mundy knew that his mother wasn't at home. She was at Koskinen's farm, and he would need to make coffee, if they had any at all, because Koskinen had been dipping into their supplies.

He hung a pail of water on the hook over the fire pit, when one of the strangers broke off from the others. He was of average height, but his appearance otherwise was most striking—red curly hair and matching muttonchops that framed a pair of piercing green eyes set too close together, and too round, like a doll's face with thick, rusty sideburns.

"Hello, son! This your family's place?" Without giving Mundy time to answer, the red-haired man sidled up to Mundy, who was on all fours, coaxing the fire with long, hard breaths, until a cloud of gray smoke bloomed before the crackle of wood fire announced that the flame had taken hold, for the wood and the air was damp.

"Maybe you can tell me what's going on around here?" He extended his hand, long, slim fingers, on a white unscarred hand. "The name's Thaddeus Colton. Here from the St. Paul Dispatch. That's a newspaper, in case you're wondering. People read it, far and wide. You can read, can't you? Well, I'm here to tell those people exactly what's been going on around here. Been some rumblings, some rumors, if you will, but we newspaper men like to get the story straight from the source."

The sound of a horse approaching made them both look up. Isabel carried Mr. Lewis at a half-gallop, right to where Mundy and the reporter stood. He slid easily from the saddle, in a hurry to gain his feet.

"Good morning, Mundy. Who's your new friend?"

"The name's Thaddeus Colton," the reporter said as he extended a hand for shaking. "Here from the St. Paul Dispatch. You the boy's father?"

"Never mind that," Lewis did not shake the reporter's hand but grabbed Mundy by the shoulder and led him behind the cabin. "This isn't good, Mundy."

Mr. Lewis explained to Mundy that word was getting around about the sermon. He said that the Buffalo paper was the first to report, but in their account, the giants had grown in both number and size: Minister Unearths Entire Village of 10-Foot Goliaths.

"This reporter and these other people," Mr. Lewis concluded. "They'll bring an ill wind, Mundy."

"What can I do?" Mundy shouted, jerking his shoulder free. He did not like being held down or held back. In him it now set off a wild, indignant spark.

"For starters, don't say anything more to anyone about the bones. I'll try once more to reason with your uncle. Maybe we can stop this." Another wagon appeared with even more people, including Uncle Halvar and Amanda. Uncle Halvar was reprising his *Mighty Men of Old* sermon from the previous week, but as soon as he noticed the red-haired reporter, he leaped down from the wagon in mid-sentence.

"Glad to know you, Reverend. The name's Thaddeus Colton. Here from the St. Paul Dispatch. I hope you'll tolerate me firing off a few questions in your direction."

"Mr. Colton, I would be delighted to answer your questions." Uncle Halvar sneered at Lewis. The edges of his wild hair caught in the breeze, fluttering like a flock of sparrows winging in the field over cut wheat.

"Unlike some people who refuse to hear the Lord's truth, your readers need first to understand the importance of this revelation. In this modern age, the people are led astray by the so-called scientists who have abandoned faith—true faith—and replaced God in their hearts with the false god of reason. Our little farm has yielded the abundant harvest for the faithful. A grim bounty that proves what science would deny: the holy truths of the scripture!"

"Let's talk plain, Reverend," Colton said. "Give our readers a clear picture. What exactly did you find?"

"Yes! Let us talk plain! Even better: let me show you!" He led the reporter toward the waiting crowd when Mr. Lewis interrupted them, saying he needed a moment to talk with Reverend Ingegaard in private, but Uncle Halvar ignored him completely.

"Yes, sir, Reverend! Seeing is believing, as I'm sure your Bible says." He clapped a hand on Uncle Halvar's back in assumed camaraderie, but

Uncle Halvar stepped clear of his reach.

"Actually, it says quite the opposite to that Mr. Colton, yet the Lord has seen fit to provide us with the 'clear picture', as you say, just the same." Uncle Halvar continued talking, leaning heavily on his most recent sermon, and soon the Reverend Ingegaard was in full voice for the benefit of the entire group as they stood waiting next to a makeshift tent that protected the giant skeletons from the elements. The group listened with rapt attention to the tale of what was found on the Nelson farm. Uncle Halvar pulled back the canvas to show the bones causing one woman to faint outright.

"Here, in the soil of my humble little farm! The skeletons of warriors eight and nine feet tall, awaiting their final judgment by a court of angels."

Mundy half expected to see Aunt Helga or Tomas arise from the pit wielding a skull like a stage prop.

"Looking into the skulls of these giants, into the faces of these mighty men who knew angels as their fathers, why! It forces any reasonable man to conclude: this is the proof that the modern age requires, that the Holy Bible is more than the instruction for a moral life! It is the true history of this world. The bones of giants, sons of the angels whose blood mingled with the flesh of human daughters in the account in Genesis."

"Or trolls," Mundy muttered, but not loud enough for anyone to hear.

"Genesis chapter the sixth, ladies and gentlemen!"

Mr. Colton seemed baffled, his close-set eyes blinking rapidly. "I wouldn't have believed it! Not without seeing it."

"It is as Jesus said to Thomas, blessed are those who have not seen but believe."

"Well, that may not be the risen Christ you've found buried in the ground, but you may have some pretty goddamned big Indians!"

The joy disappeared from Uncle Halvar's demeanor.

"You must tell the truth! These are no Indians! These are the sons of angels! These are the mighty men of old! The Nephilim! You must say this correctly." He grabbed the reporter by the collar and, himself towering a full foot over the reporter, gave an indication of the advantage those buried warriors must have leveraged against their mortal enemies.

"Reverend, I am only going to write what I see. And what I see are seven of the biggest Indian skeletons I've ever set eyes on. I'll certainly add your claims to the story. You make a compelling case." He grabbed the minister's wrists and pulled them from his lapel. "You'll have to trust that God will guide the readers to the same conclusion you have reached from your personal witness. And truly, this is quite the story! Quite the story, indeed! And now, I imagine we better be off!" He signaled the drivers to shepherd their passengers back to the wagons.

"Procrastination and bullshit won't quit this year!" Lewis bellowed, standing by the fire. "Why don't you print that in your newspaper?"

Uncle Halvar narrowed his eyes on Lewis, clearly not appreciative of the outburst.

"Mr. Lewis, things have changed. We'll not need a survey after all."

Mundy was stunned.

"Has the land sale fallen through?"

"In a manner of speaking," Uncle Halvar explained. "This is holy ground! I intend to build a shrine here to house these skeletons. The trains will bring people from all over the country to see them. A new age of Faith will be born!"

Mr. Lewis took a deep breath and looked hard at Uncle Halvar. "You've sown a seed, Reverend, that assuredly will blossom in fields you never intended to reap."

He and Mundy watched the wagons as they turned, one after the other, followed by Uncle Halvar, until they disappeared on the path to town, their conversation rekindled with new excitement at what they had seen.

"You are all now witnesses to the truth! Spread the word!" Uncle Halvar yelled after them.

"What happens now?" Mundy asked Mr. Lewis.

"The world keeps turning, and men do what men do," Lewis drained the last sip of coffee from his tin cup. "I'm afraid your uncle has cast the die for your family in a game he is certain to lose. The government men I warned your uncle about, they will be here sooner than later."

"But why?"

"There's some government men, like I told your uncle," Lewis explained. They work for an organization called the Smithsonian Institution. They collect relics, shells, and dead animals from all over the world, and they bring them back to Washington D.C. where a man named Grover Cleveland is President."

"And they take giant skeletons? What do they do with them?"

"Yes, they take these giant skeletons, too, except, unlike everything else, they don't put them on display in their fancy museum. They hide them from people, just to keep their story straight," Lewis explained. "It's the same way all through history. Your family would be wise to deny everything."

Mundy shook his head slowly after a moment's thought. "I don't think Uncle Halvar will deny it, do you?"

Mr. Lewis exhaled, looking down at Mundy with warm brown eyes.

"If there were a way to reason with a man of faith, Mundy, I sure haven't seen it. About as useful as poking a big bear with a short stick. Once I saw a fellow, a deeply religious sort, hold two rattlesnakes that were longer than his arm. I said 'Joseph, you better toss them buggers well clear of you and run like the blazes,' but he said the Bible told him to do it. Then one of them twisted around enough to bite him, and he flinched, and the other one got him, too. At first, he was holding on to them because he felt strong, protected. But then when he was dying, he wouldn't let them go, because he was afraid of being wrong."

"What happened then?" Mundy asked.

Mr. Lewis shrugged. "I shot them."

Mundy frowned, and Mr. Lewis added, "But don't worry—I ate them. They didn't go to waste."

"I mean the man. What happened to him?"

"Well, he died. Nothing I could do for him."

✳✳✳✳✳

One of the passengers from Uncle Halvar's wagon had not made the trip back to town. Mundy heard a girl's singing coming in the woods. He recognized the voice immediately as Amanda's, and she sang a sweet song in Norwegian accompanied by calls of robins and the coo of a mourning dove.

He pushed his way into the undergrowth and saw her seated atop the burial mound. She was stroking her braided hair when she heard him rustle through the trees. Her expression turned hopeful for a moment but then became crestfallen the instant she realized it was Mundy. She must have been waiting to meet Matias.

"Oh, hello, Tiddemund," she forced a smile for him, like the one she'd mustered for Old Joe at church.

"What are you doing here?"

"You know why I'm here. Wait with me, will you?"

She continued singing as he clambered up the mound and sat next to her.

"That's a nice song," he murmured after she'd finished the final note. "What's it about?"

"It's about a girl who is in love with a devious man. He abandons her and her baby, and they drown in a river."

"That's sad," he said. "I knew it wasn't a hymn."

"Maybe it's a hymn of sorts," she suggested. "A hymn to love."

"Not likely one that your father will sing in church."

"Definitely not!" She laughed. "I have to tell you something, but you must promise not to tell anyone. I mean anyone!"

"What is it?"

"Do you promise?"

Mundy promised Amanda, but after she shared her secret, he wished he didn't know.

CHAPTER FIFTEEN

SPREADING THE WORD

After that, Mundy saw Amanda next at the Sunday service where attendance had doubled, full of out-of-towners and even Catholics hoping to catch a glimpse of giant bones. Faithful members stood outside in the brisk air to hear Reverend Ingegaard's sermon through open windows.

Then it was the usual dinner at the Ingegaard parish house where his mother continued to dodge the truth about her relationship with Kauko Koskinen, even though Mundy knew they spent nearly every night together.

Mundy followed Amanda from the table as she took kitchen scraps to the chickens. She shook the potato peelings and moldy bread from her pail as she clutched her shawl around her shoulders in the frosty night air.

He said nothing, watching her, until she nearly knocked him over on her way to the house.

"You scared me!" She said sternly, picking up the scrap pail she had dropped.

"I'm sorry. You shouldn't feed chickens like that. Make them sick."

She bristled at his unsolicited advice. "No one asked you! They're our chickens, not yours."

"Sorry," he replied. "Listen, I wanted to talk to you about the bones. It's important."

"They could jump up and dance around at the next town meeting for all I care about those bones!" Amanda banged the bottom of the pail to shake loose the scraps. "I'm tired of hearing about them."

"I know," Mundy agreed. "How would you like to see them out of your life?"

"Father would never…"

He interrupted her. "Soon, he won't have any say in the matter. There are men coming to claim the bones."

He explained, as best he could, what Mr. Lewis suspected would happen, but she was unmoved. She had no reason to believe a stranger's wild tales.

"What would soldiers want with old bones?"

Mundy shivered. He'd come outside to see her without bothering to take his coat.

"They're not soldiers exactly. The point is, they want the bones, and they don't want anyone else to see them or know about them. We could take the bones away, you and me. Maybe we could sell them and then leave."

"And where would we go?"

Mundy felt a hard thud slam his head forward, and he was on his knees. He rolled over to see Aunt Helga standing over him, wielding a broom stick.

"Amanda, get in the house."

Amanda paused, looking hard at Mundy where he laid on the ground. Her lips trembled, holding back words he would never hear. She flew from her spot, running into the parish house, and letting the door slam behind her.

Aunt Helga stared at him as if he were a worm that had wiggled out of an apple.

"We have nothing to fear from the laws of men," she said, hitting him with the broom across his forehead and nose. "Not when we hold high the law of God! Steal the giant bones, will you? Steal my daughter away, will you?" In spite of the pain, he noticed the way her breath escaped in clouds, smoke signals, made in the cold air. The blows kept coming even as Mundy simultaneously tried to block them with his arms and push himself away on the ground with his legs. "It is you! You, who we drive away. You, who are planting seeds of doubt and fear!"

He managed to roll out of the broom's reach covered in dirt and pine needles, and not a little blood.

✷✷✷✷✷

The cool air of October began to press down on the cattails and burning red sumac until only gold and browns remained, the green leaves of summer now gone, hiding in the ground until spring returned. He set the hook on the bucket handle, eased himself under the yoke and stood upright so that two buckets of water floated in mid-air on either side.

A gray squirrel, rustling through leaf litter, scampered up the nearest maple tree at the sound of horses approaching. More gawkers? Uncle Halvar was already at the farm planning the shrine for the giant bones, and Mundy didn't hear the singsong of small talk that signaled the nervous anticipation of town folk come for a 'grand excursion'. There were only the sounds of hooves driven steadily on, and the creak of wagons. He hurried back to the cabin as fast as he could without spilling the buckets.

The morning swirled with dust as the hooves of four horses carrying riders, soldiers in dusty blue uniforms, and a team of four oxen pulling a flat-bed wagon approached.

"This it?" One of the men on horseback said. They hadn't seen Mundy who took cover behind the woodpile next to the cabin, crouching so he wouldn't be seen. He carefully lowered the yoke so that base of the buckets sat solidly on the ground before slipping off the yoke's wooden beam from across his shoulders. If only Mr. Lewis were here, he wished.

The plumper of the two men on the wagon replied, "Yup, that's what it says." He smacked a piece of paper with a gloved hand. He was the only one of the men not wearing a uniform, instead, he wore riding clothes like Mr. Lewis wore, and just as well-worn and dusty, but he seemed uncomfortable in the buckboard seat, wincing as he shifted his weight to one haunch before climbing down.

"You," he pointed to the first horseman. "Knock on the door. Give them exactly five seconds. You three, at arms."

As the first man leapt on the porch, the others slid out long rifles and sent bullets clicking into their chambers.

"Halloo?"

One-thousand one, one-thousand two, one-thousand three…

Uncle Halvar threw open the door, a grim look on his face.

"Yes, what is it?"

"Are you the Norwegian minister?"

"I am the Reverend Halvar Ingegaard. What is your business?"

"Are you the one who's preaching the literal truth of the Bible?"

"Of course!" Uncle Halvar brushed the air with his hand dismissively. "Every word is a truth. The Lord does not hide his truth. It shines forth all around us!"

"That's definitely him," the man without the uniform spoke in a low voice to the solider nearest him. "The man in town said he was crazy." Scattered laughter erupted but the man without the uniform silenced them before he addressed Uncle Halvar.

"Phillips is my name. I'm a field curator for native artifacts for the Smithsonian Museum in Washington D.C. We've heard that you've found some unusual skeletons."

"Yes, you could say they are most unusual." Uncle Halvar stepped toward the man who spoke, but all the rifles trained on him in an instant without the need for command. "But why have you come here with your guns drawn?"

"Let's say we're cautious around the truth," the man chuckled. "Is it fair to say that you are currently in possession of these skeletons?"

"Yes."

"Six in all, is it?"

"Seven," Uncle Halvar corrected. His face muscles relaxed, all except his eyes which alternated between squinting at Phillips who was haloed by the sun and seeing if the soldier nearest was going to make any sudden moves.

Phillips nodded, satisfied with the answer. "That was a little test to see if you were going to lie to us."

Behind the woodpile, Mundy didn't know what to do or how to help. This was exactly what Mr. Lewis had predicted. Now there was nothing to do except watch to see what the men with guns would do next.

"And they appear to be very large-statured individuals?" Phillips continued.

"Oh, yes, quite large. Reasonable men can conclude only one thing…"

The soldier nearest Uncle Halvar darted forward and shoved the butt of his rifle into Uncle Halvar's stomach, causing him to utter a loud *ufff* before doubling over. Phillips nodded to two men in the rear, and they dashed off to the barn.

"Anyone else here?"

"No, no one," Uncle Halvar wheezed. He was doubled over in pain, but he looked directly at Mundy and grimaced.

"Sergeant! Check the cabin!"

The sergeant pushed his way inside using the muzzle of a long revolver as a lever, but he wouldn't find anyone there. His mother hadn't come home again last night

Phillips's gaze fell on the tent. "I think I'd like to see those skeletons now." They pushed Uncle Halvar toward it and tore away the canvas. One of the soldiers cursed in surprise. After a few minutes of inspecting the skeletons and collecting trinkets, Phillips instructed the men to bring the wagons to the site and start loading everything into crates.

"These are prize specimens that the museum would be honored to include in our ethnographic collection," Phillips said. "We are nothing if not fair. I'm sure spreading the word of God in this part of the country isn't without cost. He reached into his vest pocket and pulled out a sack. It jingled with the sound of coins when he tossed it on the ground in front of Uncle Halvar.

"There's twenty dollars to help you fight the good fight, Reverend."

Twenty dollars! Mundy's mind reeled. That was a small fortune. He thought of all the items in the stores in town. Maybe he could buy provisions to last them well past winter and have enough for a stock of sweets from Mr. Wells.

"That would be most generous." Uncle Halvar did not reach for the coins. "What strings are you attaching to this generous offer?"

"Your silence. These types of discoveries can fire the imaginations of superstitious and ill-informed types. No sense having people fail to understand the discovery out of context."

"Silence?" Uncle Halvar raised an eyebrow.

"Yes. We're taking the, uh, artifacts with us, and you're never to speak of them again."

Uncle Halvar's face tightened the way it did before he unleashed a rein of blows on Mundy. "Take them where, exactly?"

"Back to D.C. for cataloging and further investigation. Then when the time is right, we release our findings, at which time you would be free to discuss your role in the matter. Until then, though, I'm afraid we must insist on absolute silence on this matter."

"Those are some very thick strings you're proposing."

"Any thicker and they'd be a noose, Reverend." Phillips approached Uncle Halvar and pick up the pouch of coins from the ground. He pressed them into Reverend Ingegaard's hand.

Soon the men crated the bones in straw and nailed lids on. As the soldiers worked, Phillips asked Uncle Halvar if there were any other "little Indian hills" on the property. Mundy tensed. His uncle knew about the mound in the woods, but Uncle Halvar did something unexpected: he lied. He told Phillips that there weren't any other mounds on the farm.

Once the wagon was loaded, the men rode off, bouncing down the path leading to town, the bones and beads nestled safely in straw like hens on a nest.

After the men were gone, Uncle Halvar waved Mundy from his hiding place.

"Hitch the wagon and take me to town." His voice was quiet. He'd had the wind knocked out him in more than one way.

* * * * *

At the door to the parish house, Uncle Halvar ran his hands through his hair to make it even more tangled than it was before. Mundy followed him as he threw open the front door and announced that the devil had stolen the bones. He stumbled into the dining room, and Aunt Helga guided him to a chair.

"That Koskinen has stolen them?" she asked. "Maybe he stole the altar cross too!"

"No, not Koskinen," Uncle Halvar explained what had happened with the soldiers. His voice rolled like a river over rocks, never ceasing even when pounding hard on the truth. He didn't mention that he lied to protect Mundy, and he also didn't mention the money in his pocket.

"Oh, papa!" Amanda said, her eyes moist, too. She clutched her father's neck and kissed his forehead. "I'm sure you were brave! But all those bones are really gone now?"

"Yes, they are gone, stolen by deceitful men who conspire to keep the Truth hidden and keep the world in darkness."

Aunt Helga let out a squeak, sounding as if she were beset by a sharp pain.

"What is it, Helga?" Uncle Halvar asked.

"It's just that you've touched people's hearts by showing them the giant bones…"

"It is the Lord who has touched their hearts," Uncle Halvar corrected her. "I am only His…"

"…servant, yes," She interrupted him to regain the point. "But now, the bones are gone. Now you have nothing to show them."

Uncle Halvar rose to his feet, condemning her with his eyes.

"What are you saying? Have you lost your faith in God?"

"No, not in God." She pursed her lips and shook her head. "But now, what will you show them?"

"Show them?" Uncle Halvar grabbed his thick Bible from a nearby end table. "I will show them this, the Word of God!"

"They already had the Word of God before. Now they only have the story of a crazy person waving his hands around."

Uncle Halvar raised his hand to strike her, but she lifted her chin in defiance. He lowered his hand and returned to his seat, howling over his shoulder at her.

"At least I did not lose my faith! I remained true to the Lord's path."

Amanda kneeled next to her father and stroked his face while tears sneaked out of the corners of his clenched eyes.

"Of course, you did, you poor dear!"

Tomas signaled Mundy to go outside with him, and they walked together along the main street for a few minutes without speaking. Tomas nodded to three men seated around an upturned barrel, a whiskey bottle being passed among them.

"Still keeping it dry, Tomas?" One of them called. "A little nip wouldn't hurt you. Much!" The men broke out in garrulous laughter, and Tomas laughed, too, but didn't answer.

"I bet you don't know them from church," Mundy said.

"Nope. They're definitely not church-goers." Tomas stopped. A slight breeze blew his bangs in his eyes, and he pushed his hair aside. "What happened with the bones? Is my father telling the truth?"

"He didn't lie to you, if that's what you mean. The men came, just like Mr. Lewis said they would."

Tomas nodded.

"Mundy, there's something I need to tell you."

"Who's stopping you?"

"It's just, I don't know how you're going to take it."

Mundy waited. He'd already taken plenty over the past few months.

"I know about your mother and Koskinen. Heck, the whole town knows about it, except for my parents. But they'll find out soon enough, and things are going to get ugly around here. I'm going to get out of town just as soon as I can, and you should, too."

"But the farm!"

Tomas clacked his tongue.

"They didn't tell you, did they?"

Mundy shook his head.

"Tell me what?"

"Koskinen is buying the whole farm, not just that one plot. They're going to tear down the cabin and plow it all up for fields."

Mundy's lungs burned and he couldn't draw a proper breath. Tomas steadied him by the arm.

"My father is buried there," he sputtered. "It's our farm!"

"Look, I'm sorry. Land changes hands all the time around here. There were people on the land before your family, and there'll be other people after. I imagine your mother will have to move your dad's body, that's all I know."

Mundy cried, too upset to care how weak he might appear to his cousin.

"There's something else, Mundy."

Tomas pulled out a piece of paper from his coat pocket and smoothed it open.

"I talked to Mr. Lewis last week. I told him I changed my mind about the apprenticeship, and he gave me this."

"So?" Mundy pretended to be uninterested. "What is it?"

"It's a letter of introduction for Mr. Lewis's new survey project. I go to St. Paul first and get set up with his partners, then I head south to meet up with Lewis in Missouri." Tomas's expression lost its veneer of concern filled with buoyant optimism. Missouri! Can you believe it? Maybe I'll find more giant bones and send them back to father!"

Mundy should have been happy for Tomas, but he wasn't happy for anyone just then, least of all himself.

"When do you leave?"

"Tomorrow," Tomas smiled but realized Mundy wasn't sharing his enthusiasm. "I wanted to tell you sooner. Will you see me off at the station?"

"I don't know, maybe" Mundy grumbled and began to walk swiftly away.

"Mundy! Wait!"

Tomas ran to catch up with him, his shiny boots slapping the ground twice as he ran, first the heel and then the flopping oversized toe that flopped on its own.

"Just don't mention this to anyone. I don't want word to get around. I mean, my parents don't even know I'm leaving. I'm afraid they'll try to keep me from going, but I just need to try something big. Not even Amanda knows."

"Yeah, she's pretty busy with other things, I guess." Mundy's sour tone bristled Tomas.

"What's that supposed to mean?"

"Why don't you stay in town a few months and find out."

Tomas's face clouded with anger. "You mean she…with Koskinen?"

"According to her. Sounds like our whole family has a mess of secrets."

They resumed their walk, much slower than before, until Mundy decided he better get back for milking. He promised Tomas that he'd think about going to the station tomorrow. Mundy rode back to the farm, his thoughts heavy with despair.

*****

A fat brown mouse with glossy black eyes sped off as Mundy felt under a pile of straw for the canvas sack he'd stowed there. It was now or never to mark his father's grave, and then no one could move Lars Nelson, not with a holy symbol standing over him. He lugged the sack from the barn and slid out the cross, which gleamed golden in striking contrast to the black and gray ash around it. A two-foot-tall brass cross was sure to be noticed. Lars Nelson's grave needed something solid, something that people believed in and that they missed when it was gone. He placed it where his father's head lay buried.

A chill wind carried the cawing of a lone crow to him from the distance. There was something he was supposed to say at a moment like this, but he couldn't think of it. Sometimes it felt as if his father still was with Mundy every day, only that he stood to one side, watching to see how well Mundy would do on his own.

"Not too good," Mundy finally said.

Footsteps approached. His mother neared with a blanket draped over her shoulders, her hair tousled.

"I was looking for you," she said. "What's this?"

"It's father's grave."

"I know that, Mundy. I meant the cross. Why did you take it?"

Mundy shrugged. She should understand why.

"Oh, Mundy." She drew him to her side and draped the blanket over both their shoulders. "You need to take it back. Your aunt is very angry. If she ever found out you took it, well, I wouldn't like to see what would happen. Did you hear how she rode to the Koskinen farm all by herself to question Matias about the cross? And do you know what Matias said?" She asked, not waiting for Mundy to answer. "Matias said, I didn't steal anything. But I would have, if I'd known it was something good!"

"Then what happened?"

"Well, nothing, as far as I know. I was inside the house, and I wasn't expecting company, so I stayed put."

She had to hide from her own sister, in other words. Her own sister would never accept an attachment to a man like Koskinen, especially outside the bonds of matrimony.

Their attention returned to the little rectangle of ground where the body of Lars Nelson lay. For the moment, at least, it almost looked like a proper grave with a cross, and a wife and son standing in remembrance. A few moments passed when they said nothing. Passing geese overhead filled the landscape with their honking like trumpets announcing judgment day. She caught his hand with hers and released a deep sigh.

"Lars did his best. That's all any of us can do."

She entwined her fingers tightly in his, stroking the side of Mundy's face for a few moments before she pried the cross loose from the earth and handed it to him. "Take the cross back, Tiddemund," she whispered. "Lots more people need to see that cross where it belongs. Leaving it here, well, it just wouldn't make sense."

"Because you're going to move him, aren't you?"

"Calm yourself, Tiddemund. What did you hear?"

"I know Koskinen is buying everything and going to tear down our cabin. And you're going to dig up pa and move him to town, just like he said not to."

"The truth is I don't know what we'll do. For now, he'll stay right here, I promise. But I'll be living with the Koskinens from now on. No more going back and forth."

Mundy shut his eyes hard and pressed his head against his mother.

"What about me?" Mundy wondered aloud. It had been the question on his mind during all the uncertainty with the farm. "What am I supposed to do?"

Brita hugged him more tightly.

"You poor boy. Of course, you'll come live with us. I'll be there with you."

"And Matias," Mundy reminded her. "He'll be there, too."

"I hear he's taking that job with Mr. Lewis, so he won't be around for quite a while."

"That's what I thought, but Tomas took it. He's got a letter from Mr. Lewis and everything. He's leaving tomorrow, except I wasn't supposed to mention it."

Brita's expression lit up.

"Now that Tomas is leaving, Mr. Buri will need a new assistant! You could take Tomas's job at the store. You could help Kauko on the farm."

"You mean on our farm?" Mundy shook his head. "It wouldn't work! None of it. Mr. Buri hates me more than Aunt Helga does, and the Koskinens, well, I just don't have much nice to say about them."

"To be honest, I suppose that sentiment is mutual with them," she admitted. "Men just can't get along with one another." Her fingers soothed his cheek. Her eyes widened with a sudden idea, and she shot upright. Mundy rolled from her lap like a log onto the ground.

"Why don't you go with Tomas?"

"Go with him?"

"Yes! Certainly! Go with him on the train. Mr. Lewis could use you just as well as Tomas. We all know that boy will not enjoy working in the out-of-doors! It's hard to imagine him doing survey work, isn't it? After all, we already know Mr. Lewis likes you."

She untied a pouch of coins that hung from her dress—the coins she'd saved from selling cheese—and pressed it into his hand. "It isn't much," she gulped in a mouthful of air and drew him to herself. "But it will give you a start."

"Do you think he'll take me with him, ma?"

"He is your cousin, and he knows all you've been through." She kissed him on the forehead. They stood silently for another minute before she said she needed to get back to the Koskinens. "Things fall apart over there if I'm gone for more than five minutes."

Brita looked him in the eye before turning away. She picked her way through the ash, careful not to dirty the hem of her skirt. Mundy thought he heard her say I love you, but he wasn't certain. Her face was turned from him, but it may have been the breeze.

CHAPTER SIXTEEN

THE 12:05

On Mundy's last day at the farm, he walked from cabin to barn, to the woods, and the little pond, trying to bottle up everything he saw to carry with him. He braved a peek at the mound where Amanda had sung her Norwegian love song. If ever he returned, everything would be changed. This was the last moment the farm belonged to him.

Hardest for him was saying good-bye to the little milk herd, especially after spending every morning and every evening of his young life with them. He left them in the pasture, munching the brown stubble of autumn, and kept the barn door open for them. Now, the two calves already were bigger than they were only a few months before. Koskinen probably would butcher the steer soon for the winter, but that was no longer any of Mundy's concern. Time pressed on, and he and Cloppie needed to make one last trip to town if he was to make it to the depot on time.

He strapped the blanket to Cloppie's haunches and then heaved the saddle over her, but she gave a low whinny and side-stepped his throw so that the saddle slid off. He tried again, this time strapping the saddle down as soon as it landed. Then he tied the sack with the cross to the halter so it wouldn't sway when Cloppie did and bang her flank. She was getting old enough that her bones were probably brittle.

Mundy and Tomas traveling together and working side-by-side: that was a glimmer of hope. They'd have big adventures in the fields and hills of a new place. The stories they would have at the end of it! Stories for their own children. And the work itself, well, Mundy already was used to hard work, but he also had a real interest in what Mr. Lewis did. He'd even learn how to smoke a pipe, if that's what land surveyors did.

"Just one more trip into town, Cloppie," he urged the mare as he pulled himself up.

He used to play in the pasture with Cloppie when she was younger. She would chase him, and he would run until he fell on his hands, and she would nuzzle him to make sure he wasn't injured. Then the game continued.

*****

When they reached town, Mundy tethered Cloppie to a weathered post outside the train depot, patting her muzzle. She whinnied and lowered her head for him to scratch. He looked deep in her brown eyes, etching her in his memory, one that he could take out when he thought of muddy paths or the hard pull of the plow in turf.

The 12:05 train was coming within the hour, like clockwork, but that gave him time to make it over to the church and return the cross. He undid the strings of the sack and hid it under his coat with one hand as he hurried down the main street to the church. He pulled open the side door and peeked into the sanctuary. Rows of wooden pews were tinted in a sea of red and blue from the stained-glass windows, which translated the morning sunlight into the final hours of Christ Jesus on the cross. He entered, and he was alone.

From the sack, Mundy retrieved the brass cross and ran it along his sleeve until it glowed in the kaleidoscopic light of the stained glass. He ascended the altar platform causing the dais to squeak under his weight. This was where his uncle thundered out sermons. He might not have enjoyed the services, but he sure had enjoyed staring at the stained-glass windows during those long sermons. He set the cross carefully on the altar.

The groan of hinges strained behind him, and a shaft of white daylight fell in a long triangle on Mundy and the cross.

"What are you doing here?"

He squinted into the light of the doorway. The form was only a shadow, but the sound was his aunt's voice. Quicker than he'd ever seen her move, she ran up the aisle, the whoosh-whoosh of her dress cutting the air like a scythe cutting wheat, until she was at the altar next to him, grabbing his arm so that the tips of her fingers dug deep enough that she must have felt his bone. He held back a scream of pain not wanting her to know the satisfaction of hurting him.

"You! It was you!" She shook him by the shoulders, but he broke loose and shoved her down the three steps to the altar. "Admit it!" Aunt Helga screeched. "It was you!"

"Do you want me to confess?" He yelled, as loud as any minister. "Yes! I took the cross. I took it to mark my father's grave! I've heard your daughter's song! I've heard you lie, and I know your secrets—secrets you don't even know yet. And when you find them out, I confess they will hurt you more than I ever could!"

He was shaking with anger by the time he was through. He ran out the door leaving his aunt sprawled in a glowing patchwork of colored light on the sanctuary floor.

* * * * *

Mundy hurried to the depot and ducked against a wall under the awning to avoid the pricking fingers of the north wind. His legs were weak, but if he leaned against the depot wall, maybe the depot would hold him steady, and the wind wouldn't notice him. He forced himself to breathe deeply and regain his composure. He heard the sound of Tomas's boots slapping the platform before he saw him wearing his best church coat. His cousin dropped his travel case when he caught sight of Mundy. His face was pink from a fresh shave and the cold wind. He embraced Mundy.

"You came to see me!"

"Family is important," Mundy said into Tomas's shoulder.

"That makes me so happy!" Tomas pulled away from Mundy to scan the platform. "You didn't tell anyone did you?"

"My ma knows," Mundy sheepishly admitted, adding hurriedly, "But she has her own secrets to keep with your mother."

"I suppose that's true."

"But why I really came is to tell you I'm coming with you."

Tomas laughed. "What? With me?"

"Yes! We can both work for Mr. Lewis. I'm sure he's got enough to do for a whole of crew of young men like us."

Tomas was still laughing. "But Mundy! You're just a boy! Mr. Lewis told me he wasn't sure you were old enough to work for him anyway, so he was glad that I was joining him." Tomas patted his breast pocket. "Yes, sir! I thought, why fight it? The Lord put an opportunity in my path. Who am I to say no?"

Mundy was going with Tomas, whether Tomas liked it or not.

"Let me see the letter again, Tomas." He jabbed a hand towards his cousin's coat, but Tomas swatted it away.

A whistle sounded in the distance. Their view was blocked by trees, but they saw the white-gray smoke puffing into the sky, new clouds for the next storm. A wave of excitement surged through Mundy: an Iron Horse from Minneapolis was approaching. He had to act fast.

The platform began to vibrate with the approach of the train. Tomas looked down the tracks as a smile took over his face.

"Let me see it!" Mundy yelled with such ferocity that Tomas's playful attitude changed abruptly. He shoved the letter at Mundy.

"Fine! You can look at it, but you're not coming with me. Let's say goodbye and shake hands like friends!"

Mundy edged away from his cousin to the end of the platform for better light to read the letter. He let the toes of his shoes hang over the edge.

The train whistle blew again, only closer and louder.

"Don't crumple it!" Tomas mouthed, but Mundy could barely hear him. "That's my future!" He patted Mundy's shoulder frantically, mouthing *Give it back!*

"I want the apprenticeship," Mundy shouted, but the train was too loud. It was no use.

Much to Tomas's consternation, Mundy slipped the letter into his own pocket as the very planks beneath their feet shook. The thunderous cylinder of black steel loomed large in a cacophony of squealing brakes. Mundy covered his ears.

Tomas reached for Mundy, gripping him hard by the shoulder. He yanked Mundy toward him, but Mundy ducked and twisted away, throwing Tomas off kilter. The platform was cloaked in a storm of steam as the tip of his cousin's shiny boot, too big for his feet, tripped on the edge of a loose plank. Tomas went over the edge.

Just as his father had sprung forward in time to save Mundy from falling off the field shed, Mundy sprang forward. He reached blindly in front of him in hopes of catching one of Tomas's flailing arms. He was certain their hands touched, but it was too late. Tomas, his eyes wide with horror, disappeared into that hot, billowing cloud as the momentum of the 12:05 brought Tomas Ingegaard to his final destination.

CHAPTER SEVENTEEN
FISHER OF MEN

Colorado, 1889

Robert Stanton rowing in Glen Canyon, December 1889.

From the field notes of **Robert Brewster Stanton**, chief engineer for the Denver, Colorado Canyon and Pacific Railroad Company expedition investigating the Grand Canyon for a possible railroad line.

Wednesday, May 22

After three days of interviews, I've assembled what appears to be a crew of dependable men. I selected most of them from a large number of applicants provided by the company, except for one farm boy who has little or no experience. I took him on at the behest of Teddy Lewis of the Minnesota Geological Survey. Lewis said the boy was growing too fast and he couldn't keep up with feeding him. I told Lewis he still owed me a box of good cigars from our last poker game, and now he might as well it make it two.

Thursday, May 23

Green River Station. Before breakfast, we all went over to look at the supply of boats meant to navigate the rapids of the Colorado River. We were sorely disappointed to find they were of the pleasure-craft design and not suitable for the task. Two of them were split in the bottom, damaged in transport. However, they are what we have at hand, and we will make do with them or drown in the process.

Friday, May 24

We had a fine breakfast at the hotel of trout, strawberries, and cream. The farm boy gobbled it down like he hadn't been fed in a week. I told him to savor it as that would be his last regular meal for six to eight months. It'll be catch as catch can, I said. He said he'll eat anything except tomatoes. After breakfast, we set up camp on the Green River about a half mile below the railroad bridge.

Saturday, May 25

Spent the morning repairing boats and otherwise discovering not enough room for all of our provisions. The entire village came out to see us push off only to quickly discover that the oldest boat, Brown Betty, is leaking all the way around the top. We came ashore and the farm boy patched the leak with a combination of flour and lard. He called it chinking, and it seems to have done the trick. I told him not to eat said chinking so the old boat would stay afloat.

Thursday, May 30

We commenced the survey of the Colorado River today by taking a true meridian reading of Polaris at 3:15 a.m. After breakfast of two large fish caught on a line by Hansborough, I personally adjusted all instruments, triangulated the positions of the three rivers and began the survey.

Friday, May 31

Narrowly escaped losing two men in the rapids, chiefly Richards and Gibson, but lost a float of provisions, about one-third of our total remaining supply. I previously had instructed those men if they were caught in swift water and couldn't control their boat, to pull to shore as quickly as possible. However today they were caught in a fast eddy with both paddles pulled under. They abandoned the boat, which nosed into an outcropping of rock and shattered the hull in two. They were fighting a swift current and bobbing in the water with the rest of us out of reach. I stood useless as a third leg on the opposite side yelling my head off.

The farm boy dived in after them with a rope and tied off to a larger part of the boat wreckage. He fought the current and reached the struggling men, pulling them to shore. His actions provided the lifeline that most assuredly saved their lives.

We have dubbed him Peter, for he truly is a fisher of men. He insisted he is not a Christian, but I told him I'd never seen anything more Christian in all my life.

This was camp number seven. From here on in the rapids will only be rougher.

I rest easier tonight knowing I have good men around me.

THE END

Cloppie

He used to play in the pasture with Cloppie when she was younger. She would chase him, and he would run until he fell on his hands, and she would nuzzle him to make sure he wasn't injured. Then the game continued.

Acknowledgments from the Author

Special thanks to:

Paul Langland and **Elizabeth Langland**, son and daughter of Joseph Langland, whose poem *On the Origin of What Really Matters* inspired the title of this book, and perhaps more.

Editor **Jane Turley** who made this book better thanks to her thoughtful questions and suggestions.

Giants of the Earth Heritage Center, Spring Grove, Minnesota, for your collection of photographs and information about Norwegian immigration—and for introducing me to the work of Joseph Langland.

Pioneer Park, Annandale, Minnesota, where I apprenticed as a blacksmith when I was Mundy's age under the patient tutelage of master blacksmith Tom Latané, the Park's live-in caretaker along with his charming wife, Kitty.

The Minnesota History Center for providing one of the best research experiences with a beautiful view of the Minnesota State Capitol.

Sweet Reads bookstore of Austin, Minnesota, for supporting local writers.

The Park Avenue Authors writing group for being a strong tribe of writers.

My wife, **Naomi Stanton**. She may not be Norwegian, but she is stubborn enough to have toughed it out with me for twenty-five years.

...and to you, **dear reader**. Thank you reading this book. I hope you enjoyed it.

ABOUT CHAUNCE STANTON

I was raised in Annandale, a small town in central Minnesota, where I played in the woods, sod fields, and cricks. I fished Pleasant Lake with my dad. My mom was on the City Council, which was a pretty big deal back in the 1980s, to have a woman on the Council. I rode my Huffy dirt bike, *The Red Baron*, around town until I earned enough from working at the Dairy Queen to buy my first car—a 1969 Dodge Dart.

I imagined the future, and dreamed of the past, wrote, fell in love, got my first kiss, went to church, sang in choir, played Atari, and checked out more books than I could carry from the local library, all in a little town called Annandale.

I still dream about our house there, but as Thomas Wolfe wrote, you can't go home again. This book made the attempt, anyway.

WWW.CHAUNCESTANTON.COM

Made in the USA
Monee, IL
29 September 2020